A McDADE NOVEL

FORBIDDEN BOND

SCARLETT FINN

Copyright © 2024 Scarlett Finn
Published by Moriona Press 2024

All rights reserved.

The moral right of the author has been asserted.

First published in 2024

No part of this book may be reproduced in any form or by an electronic or mechanical means, including information storage and retrieval systems, without permission in writing from the publisher, except by a reviewer who may quote brief passages in a review. It may not be used to train AI software or for the creation of AI works.

All characters in this publication are fictitious and any resemblance to real persons, living or dead, is purely coincidental.

ISBN: 9781914517716

www.scarlettfinn.com

Also by Scarlett Finn

NOTHING TO...
NOTHING TO HIDE
NOTHING TO LOSE
NOTHING IN BETWEEN: ONE
NOTHING TO DECLARE
NOTHING TO US
NOTHING IN BETWEEN: TWO
NOTHING TO SAY
NOTHING TO GAIN
NOTHING IN BETWEEN: THREE
NOTHING TO YOU
NOTHING TO THIS PREQUEL: ONE WILD NIGHT
NOTHING TO THIS
NOTHING IN BETWEEN: FOUR
NOTHING TO DO
NOTHING TO FEAR
NOTHING IN BETWEEN: FIVE
NOTHING TO DENY

GO NOVELS
GO WITH IT
GO IT ALONE
GO ALL OUT
GO ALL IN
GO FULL CIRCLE

KINDRED SERIES
RAVEN
SWALLOW
CUCKOO
SWIFT
FALCON
FINCH

EXILE
HIDE & SEEK
KISS CHASE

THE EXPLICIT SERIES
EXPLICIT INSTRUCTION
EXPLICIT DETAIL
EXPLICIT MEMORY

THE FORBIDDEN NOVELS
FORBIDDEN DESIRE
FORBIDDEN WANT
FORBIDDEN WISH
FORBIDDEN NEED
FORBIDDEN BOND

WRECK & RUIN
RUIN ME
RUIN HIM

MISTAKE DUET
MISTAKE ME NOT
SLEIGHT MISTAKE

THE BRANDED SERIES
BRANDED
SCARRED
MARKED

TO DIE FOR...
TO DIE FOR TRUTH
TO DIE FOR HONOR
TO DIE FOR VIRTUE
TO DIE FOR DUTY
TO DIE FOR LOVE

RISQUÉ & HARROW INTERTWINED
TAKE A RISK
FIGHTING FATE
RISK IT ALL
FIGHTING BACK
GAME OF RISK

FORBIDDEN PREQUEL DUET
ALL. ONLY.
ONLY YOURS

LOVE AGAINST THE ODDS STANDALONE COLLECTION
SWEET SEAS
HEIR'S AFFAIR
RESCUED
MAESTRO'S MUSE
GETTING TRICKY
THIRTEEN
REMEMBER WHEN...
RELUCTANT SUSPICION
XY FACTOR

LOST & FOUND
LOST
FOUND

ONE

"ARE WE GOING TO run forever? Is that your grand plan, Dad?"

"I'm thinking, I have to think." In the car, since leaving Conn bleeding, cuffed to her grandfather's couch, they'd been driving around the city. Just driving. Achieving nothing except dowsing tiny, anxious glimmers of hope. "We need a car. We need a different car."

Conn deserved a chance. He'd put himself in front of her; taken that bullet for her. No one else knew what went down in that room, no one else was there, no one else saw. His survival depended on her.

"We need to call Lachlan," she said. "We need to call an ambulance. It's not too late to—"

"No! No. No. No!"

The warmth on her cheeks chilled until a fresh wave of tears escaped. "Please," she sobbed. "Please, Dad. You don't want to do this. If we go back now, if we get him help—"

"He's beyond help!"

Fear dried her throat. A world without Connel McDade? Without her McDade? She wouldn't believe in his demise until her own eyes witnessed him prone and lifeless.

"Daddy, please."

This man, the strength in him, once all bluster, had become something determined... and unsettling.

"That Irish scum doesn't deserve to breathe. You don't need him. You're a McLeod, I did you a favor. In time, you'll see I'm right."

Every time she closed her eyes, the growing blot of blood on Conn's pristine shirt poisoned her mind.

"I love him, Dad. I know you don't..." The words stuck in her throat. Though she fought to expel them, only a shriek escaped. Loud. Pained. Desperate. Primal grief commanded her senses. "God-fucking-damn you! Give me your phone!"

"No, my phone..."

Her father drove with one hand on the wheel and one on the gun in his lap. Was that how this would end? Murdered by her own father?

"If he's gone, if I've lost him..." Swallowing a dose of resolve, grief gave way to rage. "I swear to God, I will take you down and I will make it fucking hurt!"

"Watch your mouth!"

"You fucking bastard!"

She wanted her goddamn hands, wanted to punch and kick, and cause him pain. But that was nothing to her need to be with Conn, to call for help, to scream from the deepest depths of her guts. He couldn't be gone. He couldn't.

It was her fault. He'd only been at the meet for her. She should've told him to stay in bed. Left him safe in their loft and gone to meet her father alone.

"Don't you dare speak to me like that, young lady! You have done this! Caused this! Everything worked until you—"

"Fucked Ire McDade," she spat and lunged closer. "I did, Daddy. Over and over and over again. He was fucking amazing, made your little girl take it fucking hard and I begged for more! Begged him, you sick bastard!"

"How dare you!"

"How dare I?" Disgust tightened her jaw. "You're a murderer! You murdered your father! Murdered the man your daughter loves! You need help!" Though she wasn't the one who'd give it. "Take off the cuffs, give me the gun, and I'll end both our miseries right here."

"My car is too conspicuous." The bastard wasn't even listening to her pain, to her boundless agony. "We need something—Lachlan uses the motor pool."

"Yeah?" she asked, though already knew that. "Why don't you drive us there, huh? Right up to the precinct."

"We need something—no one would know we… One of your lowlife friends must—"

"Oh, sure, wait while I call my friends for help. At least I have fucking friends who can help. At least they know—"

"Kurt Stratford."

Strat. Another shiver of fear.

Anger faded to a sheer terror she didn't want her father to see.

"What?"

"What is his address?"

"I am not taking you to his place."

"His son then—"

"No! Why would I—"

"You do this! You help me or your lover will not be the only one going to hell tonight."

Gritting her teeth, the fire of anger in her belly

threatened to erupt. She'd allow it to burst, if she wasn't so damned impotent.

"I won't let you near him."

"His son—"

"No! Why would I open my network to—"

"I have the power to dismantle everything that slug built. Do you want me to make a call and bring in every McDade that walks the street?"

Yes, she sort of did, because at least then they'd know something was going on. Except if each person was brought in alone, how long would it take anyone to notice Conn wasn't among them? She needed McDades, needed them to hear her silent plea and start looking.

Niall would find him.

Though their First Team, as Conn called them, were asleep. Niall was the only hope. The guys outside her grandfather's would never enter and interrupt a meeting. The silenced shot would've passed by unheard. She and her father went out the back. No one knew her love was there, slowly bleeding to death, the cuff on his wrist preventing him seeking help on his own.

"Stag," she said. "Go to Stag, we have cars there."

"Ha!" His single beat of incredulous laughter startled her. "Don't play games with me, you think I'm that stupid?"

"I think you're that crazy." And entitled. "You said you needed a car and I'm telling you there are vehicles there."

"And plenty of men you might appeal to for help."

Yeah, rocking up with her father would be bad enough. When they saw the cuffs and the gun, and the lack of their leader…

Someone would rouse Niall, wouldn't they? Who else would be on-site? She didn't know if there were cars for the taking. Even if there were, she wouldn't know where to find keys. If she could stall—who would know her well enough to read between the lines?

"I won't—"

He raised the gun, aiming it toward her stomach. "Stop playing with me."

"Shoot me," she said, shifting her angle to give him a bigger target. "Please. Now. Just do it. Maybe then they'll find out what you're really capable of. Any man who can murder his own father can murder his daughter. You'll go to prison. Forever. Well, for as long as the McDades let you live."

"I didn't murder anyone. We already have a witness putting McDade at my father's the night he was murdered. When they find your body next to his, we'll call it murder-suicide and no one will bat an eye. Has the added advantage that Silvio will win the Harvest deal by default, and my standing will—"

"You make me sick."

They'd never got along. Once she'd been sorry he couldn't accept her. Now, glaring at his profile, nothing would erase her disgust. He hadn't accepted her? Fuck that; she'd never accept him.

"You were the architect of his demise, his and yours, if you don't do as you're told."

"Strat's," she whispered, resigned to their fate, and gave him the address.

"Good. This will be easier; I'm doing what's best for all of us."

All of us? All of him. Nothing about the situation was good for her. It wasn't good for the McDades or the Stratfords. Wasn't good for Steeple or her colleagues at The Chronicler. Most of all? It wasn't good for Lachlan. How could this play out without ultimately shattering his world? She'd already lost one man she loved, two men, losing another would finish her.

For the drive to Strat's, which wasn't far, they didn't share another word.

"Park over there," she said, nodding to a space by the building. "We're not going in. I don't trust you not to…"

If anything happened to threaten Strat, she'd provoke her father into giving her the bullet. She didn't want Conn setup to take the fall for her murder, but his people would fight his corner. She couldn't lose a friend. Wouldn't.

"You care too much about people," her father said, turning off the engine.

"And you care about no one." Not even his own blood. "Leave the keys in it."

"Excuse me?"

"Where's your phone? Loosen the cuffs and I'll—"

"No." He retrieved his phone from a side pocket. "What's the number?"

Much as she didn't want to give it, what choice did she have? He dialed on speaker. Shit.

Strat answered, clearing his throat. "Yeah?"

"Kurt?"

Another cough. "What the—"

"I need to borrow your car."

"Scamp?"

"Please just, come to the window, drop your keys down to the parking lot."

"What?" he asked again. "What the fuck is going on?"

"I can't talk." Her eyes met her father's. "Please just, drop them out the window."

"It's barely fucking light outside."

She hadn't thought about the sun. Not that it had risen yet. Not then and it never would again. Without Conn there would be no new day, no sunrise could replace what she'd lost.

"I know, I'm sorry to wake you. It's important."

"Come up and—"

"No, I'm not coming up, and I don't have time to explain." The answer would be different if she didn't fear her father flipping out and killing someone else. "I'm not alone."

"Why's Ire—"

"Long live the king," she murmured, hoping he'd remember their conversation about Ire's potential demise.

Strat was incredible at picking up her cues, at this most important moment, she hoped that skill wouldn't desert them. Though so early in the morning, he may not have flicked the on switch yet.

Her father's interjection was unexpected. "He makes you say that?"

"Superintendent?" Strat asked.

Ronald McLeod sealed his lips again.

"We'll leave the keys in this one," she said, "can you make it disappear?"

Something she'd never have said in front of her father before. She wouldn't name Ford or Jagg, Strat's boys, but once upon a time, they'd run the city's most successful chop shop.

"Scamp?"

"I know," she said, sighing at the trepidation in his tone. "Everyone is capable in the right circumstance."

He had to be listening. Please listen. Hear her. Asking him to disappear the car would betray laws had been broken. Suspicion would swing Strat's way if the superintendent's car was abandoned in his parking lot. She would not let her friend take the fall for her father's transgressions.

"Or the wrong one."

Yes! Strat's muttered words gave relief, though

she couldn't show it and reveal they were passing messages.

Her father gestured at the side door, gun against him, aimed in her direction. She managed to open the side door. The gun stayed on her, even as her father came around the hood. Weapon in one hand, phone in the other.

"What does that mean?" her father asked.

"Means I have nothing left to lose," she said, walking closer to the building after getting out.

Something she'd said to Strat when she and Conn were apart in the past.

"I value it," Strat said, adamant. Light went on above. His light. "You need me with you."

The window opened and there he was. Discerning his expression through the dim light and distance wasn't easy. Disapproval came in his tone, no concealing that.

"Not on this. Drop them." He did and they landed right at her feet. "I'm sorry, Strat. I love you."

Her father cut off the phone so abruptly, she wasn't sure the final words were heard. Ronald backed up, more brazen with the angle of the gun.

"Pick them up."

Turning her back, she braced for a kill shot as she crouched and fumbled to find them. As she stood, he ripped them from her hand and grabbed her arm.

"Dad—"

"Good. This is exactly what we need."

What she needed wasn't considered. At least she got to say goodbye to her friend. Whatever happened now, she doubted she'd see him again. Her father was off the rails and if he was adamant Lachlan couldn't know, she wouldn't be allowed to speak to him.

How the hell had they ended up in this insanity?

TWO

THEY DROVE FOR what felt like a million years. Her pleas for Conn fell on deaf ears. At some point, after the sun had risen in the sky, she gave up begging for his life. If he hadn't been found by then, he'd be gone. Her love. Her future. How would she go on? What was left without him?

No radio. No news. No music. The cuffs at her back made it difficult to get comfortable. The enveloping grief didn't subside and trickled out until her exhausted body surrendered to sleep.

Life, what they could've been, meaning and purpose, all had been stolen. What happened to her next didn't matter. She was done fighting. If she hadn't been so determined to liberate the truth, maybe people wouldn't have lost their lives. People like her grandfather… like Conn.

Her first thought when she opened her eyes? Connel McDade.

From then on, she'd wake lonely. Wake without him struck by the painful truth he would never sleep at her side again.

They'd stopped.

Light outside hurt her sensitive eyes. She hadn't figured out what was happening until her father opened her side door and dragged her out of the vehicle into a room.

A crappy out-of-state motel.

Her stomach rumbled and her eyes burned. Not that she cared about either.

Another set of cuffs appeared from somewhere and he attached one loop to the bed's headboard. He snapped the loose end to her wrist, leaving her contorted in a—he freed her from the first set. Thank God, she could move her shoulders.

"So is this it now? We're just on the run forever? Me cuffed to the furniture in motels across the country?"

Nothing. He hadn't said a damn word. All her life she'd been invisible unless acting out. If this wasn't him repeating that past, she didn't know what to call it. A midlife crisis? Murder was an extreme way to recapture his youth. Just what had he been up to back then?

Her mood wasn't helped by him pacing back and forth at the end of the bed.

"We're the only ones who know," he muttered.

Probably wasn't talking to her, but she was beyond caring about his wants. "About your homicidal tendencies or you screwing over the city you claimed to adore?" Bullshit. No one betrayed what they truly loved. For all the difference it made, her father didn't even glance her way. "Lach will notice we're gone, Ronald."

Using his name was more appropriate than giving him any familial title. Even in private, she didn't want to admit they were related, and he sure didn't deserve respect.

"I can control this."

Himself or the situation?

"Lachlan actually does have integrity and loyalty," she said. "He'll move heaven and earth to find us."

How she wished to be wrong on that. With their father so unhinged, she didn't trust him to make rational choices.

The superintendent's staff would wait a few hours, maybe a day, then contact Lachlan to report his father missing. Her brother would look in the obvious places and try cellphones. When no one picked up, he'd do rounds of the city officials. Had anyone seen their father? He'd call Steeple. And, yes, her brother would go to Stag.

What reception awaited him there? Would Conn's men think he was in on the murder? That she was in on it?

Didn't look good that the boss went out with his girlfriend and came back dead, with said girlfriend in the wind.

Silvio Manzani, McDade enemy and the don bribing her father, wouldn't be any help. Not that Lachlan would look there given he didn't believe their father's duplicity.

Might he go to Evander? Yes. And boy could that blow up in his face.

All the landmines they'd left behind. Avoiding them would take a miracle on Lachlan's part. Maybe her only chance for liberation was her sibling, though she wouldn't hold her breath he'd last the week in the wake of their carnage.

Eventually Lachlan would learn Conn was dead. May learn Evander "Vex" Manzani had been shot; he could be dead too by this point.

The only desperate hope for any semblance of help and protection would be if Lach went to Strat first. Her friend, her best friend, maybe had the privilege of being the last man to see her alive.

Would her brother put pride before sense? He may not want to go to his ex's father to ask for help. He may not call the ex-girlfriend who'd recently found new love. If pride won out, her brother would be in serious danger.

Her friendship with Strat was common knowledge. People from both factions, McDade and McLeod, had been working together at Stag. Should that make a difference to trust and approachability? Yes. Would it? With men, who could tell?

What about Strat? He wouldn't have gone back to bed and slept through the morning. He'd be up, working to help her, to save her. He might go to Lachlan. Then, hopefully, she could rely on her friend to guide her brother.

Conn.

Strat was one of the few people who knew about their loft. And he had Niall's number. If he called and got the lieutenant out of bed, they may have found Conn in time. Except who knew where they'd gone? How long would it take Niall and Strat to figure out they'd been at her grandfather's? The longer it took, the more Conn bled.

And there was the other problem, McDades didn't use hospitals with maximum resources. McDades had their own doctor. The guy had to be used to rooting out bullets and patching guys up. How was he with blood loss? If her love had—

"We can't go back." Her father's pacing continued. "We can't. Not together."

"You can't go back at all," she said. "I'm a reporter, Ronald. You think for a second I won't recount every minute, despicable detail of what happened last night? My mission, every day I live, will be to put the truth out there."

He stopped pacing to glare, ah, now that was familiar. "I saved your life."

Her mouth opened in unison with the widening of her eyes. She couldn't even—the words just—laughter bubbled out.

"Are you fucking insane? You called me! You put me there. What exactly was the threat to my life? Silvio walked out, no threat. Conn wasn't holding a gun; he wasn't the one shooting people. And I can guarantee, if he'd been armed, you'd be lying dead on that floor right now. You think I'd give a fuck? My guy would be balls deep inside me, listening to me scream for more, scream my thanks for taking your repulsive, vindictive ass off the board!"

Her guy once told her not to leave him alone with Ronald if they discovered he had foreknowledge of the Manzani attack that put her in hospital. How could she have thought, for even a second, that her father wasn't complicit in that assault?

As for the meet at her grandpapa's, her father put her in that room. He hadn't asked for Conn's presence. No, that was on her. His demise was on her.

"We have to fix this!"

"How do you want to do that, Dad?" she asked, rattling the cuff on the headboard. "You plan to keep me cuffed and quiet for the rest of my life?"

"You'll say nothing."

"Why would I keep your secrets? You're a murderer!"

"It was necessary!" And the wild, deluded light in his eyes proved he believed that. "I did it for the city! I did it for you!"

"What do you want, Dad? Huh? You want to go back there and pretend nothing's wrong? You want to stride on into your office and resume your role? You murdered your father. A city alderman. You're a murderer, Ronald."

"Because he was going to ruin everything, ruin careers, you don't know the pressure I was under. People looked to me, they begged for help, begged me to stop him asking questions."

His allies, those on the Manzani payroll. Not the kind of people Superintendent was supposed to serve. It made her sick.

"He was your father," she pleaded, but got a harsh slap as the words sank in.

Right there, in that moment, she was looking at her father. Hers. If someone put a gun in her hand, would she hesitate to pull the trigger? No. After what he'd done, how could he ever be forgiven? She would kill her father, just as he killed his. Maybe murder was in McLeod blood.

"The situation got out of hand. It wasn't meant to—if he'd just listened—"

"You deserve to go to jail!"

"And what about the man you brought to our meeting?" Either he couldn't say Conn's name or he was disassociating. Maybe he didn't see her love as worthy of a name. "What did he deserve?"

"Not death."

"Hasn't he killed? Hasn't he murdered people? Would you have put him behind bars?"

No and she couldn't deny the hypocrisy. Whatever their crimes, she accepted Conn's world and the people in it. Even Strat and his boys once lived on the shadier side of life.

"Conn never hurt anyone I loved."

"Those he did hurt were loved by someone."

Somewhere. Maybe. What about Pietro? Had he been loved? She'd stood there while life slipped out of him. What had she done about that? Nothing. She hadn't objected. In fact, she went straight to the murderer's bed.

"I figured out you were responsible for Grandpapa because you didn't care about finding the murderer. When we were in Stag, everyone else was working hard and offering help, you just sat there. Because all along, you knew who did it." She scoffed in an ironic laugh and sat on the edge of the bed. "Conn said you might not know the trigger man, but you knew more than you were letting on."

Now she wondered if he'd been protecting her from the truth.

"You talked about me?"

"We talked about everything," she said, fighting her urge to snap at his affront. "He was the man I planned to marry. The only man I'd ever consider having a family with. You took that away from me. From us."

"You grieve now," he said, calmer than before. "In time, you'll see I did the right thing. I saved you from him."

She exhaled. "Does it matter? If we can't go back to the city together, you'll have to get rid of me too. How will you explain my disappearance, my murder, to Lachlan? You won't be able to blame it on Conn now, he'll have been found."

God, she needed that to be true.

And there in lay the rub. Her father inhaled and closed his mouth, slowly letting the breath go from his nose.

"If you're going to kill me anyway, just get it over with. It doesn't matter when or where."

"I could never—you're my daughter."

She smiled, though it wasn't in happiness. "Any affection you feel for me comes from Lachlan. Somehow, he taught you that you should care, but you don't need to act anymore. There's no one here but us. You've never liked me. You say I'm too like my mother, is seeing me a reminder of what you've lost? Did you ever love her?"

"I did love your mother. Faults and all."

"You can't even do it, can you? You can't love and just leave it at that. It's always about you, what you need, what you think. How did she live with your constant judgment?

"Your mother and I were happy. She understood the importance of my work. We had respect."

"Are you sure about that? Because I've been inside now, I've seen true love from within. I was never afraid to tell Conn anything, nothing was out of bounds for us. He didn't think about what I'd done wrong or how many mistakes I made, he supported me."

"Easy for someone who sets his own bar so low."

"Oh, that's nice. Killing him wasn't enough, now you have to disrespect his memory? That gun in your hand is looking pretty nice right now. Get it over with, Dad. Put a bullet in me and go back to your life, back to your happiness."

Which definitely didn't come from family. No. He'd killed his father and intended to kill his daughter, how long would Lachlan survive?

"I don't relish any of this."

"What about Lachlan?" she asked because she had to know. "What will you tell him?"

"Your brother is…"

He exhaled and loosened.

Yeah, Lachlan was going to be a problem. One way or another, eventually, he'd uncover the truth. What would happen then?

"He's determined to find Henry's killer. Conn's death, my disappearance…" or death, if they ever found her body. "He'll start putting pieces together and will expect your support." The discerning tilt of her father's brow gave her some inkling she might be getting through. "Think about it. How will you investigate your own crimes? Throw Lachlan off the scent without him knowing you're throwing him off the scent? You might as well kill him too."

The city would notice that, though Ronald would be hailed as a valiant hero for enduring such tragedy. He'd end up in the governor's mansion if he played it right. And all it would take was the death of everyone who shared his blood.

"Lachlan doesn't deserve to die." But others did? "He'll only accept this if…" Struck by an idea, he jerked, regaining his tension. "You will tell him."

"Lachlan? Tell him what?"

"We'll come up with it together, right here, in this room."

"A story?"

A lie. A fable. An untruth.

"Your idea, you said you'd publish a supporting narrative."

"I said that before you killed my boyfriend."

"What is so different now?" he asked, lighter and more optimistic, disgusting her further. "You want to protect your brother, don't you? Any questions of my involvement in Henry's death, in the death of your lowlife lover, they'll damage your brother too. Damage the family."

She didn't care about the McLeod family name. She did care about Lachlan.

"You want me to sell a lie?"

"We'll put it together, us, in a way everyone can accept. We'll answer the questions and put suspicion to rest."

The man had a lot of faith in the power of the pen. Was it possible? Perhaps. Could she do it? *Would* she do it?

What choice did she have?

THREE

TURNED OUT IT was as easy as bribing the caretaker's kid to buy supplies.

No phones. No computers. Everything was done the old-fashioned way, long hand on legal pads. One after another, their failed attempts littered the floor in scrunched balls and torn fragments.

For five whole days, they stayed in that room, together, draft after draft, argument on top of argument. Would they ever come to a consensus? With the curtains perpetually closed and meals only arriving when her father chose to order, she couldn't identify the time of day and still didn't know which state they were in.

Sitting on the floor, back to the end of the bed, she was numb, yet still curious.

"Why did you do it?"

Her father, in the chair by the TV that had never been on, looked her way. "Do what?"

Frayed emotions settled in their intensity. It just wasn't possible to live with such angry hate every minute, especially when they were hardly sleeping.

"Silvio Manzani, was he the first? Who approached you with a bribe?"

"We met. A few years ago, by accident."

"Accident, huh?"

"We were at a city function, a fundraiser for something, I can't remember. I'd stepped out to take a call. When I hung up and turned around, he was in the office with me."

"That's not by accident," she said. "Whether you knew it was going to happen or not, that was deliberate."

"Perhaps. It was harmless conversation, at first. We talked about the city, about a vision of the future. About our differences… our similarities."

"He seduced you, told you what you wanted to hear." Flattered him, no doubt. "Gave you a sense of righteousness. Shit, Dad, you walked right into it."

"What about you?" Though rankle hid in his expression, he did a not so bad job at remaining calm. "How did Ire seduce you away from your family?"

"It wasn't like that," she said, doodling in the top corner of the pad on her folded legs. "Connel and I were entirely mutual in our attraction." Though he'd videoed them, suggesting he intended to play her from the first second. "Conn never promised me anything but truth and he never let me down."

Ronald had torn the phone from the wall on their first day there. That and the TV's power cord had taken a shallow bath, rendering them useless. Any chance of help, of learning the truth of Conn's fate, drowned with those power supplies.

"Ire McDade was a dangerous man."

Past tense. Her father always spoke of him in the past tense. Uncertainty was poisonous… and contagious.

"I never doubted that."

"He could've hurt you."

"He didn't," she said, raising her eyes from the

stag's head she'd drawn. Though smaller, it was a perfect copy of Conn's tattoo. "He'd have done anything for me, Dad. Anything. He loved me."

"Did you consider your family when you were with him? Giving yourself to him?"

"Yes," she said, fighting to restrain herself. "In fact, we broke up once because I couldn't exist in two worlds. He gave me up. He didn't have to make the sacrifice; he did it for me. For the McLeods."

"I didn't go into my deal with Silvio intending to hurt anyone."

"These things always start with one small step," she said. "Doing the right thing never starts with doing the wrong thing."

"Your brother's words."

"He's right. It's always him, don't you see? Lachlan is the best of us. Mom and Grandpapa are gone. You and I are damaged, broken. The only hope for the McLeod family is Lachlan's purity. He wants to do good, to be good."

"He was raised with integrity."

"No thanks to you," she said. "Lachlan spent most of his youth raising me. He spent most of his life setting a good example for me."

"Is that what angers you? Why you chose to give yourself to…? You blame me for neglecting you?"

"No, actually," she said, perspective adjusting. "My brother raised me with love and was an excellent role model. I adore my brother. Which you know, that's why you used him to get me into that room with Silvio. Lach puts me, us, ahead of everything else in his life."

Maybe that was it. Lachlan wanted to raise her right, so hadn't taken advantage of the easy route, the reckless route, if ever offered to him. Choice over his character, his actions, was influenced by his need to set an example for her, and the expectation of the McLeod generations above him. Had her brother ever done something for him, been his true self, or was his entire life crafted by conformity?

"Sometimes we have to value more than one thing. My work with the city—"

"If we've accomplished any kind of truce in the last five days, can we at least be honest with each other? You enjoyed the attention. It's no shame, it's allowed. You were in control at work, felt important, you got a recognition there that you didn't get with your family."

"Silvio, more than once, brought you and your brother into conversation. Your safety was a concern." Before it became about money, maybe. "A man like that can... I did stand up for you, for my family."

"Threats are one thing, but the bigger picture... Maybe now with Grandpapa gone, it's more precarious, but Silvio couldn't have hurt Lachlan. Wouldn't have. And Evander's attention, it's been a part of my adult life as far back as I remember."

"Silvio is not close to his youngest son."

The Manzani obsessed with her.

"No. You weren't close to your children either."

"I stood up for you."

"And I did the same," she said. "Maybe we both started out trying to do the expected thing, the default thing, in standing up for our family. But now..." Everything seemed warped, every memory unreliable. "I don't know what we were doing, either of us."

Giving themselves permission to do whatever they truly wanted. That's what they'd been doing. Stacking their selfish desires under a false umbrella of virtue gave them a righteous, ridiculous excuse. They weren't thinking about the family, they were thinking about themselves.

A pause lingered. Neither waited for anything, they just sat with themselves for a minute. Who was she without Connel? Her life had been molded by the men in it. First Lachlan, her work at the Chronicler, Evander, the Manzanis, the McDades, Conn… Her morals twisted in the wind, catering to whatever the moment required. It never scared her to be near Conn. In spite of what he'd done, even in her company, disgust, fear, neither visited when he was around.

Conn would never be with her again, and her grandfather was out of the picture. Who was she without them? Who did she want to be? The McLeod restraints disappeared when she admitted her relationship with Connel. Since being free of judgment, she hadn't paused to figure out if there were other facets of herself she wanted to explore.

Lach. It came back to him, didn't it? Without Conn, her life stalled. Maybe it was her turn to look after her brother, to prioritize him, like he'd done when she needed him. He'd lost so much. His relationship, his apartment, maybe that's why he moved in with her, to get away from his own grief. He'd said she needed a keeper, maybe it was him, maybe he needed one. Had he come to her for support in the wake of his heartache? What had she done? Thrown her relationship in his face and moved out. Great job, Sersha. Just great.

"I do enjoy being important," her father said, surprising her with candor. "And I never was with you."

"Important?"

"You respected your brother. Idolized him. You clung to him, hung on his every word. He got through to you in a way I never could."

"You could've tried."

"I did."

"Harder. You could've tried harder. I lost my mother. I was the only female in our family; I've always been out of place with the three of you. Lachlan was the only person ever happy to see me, ever aware of me and my safety, my comfort. He cared about me. I never got that from you, or from Grandpapa, not really."

"We're a different generation."

"That's an excuse," she said. "You gave yourself the out and put my wellbeing, my upbringing, on Lachlan's shoulders when he was just a kid himself. A grieving kid. I've always thought it must've been more difficult for him. He had memories. He missed the woman our mother was. I missed a specter, a glimmer of an illusion. My mother was whatever I made up in my head, whatever Lachlan gave me. I pieced together the puzzle from photographs and whispered lullabies."

"I never intended to do it alone. We were supposed to do it together, raise a family together—"

"You blame her?"

"No." Something wistful touched his words. "I was lost. She left me lost. And I didn't like that, I can— I'm used to being in control."

"And you were alone." She got it. More now as an adult than had been possible as a child. "You expected to be half of a whole and the other half suddenly vanished. Maybe you did deserve a better hand than you got, maybe not. At least you got the chance to be with her, to be married and have two children with her." She licked her lips. "You've taken that chance from me."

"Ire McDade was not a suitable partner," he said, stern in his disapproval, nothing new. "A life with him would've been intolerable."

"Now we'll never know." She didn't need to experience it to know she'd have been happy in a life with Conn. "Does it mean nothing to you that he showed me love? That with him, I learned what it was to be truly accepted, to be happy?"

She didn't envy his conflict. Ire McDade, as her father knew him, was the epitome of a bad boy. No father, no regular father, would want his precious daughter with such a dangerous individual. He seemed to conveniently forget that he was no regular father. And that she was in no way "precious" to him. Their relationship, though it was changing in these days they spent together, wasn't traditional either.

What kind of a daughter could sit with the murderous man responsible for the death of her love and the family's patriarch, and accept his criminal acts? She didn't accept them with happiness; no, happiness went away with Conn. But life with the McDades, the life she'd lived through her work, taught her normality was relative.

"We should get back to work," her father said. "We're close on this draft."

Inhaling a deep breath, her eyes went back to the page as she prepared to read, again, their latest—

A knock brought their gazes together.

A knock. On the door.

"Did you order food?" she whispered.

Her father shook his head, bringing the gun to his hip as he rose to go to the window.

Should she call out? Why? So her father could shoot someone else? If they didn't find common ground, a compromising resolution, only one of them could go back to their life in the city.

Though the value of her existence, without Conn, put a question mark over her desire to breathe. Without him, it didn't matter much where she was or what happened. Spending time with her father was exhausting; how much fight did she have left in the tank?

With the barrel of the gun, Ronald edged the curtain aside and immediately leaped back. "Shit."

"What is it?" she asked, probably louder than she should've. "Dad?"

"Fuck," he hissed but went to unlock the door.

"Dad, what is—" He opened it and stepped aside to show their guest. "Lach!"

FOUR

TEARS OF JOY and sorrow sprang to her eyes. Jumping up to—she rebounded to the floor, the cuff attached to the wheel of the bed pulled her down.

Lachlan immediately frowned. "What the hell is going on?"

"How did you find us?" her father asked.

"That's your first question? Why the hell is Sers—"

"Conn," she said, swiping at her tears. "Is he alive?"

"Alive?" Confusion deepened her brother's uncertainty. "Someone better—"

"Lach, please…" Her heart pounded as desperation leaped in her belly. "Have you seen him? Since we disappeared, have you—"

"No."

Air did reach her lungs, yet all vestige of hope seeped out of her. She sank against the bed again.

"How did you find us, Lachlan?" her father asked.

Lachlan stepped in and slammed the door behind him. "Maybe we start with one of you telling me what the fuck is going on."

"We've been… talking."

"Talking," Lachlan said, his attention deliberately falling to the weapon in their father's hand. "And the suppressed firearm is what? Like the talking stick?"

Why would Conn avoid her brother? He wouldn't. If she'd gone missing, and Conn lived, he'd move heaven and earth to get her back. Which would mean working with her brother who had access to police resources. That her lover hadn't reached out, hadn't contacted her brother, didn't bode well. The only explanation was he didn't make it. She'd lost him.

"We had a confrontation."

"Uh huh," Lachlan said, coming to crouch by her. "With who?"

He unlocked the cuffs and she threw both arms around him, burying her face in his neck. For the first time, her grief wasn't unjust, it wasn't a ridiculed hinderance. Support. Love. Everything her brother's presence offered, she lapped up, absorbing him, using him to keep herself breathing.

"I knew you'd come."

"Damn right, I came," he said and eased her back to check her bruised, cut wrists. "How long has she been in cuffs?"

"Since we left the city," she answered. "He cuffs me to the shower rail when I wash, and to him and the bed when we sleep."

Lachlan surged to his feet, taking her with him in his embrace. "Someone better start talking."

"I need your phone."

"No!" her father exclaimed. "You do not—"

"You can't stop me! You won't hurt your beloved son, will you?"

"Who else knows you're here?" her father asked Lachlan.

"Don't answer that." So much for their tentative peace. "Don't give him more targets."

"Targets?"

"Lach, you didn't believe me about Silvio Manzani—"

"What did you tell him?" her affronted father demanded. "You didn't—"

"Tell you the full truth?" she spat. "Of course I didn't. How does it feel to be in the dark?" She grabbed her brother's hand. "We have to get out of here. We have to—"

"Whoa, whoa, slow down."

"We can't," she yelped. "If he gets control, if he has the chance—you can't get trapped here too. I couldn't get away alone—"

"You're not alone," her brother said. God, if only she could be so optimistic. "Whatever's going on, we'll work it out."

She shook her head. "He doesn't want to figure it out. And I need to find my guy."

"Why are you so worried about Ire?"

She pushed out of his arms. "You don't think if I went missing, he'd do anything to find me?"

"Until right now, I didn't know for sure who you disappeared with."

"Dad and it wasn't voluntary." As the cuffs attested. "I don't want to leave you here. He's unhinged and—"

"Sersha! I did what was necessary."

"The truth," Lachlan said, tucking her under his arm. "Trust me, Sersh, you're safe now."

"Sorry if I find that difficult to believe. My father has held me captive for almost a week. He lured me to a meeting that he said would save your life. Instead, Silvio

Manzani walked in and Conn got shot."

"Conn? Ire? How is he involved?"

"He came to the meet with me—"

"Sersha, stop this," her father demanded, marching over.

On instinct, she put herself between him and Lachlan. "If you're going to shoot someone else, make it me. Please."

"No one is shooting anyone," Lachlan stated. "Put the gun down, Dad."

"I can't." Rather than put it away, he raised it toward the ceiling, shaking it, emphasizing his dominance. "Our lives hang in the balance."

"Why's that?" she asked. "Because you took Manzani money and didn't deliver? Or because you murdered the head of the McDade family?"

"Murder?" Lachlan asked. "He's dead? Why did you ask me if—"

"If you haven't heard from him and he's not here, death is a given." She took his hand. "We need to get out of here before we're next."

"I need to know what's going on."

Part of her wanted to run for the door, to just get the hell out of there in a hurry. Lachlan meant something to their father, father wouldn't murder son, would he? That wasn't a reliable measure. If pressed, she'd have guessed father wouldn't kill grandfather.

"We were in bed," she said to her brother though her focus was on their father. "Conn and me. It was the middle of the night. I got a call from Dad, he said I had to meet him at Grandpapas, that your life depended on it."

"Alone. I told you we had to meet alone! You brought him. He was there because you—"

"I know that! Don't you think I know that? Connel was in that room because of me. You put a bullet meant for me into him."

"Wait a fucking minute," Lachlan said, heavy anger in his slow tone. "You took a shot at your daughter?"

"It's only thanks to Conn I'm here." He'd given his life for hers. "Don't be shocked, brother," she said, folding her arms. "Turns out Ronald here is responsible for Grandpapa's murder too."

"What?"

"Sersha!"

"If you're only going to shoot me anyway, someone has to know the truth. Yes, Lach, our father killed our grandfather; that is why I want to get the hell out of here."

"No, no, it can't…"

"It can," she said, not envying Lachlan the shock. "Please, trust me."

"I trust you, I can't…"

As Lachlan dropped to sit on the end of the bed, she missed the stability of his stable form. Throwing something like that at him, a fact that shook the foundations of his world, wasn't fair.

"Your sister doesn't know what she's talking about," their father asserted.

Sitting by her brother, she held his hand and stroked his forearm. "This is a lot, and I'm sorry, I… I learned my lesson about keeping secrets. The only way we get through this is if everyone knows everything. And now I know I can't trust him, I don't want you to take the risk of doing the same."

Her brother's head came up fast. "Sersha's attack, did you know?" The gun in their father's hand descended to his side as the man averted his gaze. "You did, didn't you? Everything Sersha said was true. You tried to get that information from her for Silvio Manzani. When that didn't work, he sent his guys after her. You let me think it was—you put it on Ire—"

"It was his fault! She was in his territory!"

"You didn't know about their relationship then," Lachlan said. "You didn't know she was under his protection."

"No one was supposed to touch her there, it wasn't meant to happen that night. That wasn't the plan." That there had been one at all was shocking enough. "Silvio had people watching her, monitoring her movements, who she talked to."

Because watching her was easier than following Ire McDade. She'd been the oblivious fly caught in Silvio Manzani's web.

"What changed?" Lachlan asked. "What did she do to deserve—"

"She was refused entry that night. At Stag. They turned her away. We didn't expect that." Both men looked at her though her father quickly returned his appeal to Lachlan. "The McDades blocked her… Silvio's men told him what happened and he decided that was the time, the moment. I wasn't consulted. Silvio Manzani doesn't ask my permission before making decisions." Though her father wouldn't mind people thinking he had that kind of sway. "I asked, I demanded to know what happened."

"And?"

Their father exhaled. "That was an opportunity they couldn't pass up. With the McDades rejecting her entry, she would be angry, maybe she'd seen more than they wanted her to see. The only way to—don't you see they only wanted words, names, why would she endure—"

"They didn't care about names," she murmured. "Not as much as you want to think. Men like that don't have finesse, they don't have patience. They think with their fists, with their dicks, and that's exactly what happened."

"You weren't raped," he sneered, diminishing her trauma.

Was that meant to be a comfort? Odd the justifications her father could make. Maybe they were all guilty of it, believing what they wanted to believe just to get through the day.

"You let them put their hands on her," Lachlan growled. "She could've died!"

"Not if she'd answered them! I was sure she would! How could I know she'd been seduced by that animal? That he forced himself on her?"

Lachlan whipped around fast. "Forced?"

"Connel never forced himself on me," she said with renewed anger toward their patriarch. "Which I told you, Ronald, you know that."

"He made you think you had a choice." That her father could be so dismissive hurt more with the knowledge he'd just as easily shrugged off Conn's life. "You've never been strong. Not strong enough to—"

The door opened. No knock this time, just a man filling the frame.

A man who breathed new life into her determination.

Without the cuffs hindering her this time, she leaped up and ran to him. "Strat!"

"You wanna watch your fucking mouth, Superintendent. You have no idea about her strength," Strat said, locking an arm under her ribs to pick her up and carry her inside. "You don't have a fucking clue!"

"Who are you to speak to me like that? You don't know my family! How did you find us?"

FIVE

"I WOULDN'T HAVE found you without him," Lachlan said. When Strat put her down, she came up against her brother who'd come to join them. "We found her together."

Her? Had they been looking for Ronald at all?

They must've known father and daughter were together. Strat saw them together in his parking lot.

"You have no idea how amazing it is to see you."

Burying her face against Strat, the tears that warmed her eyes were far more vulnerable than before. Her brother gave her security, safety, but Strat gave her acceptance, support. She didn't have to wonder if Strat would let her grieve, approval and latitude were absolute with him.

"Conn," she whispered, probing the new source. Laying a hand on Strat's chest, she pushed back. "Have you seen Conn?"

Strat shook his head. "Haven't seen him since before you ran off. You think he's dead."

"Can I have your phone?" She didn't want to confirm, or even acknowledge, her fears. "Did you call the boss?"

"Called and called, voicemail every time. No one's picking up."

What happened when the leader was snuffed out? Where did that put Niall, the lieutenant, and those loyal to him? More than not picking up, if the phones were going direct to voicemail, they were off, that meant tracing them wouldn't be possible.

"Did you go to the club? To Stag?"

"It's open. Business as usual. On certain floors."

"Did you—"

"No business there, club only."

And she couldn't press for details with her father loitering over her shoulder.

"He shot him," Lachlan said while she and Strat spoke silently with their gazes. "You did shoot him, didn't you, Ron? Did you murder Ire McDade like you murdered Henry?"

That truth startled Strat. "What?"

"Yes," she said. "Like we thought, Henry was asking questions. Ronald here told him to stop, they got in a fight, I guess and—"

"You murdered him," Lachlan said, capturing her loose hand. "Jesus fuck, Dad. You murdered him!"

The shock was understandable, but she didn't have time to sit around and wait for her brother to process.

"We need to go," she said to Strat. "Can you hotwire your own car?"

"Why would I—"

"The keys are under the TV, and I don't trust my father not to hurt you."

"No one is hurting anyone," Lachlan said, putting himself in front of them. "Where are the keys, Ron?"

"You have to understand what you're doing.

What going back there will mean—"

"I don't have time for this." Crazy and misguided as it might be, hope found light in her saviors. "I need to know."

"Do not let her walk out—"

"We're all going together. Get the keys, Dad."

"No! We need time, look at this mess, we can't leave it here."

"What is it?" Strat asked, just like Lachlan, he inspected their littered confinement.

"He wants me to write it," she said. "Write him out of a murder charge."

"Print something in the paper that paints him as the victim?"

When put that way, the idea didn't seem so great. Her friend never did pull his punches when it came to her father.

"Trash it or bring it," Lachlan said. "Give me the gun, Dad."

"No."

"Are you going to shoot someone?"

Someone else, he meant.

"I have to maintain—Sersha is unreasonable."

When Lachlan took a step, panic prompted her to go too. Except Strat apparently sensed that need and tightened his hold on her.

"You're not going to shoot your own daughter. Whatever you've done, I'm sure you have your reasons. We'll talk in the car, you can't stay here."

No because they were traceable. Of all the people on the look out for them, Lachlan and Strat knew them best. Not everyone had their strength or resources. Still, it wasn't impossible other parties may be on their tail.

"You can't let her—"

"Sersha's not our enemy."

Amazing how Lachlan could stay so calm.

Creeping closer, hand outstretched, he couldn't understand the threat of their father. If he went crazy, if he started shooting, he better take her too. Lachlan and Strat were all she had left in the world. Without them, she would have no reason to go on.

"She knows. She'll talk."

"Woman keeps secrets bigger than this every day," Strat mumbled. "He's a fucking maniac."

Maybe it was in the blood.

If Lachlan hadn't been the first, if Conn found her instead, Ronald McLeod would be dead already. She shouldn't wish that fate on her own father, but what other possible resolution could there be?

"I need to find out," she whispered to her friend. "I need to know if he's alive."

"What the fuck happened?"

Raising her eyes to his, she wanted to pour out her pain. Somehow, Strat always brought her clarity. Something she needed right then; she'd needed it all week.

"Dad," Lachlan said, stopping in front of him. "Please. We need to figure this out as a family. Trust me, we will work it out."

Did he mean that? Lachlan didn't lie, he just didn't. But how could he accept their father was a murderer with barely a hitch? All that cop training paid off. That had to be the answer. This was his job, what he was good at. Keep a cool head, use soothing force, gentle direction. And it worked too because Ronald slapped the gun onto Lachlan's hand.

Good.

The only sane one among them should have responsibility for the weapon. And almost as expected, the first thing Lachlan did was rid the weapon of its ammunition. Separating one from the other gave them another line of security.

"Okay, if this paper is important, gather it up. Then we're getting in the car and leaving here. Together."

SIX

LACHLAN AND STRAT'S car was a rental. Her brother texted the agency for pick up and left the keys with the guy at motel reception.

They bundled into Strat's car, with him driving and her shotgun, and got to the highway without saying a word.

"How long will it take to get back?" she asked, calling number after number in Strat's phone. Just as he'd said, no McDade phone was on. "How far are we from home?"

"It's him. That's all you care about," her father said. "You have no concept of what the rest of us are going back to."

"Oh, I have a pretty good idea," she said, choosing to text the same numbers, just in case. She had to be doing something. "You're going back to a prison cell."

"You have no proof of anything." Good point. "I'll deny everything and people will listen to me. No one will take you seriously, there will be no investigation. You have no credibility."

Huh, yeah, if she went back shouting out Ronald's guilt, who would believe her? The woman in bed with a McDade, enemy to men like her father.

Lachlan wasn't to be underestimated. "Is the suppressed firearm the murder weapon?"

"That's proof."

"Proof of nothing. The gun isn't registered to me."

She didn't want to ask who it was registered to or how he'd come into possession of it.

"I can't believe this," Lachlan murmured. "I can't believe any of this." Her heart hurt for him. "I told Sersha she was full of shit when she told me about you and Manzani, but it was true, wasn't it?"

"You shouldn't believe everything your sister says. Ire has been pouring poison into her for weeks, months."

Strat glanced at her. "Take it things went the McDade way?"

With the Harvest deal. Had voting been that week? Maybe.

"For all the difference it will make if Conn's gone," she said. "I don't know how the cards will fall without…" Her voice cracked, so she cleared her throat. "Sorry."

He reached over to squeeze her hand. "That fucking bastard won't die so easy. He's out there."

She hoped so.

"Have you tried hospitals?" Lachlan asked.

"He wouldn't go to a hospital."

"Where would he go?"

She twisted to glare. "You better not be pumping me for information with ideas of bringing down my guy when your own father is a murderer. Whether Conn is alive or dead, our father killed our grandpapa, he did. Can you believe that? I couldn't… Let it sink in. It's all about Manzani. About power. Greed. Money. Our father killed our grandfather because he promised Silvio Manzani votes. Henry was smarter than him, smarter than both of them, he was asking questions. He knew something was going on, something was happening, and he wanted to stop it."

"Did he know?" Lachlan asked, though not of her. "Did Henry find out you were working with Manzani?" Ronald said nothing. "I'll back her. Don't doubt it, Dad. You can dismiss Sersh as crazy, deluded, whatever, but I'll be with her. You better be ready to trash both of us."

He'd stand with her because it was the right thing to do, because it was right for their grandfather's memory.

"I already told her if she comes for me, I come for the McDades."

"Then you better hope Ire is alive," Strat said. "He's the only one who'll listen to her, and she's your only chance of getting out of this with your life."

"The McDades will come for him." She exhaled and settled in her seat again. "I guess it's all moot. Why shout about his crimes to the authorities when the families in the city will run him out on a rail? He took the money and failed to deliver. He put a bullet in one McDade and held another captive for almost a week."

"Not much of a future."

"You threaten me while allying yourself with a criminal."

"Who's a criminal?" Strat asked.

"Ire! Ire McDade!"

"Oh, really?" her friend played it straight. "I didn't know that about him." They shared a smile. "I'd love to see the proof of that."

If the authorities had enough to bring down

Conn, they'd have done it. Just like her father claimed now, that she had no proof, he wouldn't have sufficient proof to back up his claims either.

"You're both hypocrites."

Her friend's wrist slid to the top of the wheel. "Say that's true, we're hypocrites and you're both murderers, you and Ire, like say, hypothetically, it's true. There's still one major difference."

"What's that?"

"Ire loved her, loves her." More support from her friend. If she wasn't ready to accept Conn's death, Strat wouldn't either. "She is loyal to him and his people because they all love her. She's one of them. One of us. She isn't on the outside, she isn't judged. Sersha cares about people. You have no fucking idea how far she's gone to protect the people she cares about. People I care about. Hell, to protect practical strangers. And that's without breaking the law." Though could be classed as the gray zone. "Your daughter is an amazing woman, strong and virtuous…" maybe, sometimes. "You should be proud of her, support her. Maybe if you had…"

She wouldn't have ended up in Conn's bed? They wouldn't be in this mess?

"If she comes for me, if any of you come for me, I guarantee I'll be the last one standing."

"Because you'll abuse your position. Just like you abuse the city's faith. Like you abused your father's trust."

"I won't take this. You class yourself as a McDade," her father said. "Judge one by one measure and use another for others? I won't take it. It's a double standard." The truth, unfortunately. "You have no proof of your claims, and I control anyone who might investigate them, which means, like I said, no investigation."

"Resign." A single word from Lachlan, who'd

been quiet for a while. "Resign your position." In silence, they reflected on the suggestion. Well, she did, her father was probably dumbfounded. "Today. Right now. Email in your resignation."

"I will not! Why would I—"

"Because you're not the right man for the job, you don't understand it. Proposing to use your position in order to free yourself from a criminal charge proves you don't understand it. Henry would've insisted on this. You know that. You know he would. That's why you shot him, why you killed him, right? He found out you were in Manzani's pocket and influencing others to accept his bribes? There are repercussions for that, for what you did. You can't just get away with doing what you want and lining your own pockets."

And that was before addressing him being a murderer. Ronald seemed to be taking the fifth.

"I agree," she said, backing up her brother. "Resign. You expect us to cover up your crimes? To stay silent? You can't walk back into your life like nothing's changed."

"No one would believe it. Why would I suddenly give up a role I value? I excel in it, it's my life, my purpose—"

"Your family," Lachlan said. "You're giving it up to spend more time with your family."

"People would believe that," Strat offered. "You did just lose someone. Puts things in perspective."

For some people, not the one holding the gun and pulling the trigger, apparently.

"And you don't excel in it," she said. "Your job is literally to uphold the law. Didn't Conn remind you that you're supposed to obey it too?"

"How could you do it?" Lachlan asked. "Henry was—he didn't deserve—I can't believe you'd walk in there and shoot your own father. He wouldn't have seen you coming, wouldn't have thought anything about letting you in to talk. You took advantage of his trust."

Exactly what she'd said.

"Ron's not the man we thought he was," she said.

"You've been telling me that for years. I should've listened. I'm sorry I—"

"It's not your fault that you wanted to see the best in him, Lach. You idolized him. We see what we want to see."

"I'm not a monster," her father hissed. "Neither of you understand. It wasn't meant to—I didn't mean to… I didn't go there intending to hurt anyone."

"Except you took a gun, one not registered to you," Strat said. "Kinda kills that argument. Why go armed if you didn't intend to hurt anyone? And if it was for protection, in case laws were broken, don't you have a service weapon?"

"This has nothing to do with you!"

Oh, her father was getting catty in all the wrong ways. She twisted, grabbing the headrest to get a better look at Ronald.

"I would walk into fire for Strat," she said, narrowing her eyes. "I haven't even decided if I'll let you live yet."

"Sersh," Lachlan warned.

"Accidents befall people all the time, Lach. Especially out on the open road."

Strat's warm laugh appreciated her.

Lachlan's scowl did not. "Sersh."

"Okay," she said, holding up her hands as she bounced back in her seat. "I'll behave."

"Never do for anyone else," Strat said from the corner of his mouth and winked her way.

SEVEN

THEY DROVE THROUGH the night and stopped for gas at first light. Strat got out and she wasn't far behind.

"Stay here, Dad," Lachlan said as her door closed, then followed her out. "Sersh, we have to talk about this."

"Not where he can hear us." She went to stand a couple of yards from the hood, her brother on her heels. "What do you want?"

"What do I—don't start giving me the attitude."

She exhaled and took his hand. "I'm sorry, I don't mean to… I've had a pretty shitty week."

"Sounds like it. You really think Ire is dead?"

"I think I'm going crazy not knowing. I know you don't like him, Lach. You think he's wrong for me, that he's caused problems, and—"

"What the fuck do I know? I trusted our father. Clearly, you're a better judge of character than I am."

"Don't think that way, everyone trusts their parents."

"You didn't," he said and scrubbed a hand

through his hair. "We could take him in."

"And then what? He said it, we have no proof."

"We could get him on tape."

Ironic that the suggestion put a bad taste in her mouth. "I want him to rot in hell for killing Henry and shooting Conn…"

"But…?"

"A trial? What else will be dragged up?"

"You mean about us?"

"I mean about him," she said, lowering her volume. "Do we want the world to know he's in league with Silvio Manzani? The don, Lach, how long has it been going on? What else might they have done?"

"Every prosecution he's ever been a part of will be scrutinized. Every exoneration too. They'll reopen cases—"

"Maybe let worse people out in the world?"

"Would everyone believe we didn't know or will they assume…? My investigations could be open to inspection too."

"You do good work. And though our father is the lowest of the low, I'd like to think that at some point in his life, he put away people who deserved it."

"I'll support whatever you want me to support."

That was… "You will?"

"He deserves to go to prison for what he's done, but bringing a cloud over our family, over all the work we've done… and Henry's memory too… I don't know, is that right? And we'd have to testify." Did either of them want to do that against their own father? And Conn, if he was alive… "They wouldn't miss a chance to put Ire on the stand either."

She held her breath for a second. Man, her brother really was good at his job.

"He'll plead the fifth," she said. "We'll all plead the fifth."

"Then we might as well join Ron in custody. You know what's inferred from a Fifth defense."

Shit, thanks, Dad, they were painted into a corner. It was inevitable they'd be dragged down with him if they tossed him to the authorities.

"I can't believe this…"

That their father's misdeeds brought them to that point. That untenable point.

"All the evidence we gathered." Lachlan seemed bewildered. "The statements we took and footage, how did we not know he was at Henry's that night? Why didn't anyone mention him?"

"Lupe wasn't there. Sneddon was the only one in the building."

"And he's the type of guy who wants the superintendent to owe him."

"That and there's the tunnel."

"Tunnel?"

"See!" she exclaimed and socked his shoulder. "I didn't know about it either!"

"What tunnel?"

"From prohibition days apparently. It's how Dad brought me out of the house without Conn's guys seeing. Must've been how he got in to visit Henry the night he killed him too. Lupe was the only one with a key. We thought Lupe was the only one with a key. I don't know how or why dad got one."

"We have to decide," Lach said. "Are we taking him in?"

Without proof? "We could talk to Lupe again, Sneddon, see if they'll be more honest now we know what happened."

"If they truly didn't know anything, we can't ask them to embellish their statements just because we've identified the guilty party. We have the murder weapon."

Which was just disgusting. "With your prints on

it too. They can't test him and his clothes for gunshot residue, it's been too long."

"Ballistics will match," he said. "The gun to the crime, not the crime to the man. Though if he did kill Conn with it."

She flattened a hand on her stomach. "I can't even think about it."

Lach pulled her into a hug and kissed the top of her head. "This is difficult for me."

"Dad was your hero. I understand that—"

"No," he interjected. "Seeing how you love him, how much you love him."

Conn.

Her eyes closed. "Sometimes it hits me and I feel sick. I don't want to go on, I want to lay down and…" Pushing out of his arms, she wiped the moisture from the corner of her eyes. "I told myself I wouldn't believe it until I saw him. Until I actually lay eyes on…"

"Ire's a tough sonofabitch."

"You better believe it." Because she did. "You know you have a lot in common. He lost his mother young, around the same age you did."

"Conversation tips?"

"Very funny." Like tragedy would be something the men could talk about and bond over. "They may not be the same as yours, but he's a man with morals and integrity. You look at things from different angles, but there's a lot of you in him."

"I don't wish him dead, if that's what you think of me."

"You wouldn't wish anyone dead, Lach. No part of you could—maybe that's the worst thing."

"Worst thing?"

"About what Dad's done. Killing Henry was— it's abominable, unimaginable, but I hate him more for letting you down."

He touched her cheek. "I'm not as perfect as you think."

"I don't think you're perfect, no one's perfect."

"I'll get over it. You think I've never been let down before? The two of you always butted heads, which put me in the middle. Dad expected a lot, expected me to be a certain way. Now it's almost as if…"

"The chains have come off," she said, her smile tight. "It's how I felt after admitting I was Conn's alibi. I never wanted to hurt you; I didn't mean to fall in love with him. But being without him, existing every day apart from him… After telling the truth, I could be me, the truest version of me."

"And Ronald's struggled to accept that."

Their father's morals had never been hers. Obviously they hadn't been her father's either. Maybe it all came down to Henry. They each tried to make him proud with their grandfather's impetus.

"There's something to be said for freeing yourself from other people's constraints."

"Don't you have new ones? Identifying as a McDade puts a different pressure on you."

"No." She shook her head; her smile loosened a little. "Maybe it's because I'm at the top or because he loves me, but the McDades accept everything, Conn accepts everything. Everything about me, Lach. The worst of me, the mistakes, the lies and the truths, I tell him everything and he never judges, he never punishes, he supports me. More than that, he helps me, encourages me."

"Maybe all this has taught us not to be so quick to judge by what's on the surface."

"He's no saint."

"Are any of us?" he asked and put an arm around her. "Dad has to give up his post."

"For family. Yes. And we don't take reporting

him off the table. It's selfish, but all I can think about now is—"

"Finding Ire." And with a head bob, he guided her back to the car. "We'll get Dad working on that resignation email."

"Okay, just don't do anything final… yet." Lach kissed her cheek and got back into the car. The male McLeods could probably use a minute alone. Her focus landed on Strat. "You found me."

"Yeah," he said, gas still pumping into the car. "Don't make me regret that. Might lose you again just as quick."

"Will you help me find him?"

"You know I will."

"And if he's…."

"Whatever we need to do, we'll do, Scamp. What were you and the cop talking about? Daddy?"

"I can't think straight about anything. Lach's right that Dad has to give up his job. You can't be a corrupt murderer and run the city's police department, that's just crazy."

"You're hesitating because you want to talk to him," Strat said and their eyes met. "Ire, you want his take before settling on a plan."

"Is that such a bad thing?"

"No. Providing your brother knows this is a three-way decision, it's not just you and him."

"It's a decision for all the people who know, Lach, me, Conn—when I tell him, and you."

"I don't want the decision." He took the nozzle from the car and hung it up again. "After this week, I'm taking a vacation."

"A vacation? Where?"

"My apartment."

She laughed. "Haven't you missed my craziness this week?"

"That's one way to put it." He went around the back of the car. "Want anything from inside?"

"They'll be coming for me, you know." Strat stopped. "The Manzanis. They might want my dad for failing to deliver, but they'll be coming for me too."

"And they're already gunning for the McDades." If only she could talk to Whisper, find out what happened at the prison with Biz. "This is good."

Startled, she blinked at her friend. "Good?"

"They're spreading themselves thin. Silvio's got an idea what he's doing, but he can't rely on Vex to back him up."

Evander "Vex" Manzani, another potential corpse on her conscience. "You heard anything from Evander this week?"

"Vex doesn't usually check in with me." His chin rose as his focus narrowed. "Why?"

"You don't want me to answer that question. You'll thank me for the ignorance one day."

"With you, Scamp, these things always come out in the end."

Maybe. "We'll find Conn, get drunk, and then decide if you want another crime on your rap sheet."

"There's one up side."

"What's that?"

"Life in prison's a shorter stretch for me than it will be for you."

She laughed. Trust Strat to be the one brightening her day.

"I'm coming in with you," she said, coiling an arm around Strat's to walk across the forecourt with him. "I haven't eaten properly in days."

"You buying?"

"IOU," she said, peeking up at him. "My purse is still in the back of Conn's car somewhere."

Though her wallet itself was at the loft. They'd

left their bed, their room, their home, believing they'd be back in an hour, maybe two. Would everything be as they left it?

"What you thinking about?"

"The loft," she said, ducking under his arm when he held the door open for her. "Did you go there?"

"No answer."

Didn't mean there wasn't anybody there. Strat wouldn't get inside on his own. As far as she knew, he'd only been there with other McDade men, people who'd likely have the code, or had the door opened for them.

Though what reason would Conn, or any McDade, have for barring her friend? Strat was one of them and could be key to tracking her down. As evidenced by the fact that he did.

"He's out there, isn't he?"

"We'll find him, Scamp."

Maybe, but what state would he be in when they did?

EIGHT

THE CLOSER THEY got to the city, the harder her heart pumped. The increasing darkness cocooned them, deepening with each minute that passed. Welcome darkness. Night meant activity, meant hope. The people she needed to see, the man she needed to see, thrived in the dark.

"Where am I going?" Strat asked from the driver's seat. "Yours, mine, the cop's—"

"I'll take Dad back to mine," Lachlan said. "We need to talk."

Have at it. She'd gone beyond her tolerance level for "alone" with their father. Lachlan deserved his own stretch. There would be a lot they'd want to say to each other that she didn't need to hear. Besides she wanted to get alone with Strat. And alone with her guy, wherever he was.

"That's your old place, right?" Strat asked and she nodded.

"You live with him? McDade?" Ronald demanded with pure outrage. "Permanently?"

"That's a good way to define it, yes."

Her jaw pushed forward. All she had to do was get through a few more minutes. Thank God she wasn't armed. Though the club, Stag's basement, sprang to mind. What would her guy do to get some time alone down there with the good superintendent? What would she do for the same? If any of her people, those that knew her, were in there… God, she needed them to be.

Conn told her she'd never be refused entry to Stag again. What if he was gone? What happened then? Would whoever assumed control grant her access? Would she ever know the truth? This was what she did. Inhaling determination, she had to hold on, couldn't lose it, not yet. Not until he was with her, until they were together again.

"Every minute I learn—"

"You don't learn, Dad," she said on a sigh. "You haven't learned. Still you sit there judging me. How is me living with the man I love worse than you selling out every citizen of this city?"

"You believe the McDades deserved to win that vote; that their vision for our home was better. I believe the Manzani vision is more appealing."

"Is there anything you don't tell yourself to justify your betrayal? You sold your soul to the devil for nothing."

"What did you sell yours for?"

"Ask me again tomorrow."

Strat stopped the car at their destination, which couldn't have come quick enough.

Lachlan's head appeared between them from the backseat. "You staying with her tonight?"

"I'm staying with Conn tonight," she said before Strat could answer.

"Checking you'll be safe, sister, not trying to chase you off your hunt." He kissed her cheek quick.

"We'll get you a phone tomorrow."

"You can call Strat if you need me. He'll know where I am."

"Yeah, I've figured that out about him." Her brother actually smacked Strat's shoulder like they were buds. "Keep me in the loop." Her brother urged Ronald out. "Let's go."

They sat there in the car, her and Strat, even after father and son had gone inside.

"You sure you want to do this tonight?" Strat asked. "It's late."

"The club'll be open."

"I know—"

"No, I mean…" Her focus tracked to him. "I need the club first. Please."

Her sanctuary. The place he'd taken her to find her equilibrium when she'd spiraled before. Without question, Strat peeled away from the curb.

"If he's hurt bad—"

"I can handle it."

"You gonna let me finish a sentence?"

Sealing her lips, she pushed them to the side. Yes, adrenaline coursed through her. Fear, hope, anger, need, so much of it swirled in her veins, she couldn't settle on exactly how to feel.

"Sorry. Go on."

"Okay. We have to think about this is all. If he's hurt bad, he won't be anywhere the other families can get word about it."

Because losing Conn damaged the family. Weakened their position, unless someone else had taken the wheel. Conn would want the family strong. Any inference of the opposite would stoke his short temper.

"No," she murmured. "They'd keep him out of view, off the streets. Only those closest to him would know…"

Not only where he was, but how bad he'd been hurt. She couldn't say the latter out loud, it might jinx them. If she believed in that. Her faith in the man and the myth ran deep.

"Step by step," Strat said. "We take this one step at a time."

Yes, good, she could handle that. "After Ronald and me left your parking lot, you went to the club?"

"I went to the loft, where you were supposed to be, where Ire was supposed to be."

Where they had been until her father's call. Would she ever forgive herself for dragging Conn along?

"You couldn't get in."

"So I went to the club. Was closed by then. A ghost town."

"Could be everyone was just asleep."

"Maybe, I didn't feel like breaking in to find out."

"Then you went to Lach…"

"If you were in trouble, in danger, Ire would fucking gut me for not going to him first. When I couldn't find him… any of them…"

She squeezed his arm. "Conn wouldn't let anything happen to me."

"Sure, that's why he took a bullet for you. Thing is, if he's off the table, who's around to look out for you? You can be damn annoying, Scamp. Sometimes I want to shoot you too."

They rode a couple of blocks without words. Whatever thoughts he was lost in, she could only stick on one.

"He can't be dead. I'd know if he was dead, right? I'd feel it?"

"Yeah," Strat said. "One fucking bullet's not gonna take down a guy like Ire McDade."

"But with his cousin, Biz, the bullshit he's pulling with the Manzanis… What if they come for him? If he can't defend himself—"

"Think about it," he said and turned on the radio. "If Ire McDade had been found dead in your grandfather's house, fuck, it would be everywhere. The guy accused of murdering the alderman is taken down in the same building? Shit, Scamp. And there's you, granddaughter and girlfriend of the victims, gone."

"Does that make me like a black widow or something?"

"It's newsworthy. I don't have to tell you, this is what you do every day. You telling me if you were outside this situation looking in, that you wouldn't want it? You wouldn't think there'd be a story to tell."

"There is a story to tell. My father's been trying to get me to tell it his way all week."

"Point is, Scamp, if Ire died the night you left, if he died in that room, we'd know it."

"All week my dad kept the TV off. I had no way to know if it was in the papers."

"I'm telling you it wasn't," he said. "Yeah, me and the cop were on your tail, trying to track you down, but we were paying enough attention to know that. You and Ire's names are linked now. Even if the world doesn't know it, we do."

She tried to take solace in that. "If they found him after he was gone, his people, they'd get him out of there. They wouldn't let him be found like that, not to be a public spectacle."

"You talked about it?" Strat asked. "What's the contingency plan?"

"Closest we got to one of those was Conn making it damn clear he'd hurt anyone who tried to hurt me."

And him saying she would never go before him, that he simply wouldn't let it happen. Too bad she couldn't deliver on the same promise for him.

"If the way you tell it's right, he backed that up by taking a bullet for you."

"Yeah, but don't you see how frustrating that is? He has that power, those resources, what the hell have I got?"

"You think the McDades'll shun you? If Ire's gone, you lose that connection, that army?"

"Depends who takes his place," she said and squeezed her eyes closed. "No talk of that, we're being optimistic here."

"Okay. So let's say he's alive. His people got in there, discovered him bleeding, then what? What's the first thing they do?"

"Call Niall. He wasn't there. None of our usual people were there."

"So none of the guys on the street had the authority or smarts to figure it out. Okay, that's good."

"How is that good? That means they wasted time. Valuable time. What if they couldn't get Niall on the phone? What if they waited for him to arrive?"

"They've gotta have a plan, a procedure, for what happens when McDades are hurt."

Like a SOP. They weren't exactly a corporation with an employee handbook.

"They have a doctor on their ledger," she said. "When Daly was hurt, he rested up at the doctor's."

"Where is that?"

"I don't know. I asked to visit Daly. Conn wouldn't let me. I don't know where the doc is, if he's in McDade territory, or even in the damn city."

He eased her hand from her leg, extricating her nails from the denim marked by her infuriation.

"We'll get this. We'll figure it out. Trust me."

"You know you don't have to do this. All of this, any of this. You don't—"

"Yeah, 'cause you'd walk away from me if the

situation was reversed." He flashed her a smile. "I'm in this. No matter how it turns out, I'm with you."

"You better be because I'll need a place to sleep."

Strat laughed. "Better warn my daughter in advance this time."

"How is she? Have you talked to Jagg?"

"My family drama's got nothing on yours. You think Ire's at this doctor's?"

"I'm hoping he's at the club, or at the loft. Someone will have to give us answers, won't they?"

"If we get in." His eyes cut to hers, mirroring her thoughts. "If he's in the driver's seat, you snap your fingers, you get what you want."

"Then we're fine."

"Okay," he said, bobbing his head in understanding. "If you're confident, I'm confident."

Cool air passed her lips, one breath, two. "It's just…"

"What?"

"If Conn's in charge, if he's okay…"

"How come the McDades didn't storm that motel room and take out your father?"

"Maybe he blames me," she said. Funny that it would actually be better for Conn to be mad at her than not. Mad meant alive. "My father shot him, maybe he's pissed at me too."

"Did Ire say anything? After it happened? How bad was it?"

"There was blood. All I saw was the blood. On his chest."

The slight press of Strat's lips betrayed his concern. "That's not a good area."

"I put pressure on the wound, I tried to—it wouldn't stop bleeding—didn't and—my father ordered me away, cuffed us both. Me in the corner. Conn to the damn couch. I tried to keep him talking, tried to…" The memory stung her eyes and her temples. Pain. That's what it was. Horror and devastation. "He spoke to me, like he does, in fucking Gaelic, so I can't understand it."

"Why would he—"

"It's what he does, it's…" Her inhale became a shaky staccato. "I can't understand the words, but I always know what he's saying." The truth was hail on her sensitive skin. "He was saying goodbye."

A double take. "Why the fuck—he thought he was a goner? Why wouldn't he just say—because your father was in the room?"

"I love him, I would do anything for him. If he isn't… If we find out he's…"

"I know, Scamp. I know."

NINE

IF CONN WASN'T at Stag, there were other places to check. Optimism could be a cruel miser. Losing everything while trying to stay positive and—no, she couldn't go there. Just like she couldn't think about her father.

She'd figured it out, just a couple of streets away from the club. The reason she hadn't cared much about making a concrete plan for her father's future. If Conn was gone, if her father had killed him, she'd murder Ronald herself. What future did she have without the man she loved? None. In that case, it was only right the murderer should face the same punishment.

Strat pulled up to the curb at the end of the block. "I'm leaving it here," he said, killing the engine.

They were far enough away from the door that anyone special pulling out wouldn't be hindered. Going in the back way would take too long and God knew if they'd get in there anyway. At least at the front, the open door gave them an aim.

Witnessing life carrying on as normal chilled her.

Ever reliable, Strat took her hand to help her out of the car.

Wannabe clubbers lined up behind rope, music beat from inside, men guarded the doors. Business as usual.

Strat kept his fingers laced through hers, providing support while letting her lead the way. She could queue. Considered it even. That would stretch the time between her getting from here to there, to finding him or not. But she couldn't draw out the torture like that. She also needed to know. Conn said she'd never be turned away from Stag again. Never.

Fifteen feet from the car, she stopped. Strat stayed with her.

Closing her eyes, she breathed. If she stopped overthinking and just felt the moment, it could almost be okay. The sounds, the scent, Stag delivered her to a time without fear, one that included Conn in his office in that building. Her man. Her place. Her home.

Strat kissed the top of her head.

She exhaled, raising her eyes to his. "Sorry."

"Don't apologize. I'm here for whatever you need."

And the only way she'd identify that was by going inside.

On the approach, the guys on the door weren't familiar. Not all of Conn's guys were, there were so many that it wasn't possible to know every single one.

Strat's hold on her hand tightened as her breathing slowed. Up ahead, ten paces away, the guys didn't move. Five, four—they moved. Oh, shit, she nearly screamed. The guards each took a sideways step away from each other, opening up a clear route inside.

Always really did mean always.

Over the threshold, the heat of the club beckoned, but she stopped. "I'm going upstairs."

"Want me to check down?"

She nodded. "If the guys are there and you get the story, come up." Because if the guys were present, she still held some position. "If you don't…"

"I'll check here or get you at the car."

If Conn wasn't upstairs, if he wasn't in that building, she wasn't stopping there. Hopefully, someone would point her to him, give her an address, a clue, a next step.

With a single nod, she walked away. Strat stayed behind. The why was obvious, she still had to get upstairs. Men stood there too. Once upon a long time ago, she'd refused to ascend those stairs and been compelled to go up against her will.

What she wouldn't give to go back and do it all over again.

These men didn't move. Not at first. She held her ground. They glanced at each other, said nothing, then shifted out of the way.

Were they unsure of her identity or afraid what she might see? Death? Carnage? Heartache? Whatever it was, she'd have to face it sometime.

The stairs were clear. Not a good or bad sign. Could go either way. At the top, she lingered a second before opening the door to go inside.

She stopped short.

There were people there. Two, to be exact, a male and a female. She immediately recognized the first.

"Play," she said.

Having spent a lot of time looking at pictures of Doran "Play" McDade and his relatives, it wasn't hard to pick him out as another of Conn's cousins, younger brother of Score, Raze, and Biz.

"Bluebell," he said, a half smirk on his face.

Oh, she was interrupting. She'd been in that place. Up against the man propped on the table, nestled in the vee of his thighs, his hands on her hips. Different McDade, day, and woman, but it piqued her longing.

"I'm pleased to meet you." This not from Play, but from the tall, gorgeous woman he'd been entertaining, or about to entertain on Conn's desk. "You're an intriguing woman."

She continued a few steps. "I'm an intriguing woman?"

"Yes," the beauty said and offered a hand. "Madison Byrne."

Yeah, she'd known that, just hadn't wanted to get too hung up on it.

"Happy to meet you too."

Though happy was the wrong word for the unexpected encounter.

Madison slid a possessive hand up Play's thick upper arm. "I'm sorry for your loss, Miss McLeod."

"My loss?" she asked, unsure if her heart stopped or leaped out of her chest. "My loss?"

"Yes," Madison said, drawing her eyes away from her fawning. "Didn't you lose your grandfather recently?"

Oh, relief came out in a sharp exhale. "Yes, my…" She almost smiled. "I lost my grandfather."

Minor heart attack averted, her eyes cut to Play's. They'd never met. Didn't know each other. Though not introducing himself sort of implied to Madison they had. Family secrets stayed close. She couldn't blurt out her questions or beg for answers while the Byrne woman stood there bearing witness.

"Play, do you… have a minute?"

"Don't need one." He swept Madison's hair from her shoulder. "You know what to do, Bluebell."

Knew what to do? Not descriptive, but as much as she'd get.

"I'll…" She gestured toward the curtain. "Leave

you alone."

She hurried through the heavy drape and up the stairs into an empty apartment. No one. Maybe the bedroom? No, that was empty too. No people and so many questions.

The closet was still full of their things. Hers and Conn's. Catching a sleeve, she pressed it to her nose, inhaling his sent. A sharp pain between her eyes preceded tingling grief. Everything would be okay. If she could be with him, lie with him…

She didn't know Play. Would he understand her desperation? Would he come up to see her? Not if they wanted to keep their poker face in place. Everything normal. Everything was just the way it should be.

She searched. Everywhere she could think that might hold a hint as to what happened. She came up with nothing. Not a damn stitch out of place.

No, she wouldn't be dissuaded.

The night wasn't over yet.

Grabbing Conn's suit jacket, she tossed it around her shoulders and slid her arms into the sleeves. Her evolving plan needed one tool she could get there for sure. Running down the stairs, she pushed through the curtain and headed for the desk, ignoring that Madison was now the one seated on it with Play between her thighs, dress pulled high.

"Condoms are in the third drawer," she said, scooping up the cigar box, then swinging around for the door. "Play safe!"

"Like I never heard that before," his charmed voice followed her as the door closed and she was descending again.

The last thing they needed was a McDade-Byrne baby, though God knew what plan had been conjured up since she left.

Strat waited for her at the bottom of the stairs.

"Anything?"

She shook her head and linked their hands again. "Play's up there, with Madison Byrne."

"Yeah." They went back out into the night. "Dasha and Darla are downstairs." She caught a quick glance. "They don't know anything. Only about a dozen guys down there, none of them know a thing."

"Something's going on," she said.

Strat opened the car door for her and went around to get in himself. That was when she opened the box and took out the heavy weapon.

"Wow, okay. What do we need that for?"

"Plan D," she said, carefully tucking the box under her seat before checking the chamber.

"Plan D? That's good. Do we have a plan B through C?"

"Yep." She put the gun in Conn's pocket, keeping its reassuring weight in her grip. "Go to my grandfather's."

She'd been avoiding it. Sort of. The notion of going was far less appealing than the club, but they'd struck out there. Strat already struck out at the loft, though that would be next on the agenda.

"What do you think we'll find there?"

"Evidence."

"Of what?"

"The amount of blood, the direction, pooling. Unless someone has cleaned up," because who would? "If they haven't, there should be evidence of medical intervention too."

"They didn't call nine-one-one."

"No. But if their doctor is decent and Conn was that bad, wouldn't the doctor have come to him with supplies?"

"Isn't the plan to find Ire first? He'll tell us all that."

What was her thinking? That was his unasked question.

"It's also the last place I know Conn was alive. Just like we did with your search, took it step by step, we have to do it with this too. If Conn was hurt and they needed to take him into hiding, he might have left something, a note or an address, anything that would point me to the right place."

"The last he saw you, Ronald was dragging you off, don't forget."

How could she? "One of us would always have to find the other. Something has to give."

Something. Yes. But what? And what did Play mean? She knew what to do?

"Okay, your grandfather's it is," he said, already driving that way, "will you get in?"

"We can go in the back way. I know where the tunnel is now."

"Tunnel?"

"Yeah, apparently Henry's house is like a secret location for Indiana Jones or something. It's the way my dad got in."

Not that he'd been explicit about that.

"You have a key?"

"I have you," she said, widening her smile when he glanced her way. "You're my lock pick."

"Nothing shady about that," he said, "us sneaking into a dark, shadowy place to start picking locks."

"You know, getting arrested wouldn't be the worst thing."

"For who?"

"At least then Conn would know where I was."

Just like Strat said, the superintendent's daughter being arrested was newsworthy. What better beacon was there than the cops? They had, inadvertently, outed their relationship after all. Law enforcement had its uses.

"Let's call that plan E… or Z."

She inhaled and repeated his words. "One step at a time. One step."

The truth would find her eventually. The only concern was whether she was ready to accept it.

TEN

NOTHING.

Not a speck of blood, not a clue.

They'd been at her grandfather's and left again, none the wiser.

Back in the car, Strat drove without aim. "You're quiet, Scamp."

"Of course I'm fucking quiet," she said, her arm dropping from its place holding up her head, elbow on the doorsill. "It's like I made the whole thing up. Am I delusional?"

"Probably, but that doesn't mean you made it up."

Ha-fucking-ha. "Strat—"

"They wouldn't leave evidence." *McDades are in the business of reducing our criminal footprint.* "They don't want anyone to know a McDade spilled blood. You said Silvio was there, right?" She nodded. "So he knows exactly who was in that room. If blood was found there, reported, The Director would know who it belonged to."

"None of us have been seen around this week.

Any of the three of us could've bled out."

"He couldn't know who."

What had been her father's intended grand plan? What was supposed to go down that night? Someone could've lost their life. If Conn wasn't with her and she'd been alone with her father and Silvio Manzani… God, it didn't bear thinking about. Death was one thing, death by complicit father would be something else.

"There wouldn't have been enough blood," she said. "For it to be all of us. And it would've been concentrated, right? Just wherever Conn sat."

"I don't know, Scamp. What does it matter? The McDades must've cleaned the scene."

After their leader was taken care of.

She exhaled; her fingers curled into fists against her thighs. "I'm going to kill him. Me! I'll take down goddamn Connel McDade myself. For putting me through this? I'll wring his damn neck."

"That's treason," he teased. She'd accused him of that not so long ago. "How'd you find out?"

She grabbed Strat's phone. "Find out what?"

"That your dad killed your grandfather. Did he tell you?"

"He was rambling, frustrated, pissed off, saying how Henry should've listened to him and it shouldn't have happened that way. I just… knew."

"Not like he's denied it either."

No. Someone should be vehement about their innocence of such a heinous crime, of any crime, if the innocence was genuine.

"He wasn't thinking straight when it came out."

"Yeah, no shit," Strat said. "You sure he doesn't have a habit?"

They'd investigated Henry. Had anyone thought to background check her father?

"You think he helped Silvio under duress? That

he owed him something?"

"Not what I was getting at but, sure."

She shifted to examine his profile. "What were you getting at?"

His hands skimmed to the top of the wheel. "If the guy's twitchy, maybe he's not getting his fix."

Shock opened her mouth even before she got to gasping. "My father would not take drugs!"

Was she defending him?

"You defending him?"

Her chin hitched to the side. "No, I just can't even… though I guess I 'couldn't even' before and it turned out he was a murderer." She shook her head. "But, no, I've been with him for days, I haven't seen him take anything."

"Only takes a second, kid. Addicts sniff it out anywhere." Hmm. "Doesn't have to be drugs, some guys get addicted to horses, pussy, cock fighting—"

"My father was never much of an animal lover."

Okay, maybe she was getting her sass back. Except the knife still twisted in her gut. Every second without him tore at her heart. Soon there'd be nothing left of it.

"Scamp?"

How long had she been sitting there staring at nothing?

"I was addicted, am addicted," she whispered without moving. "I won't survive if I have to exist without him."

"Don't give up hope yet."

"It's not about hope, it's about…" Her eyes closed, trying to blind her regret. "I wasted so much time. I don't deserve him."

"You do."

"His whole life, he's lived this. He told me he came to terms with how his life would end. That the only fear he'd ever experienced was after the attack." Opening her eyes to his glancing her way, what she needed was more than anyone could give. "Me. I was the only fear in his life."

"I don't doubt he loves you, kid."

"He's this… So strong, such a beacon to power and determination. The McDades look to him, give him loyalty. Others fear him. He's more than a man, more than just a person."

"He's an emblem. A symbol."

"Yeah."

When she didn't continue, he stole another look at her. "And…?"

"Every room he walked into, he was the most powerful. Invincible… Nothing could take him down. Nothing… Until me."

"Scamp, you don't—"

"If he didn't survive this, if he's hurt or in pain, that's on me."

"That's on the one holding the gun, your father."

"Conn wasn't supposed to be there," she admitted, feeling the full force of guilt. "My father asked me to come alone."

"Ire would never have let—"

"He gave me the choice… I asked him to come. I asked him to be there and… The notorious Ire McDade survived the streets and the family, the in-fighting, the external threats, and he was there, taken down by a McLeod. Because another McLeod killed him. It didn't matter who he was to anyone else, or what he was in the world. In that minute, walking into that room, taking that bullet, he wasn't a mob boss or a symbol on the streets, he was my boyfriend. The man who loved me."

"What's so wrong with that?"

"Love shouldn't kill."

"Love always kills," Strat said. "Sometimes with a bullet, sometimes with a thousand needles. Sometimes it wears you down, sometimes it lifts you up."

"But—"

"People murder others for money, greed, hatred, the list goes on and on, all of it is love. Whether it's someone loving something more than the person they're taking down, or they love themselves too much. Love is the motivation for everything."

"Love put him in the path of a bullet. Dead or not, he shouldn't forgive me for that."

And maybe that was it. Why her people couldn't get through to Conn or the First Team. Ire McDade didn't stand for such an insult, an injury like that. And it was her fault.

They pulled to a stop outside the loft building. Going in there could be the relief she needed. Going into their bedroom, being there, if she didn't find him waiting…

Waiting… Goddamnit.

"Any shit goes down, you get your ass to our bedroom and wait for me. Understand?"

His words. The plan. The contingency. The instruction her love gave, the order. If she couldn't find Conn, he'd have to find her. Shit, knew what to do. That statement didn't come from Play, he was repeating something he'd heard, maybe something he'd been told.

Yes, she did know what to do.

"Better if I park around the corner?" Strat asked.

"No," she said, her fingers curling around the door release as her eyes fixed on the entrance. "Stay here. If I don't come down in ten minutes, just go."

"What?"

The severity of his tone attracted her attention. "He's up there or he's not."

"Yeah, and if someone else is up there?"

"The only people who know about this place are trusted."

"Huh, and no one ever learned something they shouldn't? If someone was leaned on—"

"What's the worst that happens? Someone puts a bullet in me?" She smiled as her head relaxed to the side. "You know my perspective on this. To fight for your life, you first have to value it. If they want to take me down, they can do it. What do I have left to lose? If there's trouble up there, I don't want you anywhere near it." Tears threatened again. "You're all I have left, Strat. I would never survive you being hurt either. Let them end it, they'd be doing me a favor."

"I don't accept that. Just because he's not here doesn't mean he's not anywhere. What the fuck do you think he'll do to me if I let you go up there alone?"

"I'm only following his orders."

"What orders?"

"If shit goes down, I get to our bedroom and wait."

"Really?" he asked. "That's the plan?"

What else could she do but follow orders and hope he found her?

"Yes, so go home, Strat. Get some rest, you deserve it."

Rather than agree, he loosened his seatbelt. "Thanks, I'll pass."

"You can't—"

"He's there, I'll split. He's not…" God, she really didn't want him to finish that sentence. "There's liquor and guest rooms, right?"

Her friend got out of the car and came around to open her door. Why should she fight with him? Okay, so she did feel bad about the stressful week he must've had. Shit, she hadn't even thought about how him and Lach managed to get through it without killing each other.

They went inside and up in the elevator. No one lingered outside in the hallway. If Conn was there, shouldn't there be security? Yes, and there should be cars in the street too. Though they did tend to park in the alley if the boss was home for the night.

Her print, her code, it worked, and the door popped an inch. "He told me I was never alone. That our army would always raise me up."

Strat squeezed the back of her neck. "I'm an army of one and you've got me at your back."

How would she ever repay his courage? His loyalty? Of everyone in the world, only him and her brother dedicated their lives to finding her. No one else showed that determination. That commitment.

Breathing out, she went inside. Nothing out of place. No hint of movement in the air. Empty? By all outward appearances.

She pointed to the hallway. "Guest rooms are down there. Whisper might be here; I don't know where Play's staying either. Here or at the club, I guess."

"I'll check it out."

Strat disappeared, taking her hint that the big task lay on her. She didn't check the kitchen. A glance told her the place was in order, no clutter or evidence of habitation. Ignoring the room, though there was more of it, she ascended the stairs to the bedroom.

That was the real test… and the last hope.

No whisper of sound, no breathing, no movement. At the top of the stairs, she hesitated. If he was in there, she could crawl into bed beside him, and they'd finish their night the right way. Pretend none of this happened.

Somehow, even before going inside, she knew he wasn't there. The sense in the air didn't feel right. Something about the aura was off.

It smelled of him. Of them. When she passed

through the bedroom into the closet, their essence was there. Yet it was fractured. The bathroom was empty too. How many times had they stood in there together, naked, exposed, alone, in love?

Laying both hands on the glass of the shower screen, her forehead found a cool space between them.

He wasn't there.

"Scamp!"

Strat's call forced her to return the way she'd come, to the open landing at the head of the stairs overlooking the living room.

"Anything?" she asked.

"No sign anyone's here or been around recently."

They'd tried to call every number they had. Strat didn't have Whisper's number. She didn't have a number for Raze, or Nicki.

"Nicki," she said when it hit her.

"Scamp?"

"I have to stay here, I'm going to stay here…" Leaning back into the room, the hemisphere camera was out of its hidey-hole in the ceiling, though the red light wasn't on to indicate anyone may be watching. If the cameras at Stag were motion activated, maybe theirs was the same. "Just in case he was waiting for me to show up."

Could be she was kidding herself. But if they were both trying to find each other, one of them should stay put and give the other a chance to catch up.

"You think Nicole McDade knows something?" Strat asked.

"I think she's in the Grand Hotel, room eight thirty-two."

"How do you know that?"

"Because I do," she said. "Will you swing by, check it out?"

"Why would they tell Nicole—"

"I don't care about Nicole; I care about the guys watching her. This is family. Niall commands the rotation. Doesn't that mean he has to be in touch with them?"

Strat freed his phone from his pocket to dial. "Okay."

"What are you doing?" she asked when he raised it to his ear.

"Calling my boy."

"Why?"

"Because if I walk out that door, there's no telling if you'll let me back in."

"Why would I keep you out? That's just—"

"Sane," he said and turned his back to talk on the phone. "Got a job for you… Yes, at this time, boy… Shut up and listen."

His family, their resources, nothing was hers, yet Strat put it at her disposal. More people would get hurt before the end of this. Please, God, let it be those who deserved it.

ELEVEN

"YOU SLEEP IN MY BED. Where you're safe."

Connel's words played in her dreams. The first real good night's sleep she'd had in a long time came in their bed. Until she woke lonely.

Leaping out of their sheets, she couldn't believe she'd slept through to the afternoon. Where was Strat?

First her guy, then her best friend. Not in the kitchen, the living room, Whisper and Raze's room.

"Strat!" she called, throwing open the door to the opposite room.

Sound drew her in, and she pushed open the bathroom door. Shirtless, bent over the sink, he spat toothpaste and straightened up.

"You know there's new toothbrushes in here?" her friend said, opening a drawer in the vanity. "Deodorant, cologne everything."

"That's what you say to me?" Stomping over, she socked his shoulder. "What happened at the hotel? Did Ford go over? How could you leave me sleeping?"

"You needed it. And I'm not totally clear on the

rules of admittance to Connel McDade's bedroom." He wiped his mouth with a towel. "Nothing at the hotel."

"Nothing? What's nothing? And it's my bedroom too, by the way."

"Guy at the hotel told Ford to get lost."

"And that was it? He walked away?"

"With Jagg at his side? No fucking way."

On a groan, her head flopped back. "Please don't say there was a brawl in the hallway."

Or arrests made in the McDade name.

"No brawl, mighta went that way but my boy used his head." None the wiser, she shook hers to prompt him. "Used your name, Bluebell."

Ah, her breath bated. "Fuck."

"And it worked, which has gotta mean something."

That her name still held sway? Yes.

"What did they learn?"

"Jack squat." They went to get his tee-shirt from the bed. "Guys worked in rotation with four others, schedule hasn't been changed up for two weeks. Which is…"

She blinked. "Which is what?" Except she already knew. "Not like Niall."

Not like the McDades in general.

"No, Scamp. Don't think I have to tell you Ire McDade—"

"Believes in rotation. All guys know all sites and positions."

"Never know when any situation might need reinforcements."

If Niall wasn't following business as usual, something was wrong at the top.

"What did Nicki say?"

"No one's allowed to talk to Nicole McDade, are you crazy? She's the enemy and on the top tier. Niall doesn't want her to manipulate the guys." Or seduce them. "Which works for her, she doesn't associate with the help."

Hmm, yeah, she should've guessed that.

"I should call if—"

"No calls in or out."

"I'm Bluebell."

He snickered and moseyed on by. "That's not what I meant."

"What?" She trailed along behind him to the kitchen. "You think I'm barred too?"

"I think you're giving Nicki too much airtime. What do you think she'll know?"

Good point. If Conn wasn't chasing her down, he wouldn't be racking up a phone bill with his cousin's adulterous wife either.

"If he was okay, he'd be here by now."

Strat opened and closed cabinets, looking for what he needed to put on coffee.

"Might not know you're here."

"He knows." Going to the window, she gazed at the street below. "Where are you, Mo Grá?"

Somewhere out there. Dead or alive, her man was out there.

"What's the plan today? Get supplies? You need to eat." That was the last thing she cared about. "Where's next on your hunt list?"

"This is it." She spun around. "I go to our bedroom and wait." Strat prickled, gaining mass with solemnity. "I exist beneath him. I don't think. Don't make decisions."

"Is that his rule?"

"It's my oath." Happy to take ownership of it, the directive gave her strength. "I yield. Surrender."

"And you're so sure he'll come through?"

"Yes," she said. "You can go."

"Not a chance I—"

"I want you to go. You have a whole life out there to get back to. Tell Lachlan I'm fine, don't tell him where I am. Don't tell anyone. This place is secret. No one can know."

"If you're gonna be holed up here—"

"Only until he comes back."

"You don't even know he's alive."

"Alive or not, he'll have a plan. He takes care of me like no other man can."

"Your brother will want to see you."

"I can't leave, wait in our bedroom, that's the rule." Not that she'd signed a contract or anything. "I'll be fine."

He did a quick run through of stocks. "There's nothing here to eat. Nothing to—"

"Don't worry about me. Go check how Lach's doing with the superintendent."

"Your father. You should be there."

"Soon as Conn is back, I will be."

"Scamp…"

Done with the conversation, she departed the kitchen. "I'm going upstairs to take a bath. See yourself out. Strat."

TWELVE

A BATH. A movie. Alone. She didn't want to be alone but did want to follow orders.

Lying in bed, staring at the black dome above, she wanted his eyes on her. The nights they'd spent in bed there, mornings they'd woken together… The first day she'd seen that camera, he'd asked her to put on a show. If that light was on, she'd do it again, and again, and again. Anything to tempt him into showing up.

Wait in the bedroom, that was the rule.

Shit, it wasn't easy.

The investigative part of her, the curious soul, wanted to be out there pounding the pavement, canvassing, talking to anyone and everyone. Would that put her in more danger? Would Conn see it as disobedience?

At her grandfather's that night, before they'd gone inside, Conn believed she doubted him and his ability. This was her chance to show faith. In him. In the McDades. That he knew best.

Didn't help that she didn't have a phone either.

Though after calling everyone from Strat's with no answer, what would be the point of doing the same thing over again except to further frustrate her? Steeple would pick up, but what the hell would she tell her boss? He'd offered her time off to grieve. Chances were he thought that was the cause of her absence.

Oh, if only.

"Mo Grá…" On a sigh, she opened her arms, offering herself to him wherever he dwelled. "Come back to me."

The whispered words made no difference to anyone except her and—was that…? Sitting up, she listened to—shit, the front door closed.

Leaping from the bed, she ran to the landing and—

"What's up, Bluebell?"

"Up…? Daly, my—oh thank God." Pleased to see him alive, this could be, he could be, her chance to get answers. "Where is he?"

He held up a folder. "Want to come down here?"

"I'm supposed to stay in the bedroom." The landing was an extension of the room, in her head anyway. "Is he here? Is he coming to—"

"Need you to sign some things."

"You came here for… admin? What the fuck, Daly?"

"I go where I'm told."

Yeah, didn't they all. Her friend wasn't usually cagey with her. His whole mood seemed… off. Tense and awkward almost.

Sinking onto the floor, she curled her legs beside her. "What's going on, Daly? Please?"

He came to the foot of the stairs. "This is important."

Again with the folder.

"I don't give a fuck about paperwork," she said,

defiant in her frustration. "Tell me where he is. Tell me what the fuck is going on. Why is Play at the club? Madison is in town. What about Nicki? The guys there haven't been—"

"We're in a tight spot."

"What does that mean? A tight—where is he, Daly?" If she got no answer to any other question, she wanted the answer to that one. "Tell me how he is, please." God, she was already on the floor, but if he needed her to get on her knees and bow down to him, she would. "The pain, right here…" Pressing her hand to her heart, she struggled to breathe. "Daly, I need to know."

"He's in a bad way."

Her mouth opened wide, relief couldn't take root when terror still existed. "Tell me."

"He can't… None of us can…"

What was he trying to say? She couldn't blink, couldn't breathe in anything more than short, desperate pants.

"Please. Daly, please tell me." Moisture dropped from her lashes. "I can take it, whatever it is. Please I—"

"We failed."

"Failed?" He'd spoken in present tense, hadn't he? It couldn't be that—if Conn was gone… Her tongue dried while she sought balance. "Daly, is he alive? Tell me straight."

"I'm told."

"You're… told? What the fuck is—"

"No one's seen him, he won't see anyone."

Shit. "Then how do you know he's alive?"

"I've been told."

Which was completely useless. "So you don't know? No one's seen him?"

"Not since… the night."

"What happened?" That was a glimmer of hope. "The night I went missing, the night this started, what happened?"

He shrugged. "We're not allowed to talk about it. Even to each other."

"I'm not no one, Daly. I'm Cushla Machree! I'd drink acid before even thinking about hurting him." On purpose anyway. "You can trust me. Please, I need him!"

"There's a lot going on."

A lot was going on before they went to the meet with her father. So many questions. She wanted to know about Whisper, Raze, the prison meet, Biz, Score—fuck, no, truth was none of that meant anything. Nothing meant anything without him.

"All I need to know is his location," she said. "If I can go to him—"

"No," a shot of panic joined the word, "under no circumstances."

"Under no circumstances, what?"

"Are you to go to him."

What? That seemed damn final.

"Are you telling me we're through?" she asked. "No. Only I can stop this."

Wasn't that what Conn said? That only she had the ability to end their relationship. Even if they were over, she still wanted to know he was alive. Relationship or not, they were part of each other.

"I don't fucking know. You think Ire talks to me about that shit?" Daly said, coming halfway up the stairs, holding out a pen. "I'm the grunt here for your signature."

"On what?" Snatching the folder, it was possible the documents would give her an idea where her love's head was at. "They're blank."

Save for signature lines at different locations on the various pages.

He tossed the pen to her knees. "They're from Ire."

Which was supposed to soothe her? If her love put the documents in front of her, sorry, the all but blank pages, in front of her, she wouldn't hesitate to put pen to paper. Sign now, print the contracts later, they could put anything on them. The first thing to wonder was who "they" were. Were these from her man or someone else?

Narrowing her eyes on Daly, she searched for any hint of duplicity or betrayal.

"You know, you have every right to hate me."

"Hate you?" he asked. "Why would I hate you?"

"Vex's threat. Someone told you he threatened Ire's guys and I didn't tell him. Then you and Niall got hit."

"That was a million years ago, Blue. You think I'm conning you? Playing both sides?"

His affront was potent, yet she couldn't pass up the opportunity. "Tell me something."

"Tell you what?"

"You want me to sign these?" She shook the folder in the air. "I'll sign 'em. If you show trust in me, tell me something."

And his offense disappeared in a sigh. "You don't doubt my loyalty, you're manipulating me," he said, to which she smiled, for the first time in a while. "You won't sign unless I answer one of your questions."

"You can tell him I tortured it out of you," she said. Though if he hadn't seen Conn thus far, she doubted he'd be running back to an emotional reunion. "All I want to know is if he's okay." And why he was insisting on distance between them. Why he hadn't looked for her. Why he wouldn't talk to her. "I won't survive without him, Daly. Every breath hurts. I need to know. Give me some hint he's… that he's okay."

"In a bad way" suggested otherwise. Was it a bad

way like he was in pain, or in a bad way like they still didn't know if he'd make it alive? And how had they failed? Who failed? At what?

Daly's shoulders descended as he propped a forearm on the banister. "Niall's with him."

Okay, that was good except… "Does that mean you're not all at the same location?"

"There's a trusted few. Those who know the site anyway. We drift in and out when he needs us."

"Which you know because Niall tells you?" She exhaled as he shrugged. "Not exactly a revelation that Niall's the one closest to him. Has he told you about his—"

"Sign."

Daly had been with her since the start of this. Since the very first night she'd been dragooned into Connel's office. God that night… Their time together could've been so different. Strange just how much one person could change. Something once meaningless had become her reason for being.

Signing the first page and the second, each new line felt like one closer to losing her connection to him. Daly would leave and then what? She'd just live there forever? Waiting? Wasting away?

She stopped about halfway through. "Why all the secrecy? He trusts me. Conn trusts me." Or he had before he got shot protecting her. "Will you tell him…?" She swallowed. "Tell him I'm sorry."

"Probably knows that. You're asking the same questions the guys have too. Think the picture's crystal for the rest of us? You're a good girl, Bluebell." Except he snickered. "By McDade standards. Night was crazy frantic, things moved fast. It felt like the whole world was on its head. Hasn't fixed itself since…" And they didn't have their leader for stability. "Truth is…" There was that spear of hope. "Most of us thought you were with him."

Right. She sagged. If they hadn't seen him, they didn't know who was with him or what went down. They may not have known she was ever at the meet in Henry's house. How could the McDade crew know if no one other than Niall was at his side? She would've been with Conn if her father hadn't dragged her out of there.

Her guy wasn't always the most forthright, had he told Niall the full story?

"I don't have a phone," she said. "But if you're seeing Niall, ask him to get in touch. Show up himself or ask one of you guys to get a phone—"

"You can't get a phone?"

She gestured at the bedroom. "I'm staying right here, where Conn wants me to be." Showing she could be trusted, that her loyalty was steadfast, was important. "Strat's the only person who knows this location and I asked him to go. Tell Niall the superintendent's at my old apartment. In case he wants to…"

Unsure if Daly was on the inside of what happened, she didn't say too much.

"I can bring you whatever you need."

"My guy." Plain as day. "He's the only thing I need."

"And he's the only thing in the world I can't drag to your doorstep." His sympathy was sweet. "Food, alcohol, books, or…"

"Just my guy."

"You have to eat."

She exhaled. "Not as much as I need him."

When was the last time she'd eaten? Didn't matter.

"Got a few pages left." Right, the papers. "You trust the boss? Sign it?" Trust? Desperately. Need? Even more. Miss? Without question. Waiting wasn't her strong suit. "Don't worry about it, Bluebell. He'll get patched up in no time."

And that took her eyes to his in time to see a wink. Patched up. The doctor. Yes, she'd figured Conn might need medical help. But damnit, she didn't know where to find the McDade medic. How could she get to the doctor…?

THIRTEEN

LIKE A BOLT of lightning, it hit her. How the fuck did anyone get to a doctor? Stupid, stupid. She'd told Strat the doctor existed at an unknown location. One she wouldn't need to hunt down herself, if in need of his services. That was the quickest way, the only way, to learn the where without someone giving her an address.

Putting so much faith in someone was risky. When it came to her guy, trust was absolute. But he wasn't clairvoyant.

Daly left hours ago. Would he go back to the secret base? Had he seen Niall?

Night cocooned her. Stag would be open. Out in the city… Was she going to live at the loft forever? Starving herself, avoiding everything except the liquor from the closet? Her head burst, pain, trauma, whatever the cause, it didn't matter.

As the water drained from the tub, she opened the mirror seeking help for her headache. While it pounded, wisps of a plan wouldn't knit together. Acetaminophen or—pain pills. Her pain pills from the attack. There were other bottles in there too, some labelled, some not. The names didn't matter, of the drugs or the patient, pills… They'd be better than blood. Blood meant pain.

Snagging the whiskey, she grabbed out two pill bottles and went to dump everything on the bed. Naked wouldn't be a good idea. She put on panties, one of Conn's shirts, and a suit jacket.

Having a purpose felt good. Even though it was a terrifying, possibly final, purpose. What did that matter? She still wasn't a hundred percent sure Conn was alive. Niall could be the guy behind the curtain, pulling strings without the truth being known.

Okay. Sitting in the middle of the bed, she took a long slug of her liquor, then popped open both bottles to pour out the pills inside.

Was he watching? The light wasn't on, but… scooping some pills into her palm, she raised them and the bottle to the camera.

"Sláinte."

Tipping them into her mouth, she swallowed them down with the burning liquid. The McDade world demanded extremes. Their world took loyalty seriously. And shows of faith… More pills, more liquor. The gateway to truth.

Good thing Strat was averse to coming into the bedroom. If this didn't work, she didn't want him to find her.

Who would?

Only a select few had clearance to enter the loft at all. Daly? Maybe. Whisper? What a stupid thing to fixate on.

Pills.

Liquor.

They were her whole world. He was her whole world. Without one, there wasn't the other. Without him, existence became inconsequential. The warmth of tears on her face quickly cooled in the forlorn air.

What did she have left anyway? Maybe this working meant something else. Freedom for those she cared about. Strat would be better off without her polluting his life. Time and again she dragged him into danger. Against his every warning, she'd throw herself into these things, and he never once said, "I told you so."

And Lach? God, the guy had been through enough already. Without the constraints of their father's influence, and with their grandfather gone, maybe he could find his true potential. Without a little sister to care for, or set an example for, he could thrive with nothing but hope in his future.

That was it, wasn't it? Selfish meant nothing to her. He'd held the burden for them all. And it wouldn't be a burden anymore. She wouldn't be a burden.

Conn. He could be alive, or not. The truth awaited her on the other side. What if he found her? If he was alive and the only one allowed in the bedroom… She didn't even know for sure he had access to the camera. Her father destroyed Conn's phone after the shooting. A man like Connel McDade wouldn't usually cut himself off. What did it say that only Niall had access to the leader? Something was going on. Her guy was hurt bad, or dead, and Niall was covering.

"Mo Grá," she said to no one, unaware if the camera had audio. "Know my last thought was of you."

Closing her eyes, she sank onto her back, holding the hope of oblivion. Feeling nothing was better than the numbness of boiling fear. Love. Strat was right. Everything was rooted in love.

Tears, the last vestige of herself, seeped out onto their sheets. Their happiness, their pleasure, there wasn't a better place to surrender. Her life was his. She was his. In life… and whatever came next.

FOURTEEN

HEAVY, her mouth was dry. Peeling her tongue from the roof of her mouth, the aching sting in her throat demanded a cough, but that was too much effort.

God, her head hurt. Her sinuses burned. What was—

"Try not to move."

A voice. Who the hell said that? Opening her eyes was difficult. When she tried, the heat of light closed them again.

"Who is that?"

"You're safe, Miss McLeod."

Not if she didn't know who was with her.

Conn's room at the loft was never bright, not like this, except… Memory returned slowly. Not that details mattered. Only one thing counted.

"Conn," she whispered.

The voice wasn't his. His brogue was one she'd recognize anywhere, and it definitely wasn't in that room with her. If he wasn't there, if she wasn't…

Forcing her eyelids apart, she didn't see anything

familiar. White walls, an overhead light, rolling her head on the pillow sent another shot of pain in every direction. Wincing against it, she couldn't give into it, she could be in danger, vulnerable…

"Please stay still."

"Who are you?"

The guy at her bedside was writing something on a clipboard. Was this a hospital? No, there was a mirror on the wall and a dresser in the corner by a long window, pale curtains closed over it. Was it night?

"I'm looking after you," the stranger said, putting the clipboard on the nightstand.

"Where am I?"

"Still in the city, don't worry. We needed to bring you here for—you're safe."

"This isn't a hospital."

"No, but we are taking care of you."

"Who is we?" she asked, fighting the pain to sit up.

When he tried to pressure her shoulders back, she batted his arms away.

"Please, you're still weak."

Weak, yeah, still had some fight in her though.

"Not too weak to blast out of here."

What was obvious to her? Wherever she was, Conn wasn't there.

"No, but Miss McLeod—"

"Stop using that word, I don't want to hear that name." Strange how nauseating it was to hear the name she'd been called her whole life. "I want to get out of here."

The tube in her arm connected to a bag of liquid on a stand. Didn't fucking matter, she'd tear off her own limb before living without him for another second. She dragged off the tape.

"Don't!" the stranger insisted, fighting against

her as she tried to pull at the tether. "Please, Miss McLeod, you'll hurt yourself."

"Leave me alone. Stop touching me." She swatted at his hands. "Let go of me!"

"You heard her."

And just like that her heart shattered. Whipping around, she couldn't breathe in the unknown reality.

"Mo Grá," the whisper crossed her lips, mired in disbelief.

It wasn't just that her guy was there, he stood tall, alive, astute, exactly the man she remembered. Every bit as delicious and intimidating.

"Split, doc," Conn said, his eyes settling on hers.

Doing as told, the stranger, the doctor, left, closing the door behind him.

"I need to get this thing out—"

"Hold," Conn said.

She stopped to look at him again; that glare wasn't usually fixed on her.

"I did what I was told," she said. "Went to our bedroom and—why didn't you come to me, Mo Grá?"

"I don't answer your questions."

Something was different. Something was wrong. Wrong beyond the point of unsettling. Why was he still over there by the door?

When her eyes closed again, she didn't want to open them. "At least I know."

Hollowed out in the space of a blink, knowledge didn't always lead to enlightenment... or satisfaction. With one long tug, she yanked the tube from her arm, feeling absolutely nothing.

Clambering to her feet, the room spun, yet there he was beside her, steadying her. His hand on her arm was a bliss she'd never feel again. The strength of that grip, the security of him.

This. Him. How could she ever go on without

him?

With a yank the other way, he put her back on her ass on the bed. "Stay there."

"I'm sorry, Conn." His shirt. Her body was covered by his shirt, though it wasn't the same one she'd put on in the closet. "I know that doesn't cover it, that no words will ever—"

"The loft is being transferred into your name." He'd gone back to the door. "It, and everything in it, belong to you now. Money has been put in your bank account, and you'll get a payment every month."

"A payment every month…" Gradually, her senses returned, but they didn't help her understand. Was it a fog caused by the drugs? "Why would I—I don't understand."

"The McDades will look after you. Financially." As opposed to… "You have our sincere apologies for the failure."

"Failure…" the whisper came out on an exhale, though her eyes closed as her head shook. She squinted at him. "Baby, I don't understand what—"

"You are free of McDade constraints. Stag will remain open to you. We will never take that away from you, but… be smart with it."

Those four words were the closest she'd heard him to normality yet. "Conn…" Climbing onto the bed on her knees, she sat on her feet. "Can we maybe talk about this later?"

When up was up again, hopefully.

"Aye."

Except when he turned away, she surged higher. "Conn…" Over his shoulder, his eyes cut to hers. "That doesn't mean leave, that means come over here." Lifting her arms, she hoped he'd come to them, except he stayed put. "I missed you; I was so worried—scared, Conn. I was terrified you'd—I didn't know what happened and… You don't know how seeing you again is just— Mo Grá."

Those powerful green eyes zeroed in as he turned. "Don't you get it? You're free, Bluebell."

He'd never called her that before. When referencing her with his guys, yeah. From his mouth direct to her ears? Never.

"Free from… free from what?"

"Our failure freed you."

"Our failure?"

"My failure," he said. "We had a simple contract. The McDade shield protects you so long as we're together. It failed, I failed, you have no obligation to me or our former relationship."

"Former? This wasn't…" Shit, she couldn't believe his skewed perspective. "You didn't fail. The McDades didn't fail. My God, what have you been carrying?" Unfolding one leg, then the other, she left the bed to get closer. "Where am I always safe? With you." Nothing had changed that belief, that truth. "You didn't fail, you proved yourself." His frown deepened. "Not only was I safe with you, you gave your life for mine. The McDade shield didn't fail, I failed it by letting a McLeod threat through. This wasn't McDades' fault. It was mine." Sliding a hand up the center of his body, it ascended to his jaw. "Mo Grá." Didn't he see it? Feel it? Understand nothing could ever part them. "I'm yours. Forever. I've never been prouder of you, safer with you, than I was in that room. Though…" Her hand dropped to her chest in a fist. "I can understand you may never forgive me. I put you there. Put you in—you took that shot for me, and my father—this was my mess, my doing and you—"

He grabbed the side of her head, his fingers biting deep, silencing her. "This is your kingdom."

Yanking hard, he stole her mouth with his, the

sweet pressure of his desperate need proved just how much he'd missed her. He'd been in pain too, just like her, physical, emotional, whatever it was, their need gave them life.

Locking an arm around her waist, he carried her to the bed, legs dangling. As he laid her down, he loosened his belt and with their eyes locked, he plunged inside her.

Body bucking, she called out. Tears instantly wet her eyes. Not tears of pain or sadness, gratified, complete, wonderful tears that kept flowing even as she smiled and moved with him.

His cock filling her full was the link they'd both missed. Neither could be whole without the promise of this union. Yes, it was about pleasure and desire, but the need between them was deeper. She'd almost lost him, could've lost him, and she could only be certain of them by experiencing this.

"Conn…" she whispered, writhing with the thump of pleasure beating within her.

The word, his moniker, sped his thrusts, and her calls. She didn't know who was close, even who was on the other side of the door. It didn't matter. This McDade, her McDade, prioritized her safety.

Had he really believed he'd failed her? Shit, he must've been in agony. Though it wouldn't have matched hers.

"Yes," she whispered, her panting became quick, short gasps. "Yes, Conn—baby—Mo Grá."

Love wasn't enough, orgasm wasn't enough, every whisper of need pulled and tugged, twining against him, around him, pulling his own climax with hers, demanding they both yield, surrender to the inevitable.

When he peaked, he slammed her over the line again. A string of foreign words leaped from his strained throat, through his gritted teeth.

Yes, this was her man, her completion.

FIFTEEN

CONN DIDN'T PULL out, he stayed inside her, exactly where she needed him, he knew, he remembered.

Pushing her hair from her face, he forced her chin up. "You will never do that again." Such stern, severe words in that moment of post-coital bliss jarred. "Do you hear me, Cushla Machree?"

"Baby, I don't—"

"The pills, the liquor, what the fuck were you trying to achieve?"

"This," she said, stroking his still clothed body. "I can't survive without you; I wouldn't have made it another day."

"How did you know I was watching?"

"I didn't. There's only so many hours I can live without knowing you're alive. Either you were watching, or I was coming to meet you on the other side. Did you get a new phone?"

Stupid question, he must've. His hand went to a rear pocket, then he held something in front of her face.

Slowly, her smile crept higher. "That's my

phone."

The only phone, other than his, that had access to the camera in their loft bedroom.

"Mine now," he said and sat up to put his dick away. "We have to get the doctor back in here."

"I don't want the doctor back in here." When he tried to move one of her legs, she clamped it tight again. "I want you…" Raising her hips, shifting a thigh, she presented a prime pussy shot. "Back in here."

"Again?"

"Oh, Conn…" Sitting up, she wrapped her arms around one of his, resting her face on his shoulder, rubbing herself against him. "I was so scared. I can live with anything, anything at all, providing it's with you." She propped her chin on his shoulder. "I love you. And I was grateful I'd said my goodbyes but—"

"What did I tell you? You won't leave this life before me. I won't let it happen."

Another promise he'd kept.

"Did you really think we were over? That I blamed you or—I was desperate for you. The only thing I blame you for is putting up with me."

"Giving you too much latitude," he said, guiding her forehead to his lips. "That will change now we're back in it…" He raised his brows in question. "Hmm?"

"No." Her head shake quickly gave way to a smile. "We're not *back* in anything, I never left." She squeezed his arm in her embrace. Pleasure was still on her mind, but she took a deep breath and straightened her spine. "You want to tell me what's going on? No one's seen you, Play's at the club—"

"Not here," he said and kissed her again.

"Complete the circle."

"Aye, after you complete your side." He got up and she tried to follow, except he put a firm hand on her to push her down. "Stay here, Macushla."

Sometimes manipulation felt good, even on the receiving end.

"For how long?"

"Until I say." Checking his phone, he swiped something and frowned at something else. "Get some rest, then you need to eat. When was the last time you ate anything?" When she didn't answer, his attention rose from the screen. "Macushla?"

"I swallowed a bunch of pills, does that count?"

"No, and that's the last time you'll make a joke of your stupidity. Mention it again, you'll wear chains the rest of your life. You have no fucking idea…"

"Yes, I do. It's what I've been going through since that bullet left my father's gun. He's at my old place, by the way, I don't know if Daly told you."

"Daly told Niall, old information."

"Old—"

"Your information was old. Your father is not at the apartment."

"Where is he?"

He crooked a brow. "You trust me?"

"I trust you, though I'm getting the drift it's not mutual."

Another scowl. "Who the fuck do you think you're talking to?"

"You don't trust me to know anything, wouldn't let me see you. The guys thought I was with you. Daly said—"

"More than he should have, and there will be repercussions for that."

"No," she said, leaping off the bed. "Daly is my friend and he's loyal, so loyal, to us. That kind of commitment is something we should nurture and appreciate, not punish. He cares about us."

"Any of my men ever cross the line with you—"

"I won't hide anything from you…" Linking

their fingers on one hand, she drew them up until they were palm to palm. "Except…"

Snatching her chin, he wrenched her head back to a painful angle. "No caveats, no conditions. You don't hide anything from me."

"It was telling you everything that caused this. You have enough going on with the McDades. My mess almost took you from them."

"We've been through this."

No way she'd let him brush this off like it was nothing.

"How can you forgive me? Why would you want to? The McDades need you—"

"You need me."

No part of her could deny that. "I exposed you, dragged you around the McDade shield, made you vulnerable. This was my fault. I forced you through your defenses—"

"Cushla Machree…" His fingertips skimmed down the front of her throat. "How the fuck do you do this to me?"

A question he didn't want answered. It didn't have one, not that she knew. Whatever it was, she hoped to keep doing it forever.

There was so much to say. The ground they had to cover seemed insurmountable.

"At my grandpapa's—"

"Later, Macushla. Rest."

She caught his wrist. "Then take me to our bed."

No way she'd be separated from him again. It still didn't seem real that her guy was there, talking to her.

"This is where you heal."

No. "I'm cured," she said, raising his hand to her face. "Don't let me out of your sight. I am your kingdom. Please."

And that was exactly the button to push. It gave

him the permission he wanted. What she needed, and the only way she'd heal, was with him.

Snagging his fingers between hers, he led her out into a large office, desk angled to the right, double doors behind it.

A round table, couches—he guided her behind the desk and opened the double doors. A bed, black silk with the occasional spot of red. Yes, this was their domain.

Her restraint strained against its want to let go and leap on, to declare this conquered land her territory. With everything going on, and how they'd got there, too much exuberance didn't seem appropriate.

She pulled back the covers to climb into bed without letting go of him. "Can you join me?"

Releasing their connection, he grazed the back of his fingers down her jaw. "Rest."

He kissed her hairline and left her alone to scoot to the middle of the bed. He'd wanted to give her up, thought they were over. All this turmoil had a crucial consequence. When they got to talking, she'd make a few things clear.

"Mo Grá?" He paused on the threshold. "Thank you."

The curiosity in his eyes touched hers for only a moment. He went out, closing one of the doors and leaving the other slightly ajar. To ensure she didn't run away? Or to prove he trusted her to eavesdrop?

A door beyond the room opened and closed, after a few seconds, Niall's voice rose.

"Aye?" the lieutenant asked the enigmatic question.

"Aye," her guy said.

Were they really going to do this again?

The answer came in another query from the wingman. "Aye?"

Ah, but this time there was the slightest thread of something else, maybe amusement? Relief? Happiness?

"Aye," Ire finished.

"Thank fuck."

Never had Niall's accent been more welcome than right then.

"What have you got for me?"

Lying down, she closed her eyes. If her guy wanted to check on her, she wouldn't complain, but she was tired. No one would get to her, not with Conn standing in front of her. She was safe, and wasn't alone. She had her guy back.

SIXTEEN

WHEN HER EYES next opened, there was silence. The bedroom door was closed too. Sitting up, she yawned and went to explore the closet and the bathroom. The shower washed away so many troubles. The shower? Maybe the man who'd rescued her. No longer apart, all the knots pounding in her muscles disappeared down the drain.

Somehow, and amazingly, women's clothes were there. Okay, so she didn't recognize them as hers exactly, but the place was prepped with clothes in her size. Maybe they weren't for her, they could've been left behind by an ex. She still didn't know where they were. It could be the doctor's house.

The doctor, or his wife, wouldn't mind her using them, would they? It was that or strut about in Conn's shirts for the rest of time. She wouldn't complain, the guys might, and the enemies Conn intimidated. Did her wardrobe choices diminish the power of his intimidation? Having the superintendent's daughter sashaying around in barely anything had to—

The comb stopped in her hair. Superintendent's

daughter? No. Now she was what from a disgraced family? Without the law enforcement link, maybe she wouldn't be any use to Conn at all, professionally, that is. She'd be all kinds of use to him in other areas.

The office was empty, so was the small bedroom she'd started in. Hmm. She wasn't Conn's prisoner but didn't want to overstep by wandering around the unknown place.

Overstep? As the thought rose, it disappeared. Strat's attitude to her implication it was possible to overstep put hers in immediate perspective. Wherever she was, Conn was invited. Didn't that work the other way too?

Conn's phone was on the desk. His, hers, who knew anymore? She wasn't interested in snooping, so it could stay there for the moment.

Better to seek another soul before racking up the airtime. Putting her friend's mind at ease was first on the agenda. If Strat discovered her missing, if there was any hint of what happened… She wouldn't do to him what she'd just endured with Conn. By connection, her brother would get an update too, keeping everyone happy. Unlikely he'd heard what happened at the loft, though if he wasn't worrying about their father… Yeah, what happened there? She needed some updates herself.

The other double doors led to an open second floor walkway lined with balustrades. In front of her was a wide, opulent staircase. The stag symbol in the wood, and on the doors she'd just opened, clued her in.

"My God," she whispered to no one. "This is the McDade Mansion."

It still existed! Okay, its existence wasn't a shock, but that Conn still had it… Wow, that was unexpected. He'd grown up there, as had his father. She hadn't heard anything about the building for so long that she guessed it had been sold or fallen into disrepair.

Worked out even better that she'd read so much history of the family. From the reports, she had an idea of the layout, of the areas regular people accessed; connected, but not fully trusted people. The McDades would never be dumb enough to leave full architectural plans accessible or anything, but the parties…

Creeping down the stairs, the soft carpet squished beneath her toes. The clean line of the magnificent handrail aided her descent. The marble foyer floor begged attention, and every door and corner begged to be explored.

That would have to wait until after she'd connected with Strat. Why had he never mentioned the McDade house before? Did he know they still had it? No distractions, okay, the parties… The dining room was to the left, seemed like a good starting point for her hunt. The kitchen was actually on the lower floor and—

Not so swish as the old days. The dining room was huge, just like the pictures online. But gone were its formal roots. It looked more like a rec room than an opulent dinner hall. Couches, televisions, consoles, they had a coffee corner with fridges and counters. Beer. Chips. Some guys were eating sandwiches or ramen. What a life.

"Bluebell!" The exclamation brought her around to Daly coming toward her. "You found us."

"Yes, I did." She hugged him and gave an extra squeeze of stealth gratitude. "Is Strat around?"

"Not yet." Backing off, he stuck a hand in his pocket. "Heard he was on your tail. D'ya shake him?"

"He was, but…" She opened her arms. "I'm here now." But, huh? "On my tail like this last week? How do you know he was on my tail?"

"I have ears. Said we haven't seen the boss, doesn't mean we haven't heard him."

"Which boss are we talking now? My boss or

your boss?"

"Both."

If her guy was raising his voice, only one guy would be bold enough to give it back.

"He did look for me," she muttered.

"Whoa, fucking hell, look for you—"

"Daly," Hock said, strolling on up. "We got work?"

"I don't know, ask Bluebell. We have work?"

"What work?"

"We going anywhere?"

"My guy has," she said. "You seen him around?"

Both guys laughed.

The way Hock's shoulders went back broadened his already formidable chest. "No one sees Ire these days. Just Niall."

"Yeah, maybe he doesn't exist anymore."

For the duration they'd been apart, it felt that way.

"Oh, he exists," she said. "I can vouch for that. I'd submit to an exam to confirm it, but he wouldn't like that. How long have the guys been here?"

"Our numbers are growing. We're keeping things low-key at Stag."

"Because…?"

Hock and Daly shrugged.

"We're not top of the phone tree."

"Something's going on," Daly said. "Been a lot of chat, a lot of activity. Manzanis are thinking about it."

"Thinking about what?"

"Making a move," Daly answered. "Makes guys like us nervous."

And women like her too, her friends were out there vulnerable. "I want Strat here."

"We can bring him in if—"

"I'll call him before we go full deployment." Her

friend wouldn't argue, he'd want to see she was okay too. The request didn't require an abduction, just an invitation. "What about Lachlan?"

"Your brother?" The guys looked at each other. "I'd ask the boss before making that call."

She raised her hands. "This is the McDade Mansion! I had no idea it was still in the family."

"Hasn't been the base since Clancy left, way I hear it anyway."

"Do you know where Conn is?" The guys would get in less trouble if she heard this from their leader's lips too. Seeing him and hearing him were two different things, and they claimed to have done the latter. "Is he still in the building?"

"No fucking idea," Hock said.

"Word is he hasn't been venturing far. Could be because of his—"

"Let the boss talk to her about that."

"About what?"

If Hock had shut Daly up to protect the guy's hide, she shouldn't push.

"Want us to call Niall?" Hock asked.

"No, it's nothing important."

"Want to play GTA?" Daly asked, his smile growing.

She laughed. "Rain check, I have to call Strat before he goes off the deep end."

Her brother, her friend, they'd spent days tracking her. Disappearing again so soon would be kind of rude.

As she backed away, the true scope of her focus widened. Most of the guys, all of the guys maybe, had curiosity embedded in their glances and stares. Their life was in the mix, things happening at the top that they didn't understand. Could be they blamed her for the power shifts, or maybe they believed she was on the inside, aware of strategy and plans.

Power. Hatred. Pride. The dice had to be thrown before the pieces could move. What would that catalyst be? Strat would enlighten her. Or he'd tell her to keep her beak out. That was probably more likely. Didn't mean she'd follow the advice though.

Hurrying up the stairs, she went to grab the phone from the desk. Scrolling to his name in her contacts, she pressed call and dropped into Conn's seat. The smooth leather felt good beneath her. Or maybe it was the imprint of its last occupant—

"I knew you'd call eventually, Princess."

All those loose knots coiled tight again. Every muscle in her body tensed.

"Evander," she whispered to the voice at the other end of the line. "Where's Strat?"

"Right here with me, Princess. For a guy his age, he's got a lot of fight in him. Only took three bullets."

"No, Evander, please, is he alive?"

"Alive? Oh, yeah, sure, Princess, just barely."

"Scamp, you tell—"

"Shut the fuck up," Vex snapped.

The thud in the background wasn't encouraging. Nor was the silence after.

"Don't hurt him," she pleaded, "let him go."

"That's the plan, Princess. Soon as you get here."

"Evander, you don't have to do this. You don't need to—"

"You owe me, Princess. This is just the tip of the iceberg, baby. Come here, give me what I want, and Daddy goes free. Fuck me around…"

"Please, Evander—"

"That's it, baby. That's what I want to hear. Beg, Princess."

"Don't hurt him."

"Come to me, it's a clean swap, him for you."

Oh, yeah, and what did that look like? Even if Strat was given the go, even if they kicked him out of wherever they were, he'd never abandon her. No matter if she begged him to leave, he wouldn't. They could put him in a car, drive him a hundred miles away, and his first act of freedom would be to return to her.

"You think I'm stupid?"

"I think you want your special friend alive and kicking. He has kids, right?"

Kids who'd proved themselves, kids who'd helped her at her lowest, who'd supported her, worked hard for her. Everyone close to her ended up dead or in trouble. One guilt battled another.

"Where?" she asked because what choice did she have?

"You come alone, sweetcheeks; you bring the Irish, we'll have a barbecue."

"Are you afraid of him?" she asked, spiteful and helpless. "If Connel knew—"

"Ire's got his coming." The hiss of his rage screamed more than revenge. "You're gonna pay for the insult, the hurt, for the years of fucking taunting. You've got a helluva tab, Princess. I'm calling it in." Sickness overwhelmed. Terror. Revulsion. Desperation. "One hour. Hustle."

SEVENTEEN

SHIT. Shit.

Where the hell even was she? Maybe an hour wouldn't be enough time to travel—where the fuck was her guy?

Rushing through the bedroom to the closet, on the hunt for shoes, she searched the call logs and hit the one with no name. On three rings, he picked up.

"Bluebell?" Niall's thick Irish accent showered her with hope.

"I need him. I need him now. I need him, please."

"We're on our way up."

Tossing the phone aside, she dropped onto the closet bench to pull boots onto her feet. The moment she heard noise in the office, she leaped up to run through. And there he was, as promised, her guy with his lieutenant at his side.

Running to him, she pressed herself against the steadying pillar of his strong body.

"I have to do something incredibly dangerous

and insanely stupid. I have to, Conn. I have to go. I love you, but I have to go."

"Breathe." His command at least gave her an aim. "Talk."

"Strat. He has Strat. He's—" Her voice broke because she couldn't—grief didn't even cover it. "He's got Strat. He's taken him, and he—he wants me, you know he wants me. Why does he want me? People are getting hurt, so many—it's because of me, I'm a—"

"Macushla."

Right. Okay. That stability, the cool calmness, washed over her. Get it together. Where the fuck would panicking get them?

"I went downstairs looking for Strat. Daly said he wasn't here, and I'd seen the phone on the desk—I called him."

"Strat?"

She nodded. "His number's in my phone, it's in his phone too. I called, but he didn't answer. Someone else did."

"Who answered?"

Despite the question, the keen light in his eyes suggested he already knew the answer.

"Evander." Another name she'd be happy never to hear again. "He's got Strat, said he put three bullets in him." Resting her face against Conn, the tremor shaking her wouldn't subside. "He's my best friend, he'd die for me, I know. We can't let him. Please… please don't ask me to give up on him. He's looked after me, hunted me down after…" Raising her chin, her wet eyes sought his certainty. "Please, Mo Grá."

His finger slid from her temple to her chin. "Strat's proved his loyalty. It's to you first and foremost, as is the McDades. Where is he?"

"Hustle," she said. "He told me to be there in an hour." Without a word, Niall reversed to slip out. When the door closed, she licked her dry lips. "I don't want anyone to get hurt."

"Anyone?"

Was that a question about…?

"You, Niall, our people. I don't give a shit what happens to Evander," she said. "I don't want any McDades hurt. I don't want Strat hurt… I don't want you hurt."

Her palm glided down to the location of the gunshot that pierced him. Or she tried to, he caught her hand and pressed it against the family tattoo at his clavicle instead.

"It's handled."

"He said I should come alone." She'd certainly learned her lesson on that. "And he said…"

"He said what? Don't hesitate with me."

"I don't hesitate because I don't trust you, I hesitate because I don't want to say the words, face the truth. He said if I brought the Irish, there'd be a barbecue, and… he said you had yours coming." The words hurt as they passed her throat, but they just bounced off him. "Will you stay here? Please?" The angle of his head wrung a sigh from her lungs. "I know, I had to ask. You talk about keeping me in chains to protect me, while it seems all I do is put you in danger. Everyone in danger. Is this it? Will Strat's life be the cost of us letting Evander keep his? It's not fair. Was I wrong?" Her decision, to let Evander live, was meant to save the McDades paying a grave price. "I'm poison to everyone I love."

"Macushla, you need to rest."

"Rest?" Was that offense or fear? "I have to go. I have to be there. I have to be with—I can't let Strat—"

"Strat would prioritize your safety over his."

"That doesn't make it right." She tore her hands

from his. "I'm not more worthy, I'm less worthy. He has a family to protect. If either of us should survive, it should be—"

"Get back in bed. Daly'll bring you something to eat."

"I don't want something to eat!" Alarm wouldn't yield to sanity. Her blood pumped hot and there was no way to vent the steam with him being all composed and accepting. "I want to help my friend."

"You've done your part. It's McDade business." Which meant it was his duty to take care of it. "You're a good girl."

Because she again presented him with a dangerous situation with no obvious out? Was this going to be her grandfather's all over again? Maybe without her there, it would be easier for him to focus.

"I love him, you know. Strat."

"Aye."

"I love you too. I thought I lost you and—if anything was to happen to either of you… Just as it feels like I'm pulling you closer, now Evander wants to steal you away from me."

"No one steals anything from a McDade, not without consequences."

"You've been laying low here. Keeping things quiet at Stag." With one thing in her mind, she didn't want to miss other important developments. "There's something happening. You have a strategy." He didn't say anything. "What happened at the prison? With Whisper?"

"The power balance has shifted."

What did that mean? "You said that to me before. After we were out. Should I be scared?"

"You will be protected, Macushla. I won't let you down again."

"I got you hurt, that wasn't you or the McDades.

This was the McLeods, they threatened the McDades."

"And you'll have to make a decision."

"McDade," she said, curling her fingers into his shirt. "I said it that night, and will always choose—"

"Not that choice."

Niall came back in before she could ask what he meant. Her guy went to the desk, his number two on his heels. When Conn confused her, usually Strat made sense of it for her. Even if he didn't know the details, the way her friend talked to her, how he monitored her reactions and nudged her this way and that, she got there in the end. Without him… how would she live without Strat?

"Ford." She spun to the men having a hushed conversation. "Should I call to—"

"We've got it under control," Niall said.

Wasn't always an easy guy to read. Though he was right, they weren't rookies and knew way more about these situations than she did.

"Him and Vex used to move in the same circles. He might know a—" Both men's unimpressed expressions pushed her lips to the side. "Which you know, of course, and don't need me to tell you. Can I come and sit in the car?" Nothing, but nothing was needed. "How do I help?"

"You help by sitting on your arse," Niall said. "This is grown up stuff."

Congratulations, he got her from despair to offense in a flash. "And you know just the way to piss me off."

Fighting, arguing the insult, was her impulse, but she'd caused so much trouble already. Niall might be her vent, though hostility wouldn't help. They had enough of that on the outside, inside should be safe.

Meeting her guy's eye, it was easier to address him. "Will you check Lach's okay? I know you said my father isn't—I don't care about him, but my brother—"

"Is safe."

Did he know that for sure or was he trying to put her mind at ease?

"Will you take Daly? Him and Strat have worked together with—"

"Daly's job is to keep you alive."

"Hock?" When that got no reaction, she winced. "I'm sorry about this. The trouble. Again."

Her love's head moved, just a fraction, enough to send Niall trailing out of the room again.

"Front and center." Rounding the desk as he sat, she sank down onto his lap, raising her feet to the arm as he stroked her thigh. "Vex took Strat. Your father held the gun. Stop taking responsibility for other people's shit."

"You wouldn't be dealing with any of this if it wasn't for—"

"The actions of others. You're a McDade, Macushla. McDades don't apologize. Not at our level." His gaze grew acute. "I gave you an out—"

"I don't want an out. My job is to support you and all I've done recently is endanger lives."

"I am going to get your friend back. Insulting him is insulting you, and that won't fly. And if…"

She pressed closer. "What?"

"It's overdue."

"What is?"

"Vex and me got some business that needs cleared up."

So maybe walking in there wouldn't be so bad. "It's good timing?" Thinking of Strat being hurt couldn't ring any positive bells, but if Conn could kill two birds with one stone… "Please bring him back to me, and you come home to me too. I need both of you back."

"And Vex?"

It wasn't possible to convey how little she cared about his safety.

Her fingers slid down his chest. "Has whatever fate you decide. I don't care if he's hurt, I don't care if you kill him, except…"

"You worry how his father will react."

"I trust you, but I'll always worry. Living without you this week, I can't go through it again for a minute, let alone a lifetime."

"Our superior position gives us more latitude."

"You won Harvest." He nodded once, though that was a given. "Is Silvio pissed?"

Vex's father, Silvio Manzani, also known as The Director, had been on the other side of that vote. Winning it gave the McDades more territory, more power.

"He will be when I tell him about his son's betrayal."

Vex did seem to forget that he'd tipped his hand to the McDades. Sometimes he was his own worst enemy. He'd engaged with the McDades looking for help and support. But it all came down to who was packing what in their pants.

Vex, Evander, had wanted her for years. Working with the McDades, he somehow thought, increased his chance to be close to her, intimate with her. Damn, that boy could not read a room. Conn wouldn't share her with anyone for anything.

"He'll be desperate. If you shut off his Manzani support—"

"Won't matter 'cause he'll live the rest of his life in our basement."

A quiver at the back of her neck traveled to the tips of her fingers. "He will?"

"It's one insult too many. If Silvio wants his son back, he'll have to pay."

"With what? No opposition on the rezoning vote?"

"Among other things."

"I want Strat to give me away." Their eyes met. "Him and Lach. When we get married." He raised a brow. "Mo Grá."

"One spectacle at a time."

Guiding her mouth to his with a strong grip on her head, he gave her reassurance and his promise. Strat was one of them. An honorary McDade. That promised anyone who threatened him a short expiry date. She wanted to be there but trusted her guy. Would Strat trust him too?

EIGHTEEN

HER TEMPLES ACHED. The mood in the rec room was somehow both amped and subdued at the same time. Fewer men hung out than before though more eyes tracked her, if that was possible. Were the ranks blaming her for this or worried she'd pitch a fit?

"I'm going to take a minute," she said and stood.

Daly tossed the controller aside and rose to his feet. Hock, Snuff, even Biggs were right there with him.

"We're in McDade territory. There isn't anywhere safer for—you know what? It's fine." She raised the phone glued to her hand since the troops left. "Can I go stand over there and make a call?"

They all looked at each other before settling into their seats again.

She wanted to call Strat. To call her guy. To find out what was happening and whether or not they were safe. Except that was probably the worst thing she could do. They needed to be focused, to have their wits, and didn't need her interrupting.

She called Lach first, no answer. Of course there

was no answer. Her brother loved putting her on edge. That was sarcastic because the opposite was truer; he'd chased her down in the face of crazy drama. She was the trouble magnet. Her imagination might work overtime fearing her brother was dying, or stolen, or dead, but he could just as easily be asleep, at work, or out having some fun. Wouldn't that be overdue?

Steeple was next.

"Sersh?"

She smiled. That thread of wariness, the acute knowing, the intrigue, the concern, her boss, Steeple, could convey so much in just the way he said her name.

"I disappeared. I'm sorry."

"That guy came over, your bodyguard, said you were taking a few days. How are you doing?"

So her guy covered her ass by sending Daly to her boss? Though she'd have to ask Daly if that was a calm conversation or if he'd pulled out his toothpick.

"I'm okay. Getting by."

"Figured you'd call tonight."

Uh… "Why tonight?"

"You always know about this shit before the cops do. You want to write it?"

Confusion edged into dread. "Write what?"

"Shooting at that not-so-secret Manzani place, cops, paramedics—the fire department sure did their job, but it's all a shitshow. Can you ID the bodies that were pulled out?"

Hanging up, she hurried across the room. "We're leaving, job time," she barked at her boys while making a beeline for the foyer.

"What's going on?" Daly asked.

She'd guess the others were there, there wasn't time to check. "Is my car here? We have to—"

Only five feet from the front door, it opened, and there was her guy. She didn't stop and kept on going until she was right up against him.

"Oh my God, baby, what happened?"

Others came in, Stranger, Familiar, some she recognized, others she couldn't label McDade.

With a glance at her and one to those behind her, Conn's brow lowered. "Going somewhere?"

"Baby—"

"Upstairs," he said, then addressed the guys at her back. "Stow the weapons."

She swallowed. Though he gave her a kind of push, she clung to his arm. "Did Strat—"

"Miss me?"

Just at that, her friend rounded the door, held up by Niall and another guy.

"Strat!" Rushing around Conn, an emotional welcome wouldn't be appreciated by anyone, even if she felt it on the inside. The intention was to hug him, with the bruises, the blood, she didn't want to cause more harm. "Oh, God."

"It's okay, I've been in bigger messes than this."

Oh, screw it. With gusto, and little grace, she embraced his torso while the supporting guys were relieved by others.

"Get him upstairs," Conn said.

Strat winked and stuck with the men helping him to the next floor.

"Should we take him to the hospital?" she asked, wincing at each of her friend's limped steps.

"Hospitals have their own problems right now," Niall said. "And they ask questions."

Strat was alive. Conn was there. Lach was the only loose end, was he caught up in it too?

"Evander said he was shot, where did—"

"Close it up." Conn's order was accepted. Everyone else got it and scurried off to do their work, her guy, on the other hand, strode across the foyer with his own purpose. "Front and center."

Okay, that command was for her. Moving fast, she stayed at his flank as he went upstairs into the office.

"This is the McDade Mansion," she said. "I had no idea you still—" His jacket was dumped on the desk, and his cuffs were loosened next. "What happened tonight? I called Steeple and he—did we lose anyone?"

"No one important." Was that supposed to be encouraging? "You're going to write a piece."

Ah, hadn't she been trying to do that all week? Writing for Conn would be easier than writing for her father.

"Okay, what kind of piece?"

Didn't she need to know the facts of what went down? Maybe not the private stuff, that wouldn't be printed. Steeple mentioned cops and paramedics, this wasn't a quiet in and out for the McDades, there had been drama. Those were the facts the public would want to know, and they'd give some cover for anyone questioning why McDades had been around Evander's club.

In the closet, he tossed the cufflinks aside. "An obit."

Unexpected. "For…?"

"Vex."

She stalled. He unbuttoned his shirt while she absorbed the ramifications of that.

"He's dead?"

"No." That actually provoked zero emotion. Dead or alive, she really didn't care. "Wishes he was."

Which suggested he was living only at McDade pleasure. As in, Conn had him fully in control. Was he injured? Tied up? Abandoned somewhere? Did that mean their plan went off without a hitch? What did "no one important" mean when it came to murder?

"If he's not dead, why do you want me—"

"It'll have your name on it." That'll send a helluva message from one faction to the other. "We'll make sure he sees it, Silvio too."

"Won't that cause a problem? If I write it, and Steeple prints it on my word, people will see Evander in the street and…"

The sly slant to those delicious lips said so much, not as much as the darkness around him.

"No one will see Vex in the light of day again. Not without my permission."

"You got him." Unbelievable. "You actually—oh my God, baby."

The weird elation that could only be identified as joy at reprisal dwindled to nothing when he took off his shirt. And there it was, the fresh scar on his torso. A stark blemish on his enticing flesh.

"You write it, we'll handle the printing."

She didn't care about that, about Evander, anymore, not in light of the memories. Was that why her love pulled her hand away before? So she wouldn't feel it? Did it still hurt? She'd sent him out there to Evander while…

"Conn…" Going to him, her fingertips met the edge of the wound. "Are you in pain?"

"No," he said in time with opening a drawer to pop a couple of pills from a bottle. "Do you need your computer? Everything you need will be brought to you."

What she needed was a conversation with him.

"I need us to talk about this. It's like it never happened. We're out here, we haven't talked about it, now there's Evander mess. Baby, I want to know what happened the night my father took me from you."

"You were there, you know what happened."

Probably better than anyone else. She couldn't see him calling his guys in for a rundown of the evening's events. They'd have even more questions than her. If he didn't want to talk about it, that was one thing. If he was keeping specific details from the others, she needed to know, or else she could reveal something he wanted under wraps.

Okay, that sounded like a reason, it was a reason. In truth though, his wellbeing was her main concern.

"After my attack, you said I had to talk about, that if I couldn't, I wasn't dealing with it."

He caught her fingers in a fist. "Wasn't my first time, I've been shot before."

"That doesn't make it okay. The trauma of being hurt—"

"The trauma was losing you, watching him take you out of there, away from me…" He gritted his teeth, clearly still riled by the memory. "No one takes you from me."

"No one did," she said, adamant in getting closer. "Physically, he might have led me away, but I am always yours, Connel McDade. Always."

"I vowed to keep you safe."

"You did keep me safe. If you hadn't come with me, I'd be dead by now. That doesn't make it okay though. Don't you think I dealt with my own guilt? I put you in that room. You gave me the choice and I asked you to come. If I'd told you to stay in bed—"

"I wouldn't have."

Confused, she frowned. "You wouldn't?"

"Your answer to the question didn't matter."

"So why did you…? It was a test? To see if I would do the right thing, do the McDade thing?"

"The issue was allowing you to go. I should never have permitted that. It's a mistake I won't make again."

As that night had proven.

"We still have to deal with my father. To make a decision on—Lach and I thought he should resign, go into exile, I guess. We can't ask him to answer for his crimes legally without pulling everyone into the spotlight." He said nothing though his focus stayed fixed. "Is this another test? I'll do whatever you want me to do. Vote whichever way you want me to vote."

"There's no vote. I command."

And he had a knack of knowing what was best for her, even when she didn't.

"We should have dinner with Lach or something, get his view—"

"We've discussed it."

What the hell? "You've… you and Lach?"

"Aye."

That truth knocked around in her skull as he stripped her down. Only when he walked her backwards up against the wall did she focus.

"What did you discuss?"

"Your grandfather's house will be sold. All proceeds and assets will be evenly split between you and Lachlan."

"How did you get my father to agree with that? I thought everything would go to him."

"What the will says is irrelevant. This is how it's going to be."

No votes, only commands. Shit, her man turned her on without even trying.

The estate. Concentrate. There would be money. Which reminded her of earlier.

"Why would you put the loft in my name? We're not married, we don't have kids together."

"Are we going to get married?"

"Yes."

"Have kids?"

"Sure."

"Then what difference does it make whether it's now or then?"

Interesting angle.

"It's your home," she said. "This is your home too. Why have we never stayed here?"

"I try not to set foot in this house unless it's necessary. It's kept in order, maintained, always ready and available to any McDade, but I have no desire to live here."

"Bad memories?"

"This is the McDade past. It's a family home. The name is important, but it echoes when there's no life in it."

"Whisper and Razer could stay here too. Are Score and his wife safe?"

"For now."

She narrowed an eye. "Because you want them hurt, or you believe they will be?"

"That depends on Score's actions. He's not an easy man to appease, though his wife has the knack of it, I'm told."

"You think he'll want payback?"

"Clue's in the name."

The harsh edge of her guy never went far. Unless he was with her. The way his fingertips moved across her face and down her neck, his possession bled into her pores.

"You're angry," she murmured. "About what happened tonight."

"The fuck came for my family—"

"Not at Evander. At us."

"I want to lock you up and never let you out."

"Here?" she asked. "If you lock me up here, you'll have to move in."

Her attempt to boost away from the wall failed. The touch of those sure fingers bit tight around her jaw.

"Make a decision."

"Ask me a question."

"Your stake in the McLeods—"

"Is yours," she said.

In control, Connel McDade steered with confidence.

"This is not about money."

"I know what it's about," she said. "Lachlan is my brother, I love him, and I want him to be treated with respect. But for me, on my matters, and family matters, your voice is mine."

Loyalty was one thing. Having a certainty so strong, she didn't consider resisting. This was less about dominance and more about confidence. Losing him, even for a short time, was warning enough. He'd feel it even more because he was used to calling the plays.

"Do what you have to do," she said, laying her hands on him. "I'll always support you… My McDade."

"What do you do if you have a problem?"

"Bring it to you." Just as she'd done after talking to Evander. "I should go see my friend."

"The doc's got him."

His grip switched to a pinch that brought her chin upward. The press of his mouth lingered, expecting, appreciating, loving.

As she lazed in the connection, loosening, needing, surrendering, existence dwindled to—he grabbed her ass, boosting her up to take her through to the shower. He was injured, the scar was still new, probably sensitive, but she wouldn't resist. Looping her arms around his neck, she begged for more as ice-cold water hit her spine.

The water would heat in time with their passion.

"Conn," she whispered, gripping his hair.

Arching her shoulders in response to his kiss trailing lower, she lost herself in them. They'd been apart and come back together, nothing could keep them apart. Conn may be tightening his hold, forcing her close, as a response to them potentially losing each other. She couldn't argue, not when they bathed in the necessity of his possession.

The force of him propelling himself into her tightened her hold and welcomed her voice. Harder, faster, nothing slowed his hammering down. Consumed by him as her body devoured his, they were them, one unit, completion in symbiosis.

Independent woman? Yes, she'd never alter that state of mind. What Conn offered was vital, as fundamental as the air in her lungs. He didn't take her independence, he enhanced it. The McDade shield was strong, and she'd never stray from behind it again.

NINETEEN

SITTING ON THE FLOOR, spine to the wall, she switched one sentence with another. Dark mode meant light from the laptop screen was minimal. Editing, tweaking, the piece was almost—

"We got asses to kick?"

The croak of the voice from the bed raised her head. "Oh my God, Strat…" Putting the laptop aside, she jumped up to sit next to him and grab his hand. "How are you?"

"Still alive," he murmured. "All that tap, tap, tapping. What you writing?"

"An obit."

His lazy smile was a welcome sight. "Must be bad news then. The doc give me a timeline? Better just shoot me now."

"Shut up," she said, combing her fingers through his hair. "You scared the shit out of me."

"Sorry, Scamp."

Chastising him wasn't fair. Adrenaline became relief. God, it was good to hear his voice.

Took her a second to gather strength and subdue tears. "I'm sorry. I'm so, so sorry."

"What'd you do? Crash the car? We'll get another car."

His eyes weren't open, could be the meds. Couldn't be the light because there wasn't enough to hurt.

"I got you abducted, beaten, what happened?"

"Six of his guys jumped me," he said and hazarded another half-smile. "Did not bad against six roided out gym geeks half my age."

"Yeah, old man, they had it coming." Her palm slid to his cheek. "You said three bullets but—"

"Immie, Ford, Jagg—"

"Oh my God, he—"

"It was the threat, Scamp. You'd have made the list too, if he wasn't so eager to bang you."

"So you went quietly." After getting an ass kicking. "He threatened the people you love and—I've always been headstrong."

"I know."

"Stubborn."

"Roger that."

Her fingers slid between his on her lap. "In the last week… I'm putting the people I care about most in danger. How did the wheels come off the wagon so fast? And I don't know what to do, I don't know if…" She sighed. "Sorry, you don't need me rambling."

"That's exactly what I need." He took their joined hands to his chest. "Vex, the fuck, was too scared to lay hands on me direct."

Just his style. "He's always been like that. Evander doesn't fight his own battles."

"He'll have to now. Ire fill you in?"

"He's asleep. He's pissed. Like he's been pissed ever since I woke up here."

"Here?" Yes, they were in the same room she'd first woken in. "What happened?"

"It's not a fun story."

This time she actually got a laugh. "Wow, that's a surprise, our lives being so full of joy and all."

"He thought I'd leave him. That I had—the McDade shield failed me, that's what he said."

"So he doesn't know you've been living with guilt about dragging him past that shield?"

And wasn't that basically what she'd said?

"We're at the McDade Mansion."

"Yeah, the car had windows."

Ha-ha, that got a nudge of objection.

"I didn't even know it was still a thing, that Conn still had it."

"You like it?"

"I don't care about the house. I just wanted you to know we're still in the city. The doctor is looking after you, I don't know where he is now, but if you need—"

"Score McDade's on his way north."

"Here? How do you know that?"

"Wasn't just sitting around waiting to be snatched up."

If he'd been on the street, connecting with contacts, he'd know more than her.

"What have you heard?"

"Doran McDade, Play, Ire's cousin, he's taken up residence in Stag. People are worried, allies nervous."

"Is he an asshole?"

"Less than your guy."

"So why are they nervous?"

"Raze was around, now Play, we've got the big kahunas lining up. And the Doherty's inserting herself, getting way too comfortable. Manzanis don't like it. You know how it is, they front it out, but with news Score's on his way too…"

"A family reunion." At least the mansion would see some life again. "Score has a kid."

"Yeah."

"How old is—"

"Not old enough," Strat said.

"And his wife is…"

"Not from this world or any one close to it. Sure not who anyone thought a guy like Score would end up with. Doesn't matter. You know the play?"

"What play?"

"Ire's got a plan, right? That's why he's off the scene, to keep everyone guessing. Is he alive? Is he injured? Is he poised to take over the world? Maybe he's in danger, or he's lying in wait to strike. A lot of questions out there. Silvio's used to knowing the city, they call him 'The Director' for a reason. Was a time Silvio Manzani could nod and someone would be taken off the board. Anyone. There was no one out of his reach."

"His world's in motion, it's falling apart."

"And his boys, well, you've got Helios coming to the end of his stretch, Atlas, God only knows where, and Vex… that guy doesn't know what's good for him. He should be at his father's shoulder, should be listening, taking notes, following orders, that guy… Imagine what he could've had? With some sack, he could be his father's key weapon. Instead he's an embarrassment."

"Think he saw it coming? That at some point, he just…"

"You know Vex better than almost anyone. You're the longest relationship he ever had in his life outside family."

Not an accolade she was proud of. If anything, that truth was a beacon of his insanity. The longest running relationship in his life was with his stalkee. Crazy didn't cover it.

"He doesn't know what's good for him."

"No, 'cause if he did, he wouldn't be taking on Ire McDade at the peak of his power. Wouldn't be going after Ire McDade's girl at all. Guess it's not a problem anymore though."

"What's not a problem?"

Strat patted her knuckles. "Ire give you the run-down?"

"Run-down?"

"On what happened tonight."

"We haven't done much… talking."

"You get too distracted, kid."

"What am I supposed to do when he turns me on and—"

"And that's the limit of what I want to hear. Rest of us are looking to you. Someone needs to be on top of him." He dug a fist into the bed to force himself upward. "We need your voice in there."

"Don't move around," she said. Even in his weakened state, he was stronger than her. An attempt to push him down was fruitless. Not that she'd push too hard. They had a kinship when it came to being ordered around in the name of recuperation. "I'm useless without you, you know?"

"Give yourself more credit. Sersha McLeod doesn't need any guy to stand up for her."

"He was working flat out, remember? Whisper was going to the prison for Biz. Conn had a plan, and what happened with my father, it's diverted everything. We didn't need the detour. How do I know we didn't lose valuable time?"

"Now Ire has you back, he'll get things on track."

Family went two different ways. The McDades were her priority all day long. But the McLeods, actually one particular McLeod, might not be ready to get in line.

"And my father?" she asked.

"From what I hear, man's got his own troubles."

"Don't ask me, I thought he was with Lach until Conn told me otherwise."

"He say where he was?" The question lingered until her shoulder rose and her friend shook his head, amused again. "Haven't done much talking, right."

"Did the doctor say how long you'd be here?"

"I'll be good to go tomorrow."

Now who was the joker? "Not a chance. You're staying here until you're healed." Conn's threat to keep her chained up sounded like a good idea for her friend. "If anything happens to you—"

"Focus on what's right ahead of you, kid. Think Ire'll let you out again?"

He'd never ask her to be something she wasn't. "I'll support his plan, whatever it is. This week with my dad has put so much in perspective. I didn't get it. I thought I got it, but... Being part of this world, the McDade world, it has to take precedence, and everyone else has to know it."

"That what the obit's for? An ode to your former self?"

"No, Conn asked me to write it."

"For who?"

"Evander."

"Ouch, now, that'll send Vex a message. Smart." Impressed, her friend didn't seem surprised. "It'll run tomorrow? Day after? Plenty of time for Silvio to wonder about his kid. Hustle was a clusterfuck."

"Lives were lost."

"Yeah."

"How did you get out of there?"

"That's on your guy. Man didn't even flinch when he walked in there. Crowded with Vex's ass kissers, weapons, the works. Had me surrounded every which way and Ire just... strolled on in like it was a day in the park."

Never shy, and full of confidence, her guy would front it out probably until the day he died.

Fear was foreign to their leader. "He doesn't get scared."

"You told me that."

"Conn's already put a bullet in Evander's gut."

"Ah, that's what it was. They talked about something the rest of us couldn't follow. Vex didn't want to relive that night, but he sure was pissed about it. And, I'll say, he's not Mensa material, he actually seemed surprised Ire showed up."

Although Evander asked her to come alone, he couldn't really have thought she would. Conn would've put a bullet through Strat, through anyone, before letting her walk in there by herself. He'd remind her it's about pride.

"What did he think would happen?"

"You'd show up, I guess," her friend said. "Boy doesn't understand why people fear and respect his father and men like Ire."

"Because he never grew up. In his opinion, he's entitled to position and power. It's a birthright, and he flouts respect on the field."

"Doesn't understand he's nothing but a child pissing in a pool no one else is swimming in."

"Do you think he'll come for you?" she asked. The answer was kind of a given, yet she said it out loud to ensure her friend faced it. "On the street."

"No." Strat shifted higher again. "'Cause I don't think your guy will let him live that long. I'm surprised he let him leave Hustle alive."

"Killing a Manzani son comes with repercussions."

"Yeah, love him or hate him, Silvio would have to avenge his son. It'd be a sign of weakness to let that slide. People on the street, anyone in the country familiar with the family…" Which was a lot of people, probably most, some helped by her exposé. "They hear a son is dead and the father lets it go? He can't do that; he has to hit the murderer full force. The legend is, in some ways, more important than the reality."

Hmm, suspicious, she probed. "Sounds like something meant for Conn's ears."

"And this is the only way it gets there. Think he shoots the shit with me?"

"I listened to you once before about that." Drawing a knee up to the bed, she got closer. "Then I opened my stupid mouth and it came out wrong."

"When?"

"The night at my grandfather's. In the car and I, stupidly…" Almost unable to believe it was true, she scrunched her hair in a fist. "I told him if we ever had to leave town in a hurry, I wouldn't ask questions. That he should just show up and—"

"He took it to mean you had no faith in him."

"At the worst possible moment, and then with how the night ended, it was just, I couldn't tell him I was sorry."

"That's what you get letting crazy people like me in your head."

And in her heart. "I feel better that you're here."

"Not the best of circumstances. Maybe next time just give me a call."

"Tried that and Evander picked up."

The door opened, and a silhouette appeared. "Macushla."

"Sorry, yes." Leaping up, she kissed Strat's cheek and scooped up her laptop. "Sleep, friend. Breakfast's on me; I'll cook something great. Eggs?"

"Think I'd rather not wake up, Scamp."

Earning the pet name, she scurried to her guy. "Glad to know your sense of humor wasn't injured."

"Only my ego." Strat slid back down, happy to return to rest. "Night, kids."

Conn put an arm around her to draw her out and close the door. "You leave me to go to another man's bed?"

"I didn't want him to wake up alone." Going into their dark bedroom, she held her computer aloft. "And I was finishing my assignment."

As he took the computer, she stripped out of his shirt and climbed back under their covers. Sitting in the middle of the bed, knees drawn up, she watched Conn as he read her words, his face lit by the dim glow of the screen.

TWENTY

DID HE LIKE IT? Didn't he?

She'd been in the publishing industry all her adult life, some of her teen years too. Sure, back at the start, she'd been green. Almost every writer suffered imposter syndrome once in a while. For her, it hit more prominently around her time of the month. But sitting there, watching him read, the true fear was disappointing him. He'd never disappointed her; he went above and beyond for her. In this one thing, her trade, she could be useful to him. If she did it right.

He went to the side unit to set the computer down. With a few clicks and swipes, he…? What was he doing? Adding his own flair?

"You got notes?"

"I sent it," he said and closed the lid.

"You sen—to Steeple?"

"Signed by the family, it'll make the presses."

With his name at the end, yeah, she didn't doubt that.

"Did you change—"

"Didn't change a word, baby. You got it right first time."

However many drafts later, but he didn't need to know how the sausage was made. The outcome counted; the process was her responsibility. She'd been happy with it, as much as anyone could be happy with writing an obituary for someone still breathing.

"Thank you for saving Strat, for caring for him, for the doc fixing him up. Don't let him get up and out too early, he has to recover. If we let him, he'll overwork himself. He has to take this slowly."

She'd bet Conn wasn't the best patient either. In their sanctuary, they didn't need to talk about his pain, his fury, his panic.

He came to join her in bed. "I didn't have luck with that tack and you."

"Well, you know, he's more afraid of you than I am."

Lunging over, he scooped her under him into sheer, consuming bliss. "You're not afraid of me, Miss McLeod?"

"I'm a little bit afraid when you use that voice." Except her smile stayed strong. "'Cause my panties evaporate."

"You kept the panties on," he said like it was an affront. "Worried for your modesty?"

This time, when she laughed, her head dug deeper into the pillow. "My modesty never held up in your presence. Did you forget?"

He brushed his lips across hers, taking his time about easing into the contact only to inhale and withdraw, just a fraction, a whisper, less than a feather's depth. The intoxicating, faraway sense he bestowed both closed her eyes and opened her lips.

"Mo Grá."

"Things around here will get tough for a while."

Still close, tone quiet, their intimacy encompassed trust. "Situations might change fast, we'll have to adapt quickly."

"Score's on his way here?"

"Strat told you?" As his fingertips smoothed the hair from her temple, she nodded. "Word is out on the street. That's good."

"It would be easier for me to help you, and the family, if I knew what was going on."

"I'm working from the club tomorrow night."

"Okay." That was an important clue. "For a reason or just to get back on the horse? You're working with Play, right? He's not taking over."

"He's playing a role I need him to play, finetuning as I go."

"I'm not the superintendent's daughter anymore."

That drew him back enough to meet her eye. "You're not?"

"If my father resigns his position—"

"Your father's keeping his job."

She frowned. "He is? But Lach—"

"And I have developed a strategy."

Really? Her blue-all-the-way-through brother and cutthroat-crime-boss boyfriend were developing strategies in cahoots now? Shit. Up wasn't up yet.

"I guess… I always wanted you to get along." So why should she question their alliance? She shouldn't, so moved on. "What happened with Evander? What happened the night my dad—"

"A lot of questions."

"And not a lot of answers. You're stronger now, the McDades, I don't see you surrendering at all, much less surrendering when you're at the top of your game."

He frowned. "Who said anything about surrendering?"

"We're here, in hiding, and—"

"Not hiding, fortifying."

"We want the world to wonder?"

"Aye."

"And with your…" Their eyes stayed matched as her fingertips skimmed over his wound. "You needed time to heal? How bad was it? I was so terrified that you—"

"It's in the past, Macushla. What's done is done."

It couldn't be as simple as that. She wouldn't let it be forgotten like it was nothing.

"My father doesn't get a pass, shouldn't get a pass. What he's done is unacceptable. He showed no loyalty to his own father, then disrespected the McDades so horribly—"

"He doesn't get a pass. Don't upset yourself, we have this under control."

Her gusto hid an underlying fear. "How long were you there? In my grandfather's office? Alone?"

"Not long."

"How did you get out? Did Niall find you?"

"I picked the lock and got to the car," he said. "Niall was waiting here with the doc." So he'd been there the whole time she'd been away? "He'd already sent Daly and the others on the hunt—"

"We went to Strat's."

"I know. Guys showed up there less than an hour after you left. Doc put me out."

To treat his injury or to calm his temper? Maybe both. She couldn't see her guy choosing to be unconscious, but if he needed any kind of surgery, sedatives would've been the only option.

"It was Niall," she murmured. "He kept you alive."

Because if it was up to her guy, he'd have been in the car, bleeding, chasing after her. Logic didn't always feature when fear and anger stoked adrenaline.

"Not the first time he's done that."

Much as she and Niall weren't exactly bosom buddies, his allegiance to Conn and the McDades was undeniable. They should spend more time getting to know each other. Not that the guy ever seemed to have an iota of free time.

"My father drove us to a motel. We stayed holed up there drafting and redrafting a ridiculous story neither of us could agree on."

"I know."

Her head shifted. "You couldn't have got that from Strat… How much time have you spent talking with my brother?"

"Enough to know your father's debt will never be paid."

"And by extension mine. Baby, I—"

"Hush. You take your lead from me."

"Always."

"And know I could choose to take your father out any time."

Out? As in his life? Though surprised Conn was leaving Ronald in his current role, she shouldn't have been. Position gave them influence.

And the other thing? That her father may lose his life any minute? How did she feel about that? The daughter part of her recognized she should protest and defend, but it would be theater. She and her father never got along. Did she want him dead? Maybe. No, not with any vehemence, though given he'd killed his own father… Actually, the more she thought about it, the more she wanted the decision to be someone else's. Ronald killed her grandfather, shot her lover, then abducted and imprisoned her. If anyone should desire revenge, it would be her.

Objecting felt more like conforming to the

expected response. It wasn't respectful for anyone to want someone else dead, but in those dark recesses, the truth didn't hide.

"He took my grandfather down without warning," she said. "If Ronald didn't give someone else that courtesy, why should he be owed it from us?"

He kissed her slow. "Beautiful." With a single word, he lightened her burden. "He's useful for now."

"Because in his job, he can help us. What about Silvio? Won't he come after Ronald? He could want him to work for the Manzanis again."

"Silvio Manzani has enough going on. And we have his son. He'll have to bargain for him back."

"So long as we have Evander, alive, we control Silvio. Do you think he'll call Atlas back?" The middle Manzani brother. "Do you know where he is?"

"No, because I don't want to. I know people who do, that's enough. He's useless to me as he is. If that changes, I'll call in a favor."

"Who knows where he is? A Manzani who owes you? If Silvio knows where Atlas is, why doesn't he drag him back?"

Even kicking and screaming would be Silvio's style. The man didn't have any direct heir, no one who could take over quickly. Helios, the eldest, was in prison, and had been all his adult life. How much had Silvio taught his son? Was he ready to take power if the need arose? Did he want it?

"Silvio doesn't know."

"But your sources—"

"Silvio couldn't pay enough to have any of them crack. Manzani relations with the Huntsmen are murky."

"The Huntsmen?" Oh, curiosity roused with excitement. "Strat mentioned them once, said I should turn and run if they came up in conversation, that they're insane."

"Fuck, aye. You hear any whisper of them, you get to me as fast as you can. Never declare yourself to them. Never approach them. Never."

Her guy didn't seem scared, but there was definitely an edge of wary warning in that instruction.

"Never declare myself as in my name or my affiliation with you?"

"They know who you are, I guarantee it. Always assume they know your secrets."

"Who are they?"

"Nobody knows, few do anyway."

Which suggested maybe… "You do," she said. "You know who they are." He didn't confirm or deny, didn't blink either. "They're loyal to you."

"They're loyal to no one. Do not forget that." He snatched her chin to hold her head firm. "They act only in their best interest. They are loyal to no one. Say it to me."

"They are loyal to no one."

"Good." He released her. "Remember that."

"They must be loyal to each other."

Her guy rarely smiled, and though his lips didn't move, his eyes betrayed the sentiment.

"To each other?" he asked. "No. They can work in tandem, if it suits their purpose, but they're loyal to no one." What an odd, isolating life. Conn's warning should deter her, but her curious mind… "No research. You forget you ever heard of them, hear me?"

Oh, well.

She nodded. "You spoil all my fun."

"Then it's time to use you for mine."

The gentle rasp of his teeth on her lower lip heralded what was to come. The night, their lives, danger or not, hung on the thread of their relationship, and it was stronger than silk.

TWENTY-ONE

"COME ON, we've got work."

The new day started with a determination she hoped would remain until sunset. This was what she needed, energy, optimism, and a great big dose of fuck-the-bastards, which was anyone not on her nice list. Her guy was nowhere around. Typical. Even a guy who didn't leave the building could still duck out on her, that was a special skill.

Strat was dead to the world. No omen intended. And he needed the rest, so she didn't wake him. Keeping him there to heal was easier while he slumbered. Tiny win, but she'd take it.

She'd hurried downstairs and stuck her head into the dining room to call on her guys. Playing nice, following the rules, her wellbeing was one thing, knowing what it meant to Conn enhanced her need to safeguard it. And it might help Conn's decision making when it came to her autonomy. Going behind his back, sneaking around, wouldn't win her any points, or any freedom.

"Get moving," she followed up. "Chop, chop, fellas."

Her compliance did have its limits. She didn't wait. The fire in her belly begged to be stoked. No more lying around feeling sorry for herself or wallowing in guilt. The only way to get over that, and recent traumas, was to take action, follow through.

By the time Daly emerged from their pseudo rec room, she was halfway to the front door.

"Are you allowed to go out?"

"You think Conn's keeping me prisoner?" she called back over her shoulder. "If he was, my day would've started way differently."

There would be worse ways to wake up than with your smoking hot boyfriend chaining you to a bedpost. Mm, something they should try. It had been a while since they'd got any kind of freaky freak on.

"Niall didn't say anything about going out."

"Do we need him to micromanage?" she asked, tossing open the front door. "Do we have a car or will I call a cab?"

Her phone was back in her purse. The new clutch she'd selected from a range in the closet. She'd ignored the one abandoned in Conn's car before the drama. Every McDade location she visited had a brand-new wardrobe for her, accessories and all. Who did that? Knowing it came from Conn's order was hot. He wouldn't care about things, he cared about her comfort, her belonging.

When her head turned and her eyes reacted to the daylight, she blinked, and there it was, the Bentley. Her Bentley, parked with a couple of other cars at one side of the driveway.

"Bluebell, can we—"

"What more permission do you need?" she asked, gesturing at the car, hurrying down the stairs. "My car is right there. Why would it be there if not for my use?"

"It's a family car."

"You think it's parked out here waiting for someone else?" She opened the back door. "Do others use it?"

On the other side of the door, Daly's mouth opened, but a few seconds went by before he answered. "Not as long as you're here."

Not as long as ever, she'd talk to Conn about that. Though, huh, was that kinda divaish? That she expected no one else to travel in her car without her? Where was Whisper when she needed a dose of you-know-what?

"I'm safe in the car and I have my guys." Hock and Snuff lumbered over, not far behind Daly. "No shootouts or bank heists, I swear."

Her bodyguard didn't laugh. "So no fun for the rest of us is what you're saying," he said. Man had a sense of humor, that was the spirit. "Where are we going?"

"Chronicler first, Stag after, maybe my brother's," because she had to tie him down for answers. They'd be easier to extract from Lachlan than Conn. Unless her guy specifically told her brother not to share… Would that stop him? "Sound safe? If you're worried about protecting me without Strat looking over your shoulder, I can ask Conn to—"

"No one's worried, Bluebell." With a tug on the top of the door, he took it from her. "Get in and sit nice. The door shit is my duty."

Life wasn't so bad. On the way to work, she did a quick search for recent news she might've missed. And for clues on what happened at Hustle. Gunshots, fire, injuries, two bodies, no IDs yet. Hmm.

Her obit ran, no surprise, so most of the world probably assumed one of those bodies was Evander

Manzani. Except nothing in the paper, or anywhere online, stated that categorically.

Maybe her boss knew the obit was more about the message than the content. She'd ask but may not get a straight answer. From her side of the fence, the threat of her boyfriend was a useful tool. However, if said boyfriend was colluding with her boss, Steeple may be under orders to keep quiet.

Hadn't Conn been convalescing? Where had he found the time to threaten all these people into silence? Didn't have to do it himself. Her man knew how to delegate, or Niall did, the latter was usually the one dishing out orders.

Daly stuck with her in the elevator ascent. At the top, Paolo was in his booth, Lucy perched at the desk.

"Sersha!" Lucy called and leaped up. "Oh, hi! Gosh, we haven't seen you forever! How are you?"

"Good. Isn't it the weekend?"

"I love my job."

Was that an answer? The young woman didn't seem that sure, and she kept glancing at Daly. Hmm, she didn't know much about Lucy's life, anything about it, actually.

"It's busy." Lucy wasn't the only unexpected person at their desk. "A lot of people in."

"There was a big thing, I don't know, an incident at Manzani—but…" Lucy's laugh wasn't genuine, though the trepidation she pinned on Daly definitely was. "I don't have to tell you—you know the, about all the…"

"All the what?" Daly asked, provoking clear terror. "Who told you we know something?"

"Stop it," she said, using her whole body to push him. "He's kidding, he's being an idiot, just screwing around."

"I, uh," an exhale of a laugh, "didn't know they did that."

Like every thug attended the same training seminars on good goon etiquette. Better to give the woman a break than delve deeper into that stereotype.

"Any messages?"

The receptionist handed over a stack of notes and a small box. "That came today."

And she was almost afraid to open it. No return address, nothing identifying, just her name and work's address.

Evander? Maybe.

"Thanks."

"Aren't you going to open it?" Lucy asked, bouncing closer. "Is it a gift? Is it diamonds?"

"With the time I'm having recently, it could just as easily be a grenade," she said, broadening her smile while the bubbly woman shrank. "I don't know if you want to be around when I open it." In the corner of her eye, Tulip walked by Steeple's office. "Ah, excuse me."

Dashing across the bullpen, ignoring the whispers and stares, she put herself in Tulip's path.

"Sersha," Tulip said, wary or surprised, maybe both. "You bailed on me."

"I bailed on a lot of people, tough times."

"Steeple said you were on leave, grief, right?"

Somehow that came across as genuine, despite the cynicism staring at her.

"I'm sorry, I didn't mean to disappear." Really honestly hadn't meant to. "Do you want to talk?"

"Now?" Tulip looked left to right. "You want to talk now?"

Loyalty was crucial. If someone had it out for them, for Conn, she wanted to know.

"I want the CI's name," she said. "What do you want in return?"

"The price for—"

"I'll pay it. Today. Right now."

The woman's eyes narrowed. "Are you fucking with me?"

"No, I only do that with my boyfriend, he gets jealous otherwise. You want answers or not?"

This was one loose end she wanted tied up pronto. Adapt quickly, that's what Conn said. Anyone out there working against them needed to be taken down quick and easy. The witness who'd fingered Conn for her grandpapa's murder could have an agenda. Despite his new affiliation with her guy, Lachlan might still be reluctant to share the name. Her father would be more inclined to, if he thought it would save his skin, though, with him, it couldn't be her doing the asking.

The best part about it? While shuffling into the interview room by Steeple's office, with its half-glazed wall, the gawping and gossiping rose to a whispering fever pitch. Nowhere saw more intrigue and speculation than the Chronicler's investigative floor.

"Is he pissed?"

Tearing her attention from out there, she sat down with Tulip. "Hmm?"

"Ire, is he pissed?"

"Most of the time," she said. "You referencing something specific?"

"I don't get it. How can you be with a guy like him?"

"Excuse me?"

"He's hot, goddamn, he's hot. And I don't expect everyone's moral compass to be pointing north all the time, but he's… consumed by it."

"By his moral compass?"

"By his family, the business, the violence."

"Who said anything about violence?"

Tulip's head angled to the side. "Off the record, not for the story, I'm just saying, woman to woman, how do you know he'll come home to you every night? Aren't you scared witless every second?"

"That something might happen to him?"

"Yeah, or to you, Ire McDade has enemies."

"Ire McDade is a giant among dwarves. Am I scared? Only until I remember the man at my back would do anything to protect me. He's always there, always supporting me. When it comes to my safety, he's beyond passionate."

"Do you argue?" With each other? Like a couple does? Do you dare raise your voice to him?"

Yes, but *for* him was a way more regular occurrence. "Okay," she said, exhaling on a smile. "Is this an interview about my love life or did you want to talk about something else?"

"Just getting some background. How did you meet?"

"No comment."

Tulip actually smiled. "How long did you know him before you got intimate?"

"No comment."

This was good practice for any more formal situations she may find herself in. You know, like interview rooms with federal agents.

"Are you exclusive?"

"No comment."

"He ever hit you?"

"No," she said and leaned a little closer. "And, quick tip, never ask me that question in earshot of anyone else. For your own protection."

"No one's ever asked about violence in your relationship?"

"Who would ask about that?"

"Your brother," Tulip said. "Your father. Since the alderman died, your family have been AWOL in all kinds of ways."

"Grief impacts people differently."

"How does your brother feel about your relationship?"

"You'd have to ask him."

With a slight brow raise, Tulip moistened her lips. "Your brother isn't known for playing nice with the press."

"It's in his nature to be protective. With what he does, the work he does, sharing information doesn't come naturally."

"And in Ire's work, I'd guess he's the same."

Their chairs were perpendicular, so it wasn't like the Inquisition. This woman was doing her job, one Sersha could identify with.

"He's not interested in grandstanding. Nothing in his life would be of interest to reporters."

Tulip scoffed. "I know you don't believe that. Does he give you a line to toe? How do you know what is allowed and what isn't? Don't you ever want to…?"

"Want to what?"

"The things you must know," Tulip whispered with intrigue and slid forward in her seat. "You could blow the lid off the whole damn crime network, expose them all in a day, in a single article. What would he do?"

"Who?"

"Ire," Tulip said, sort of groaning the obvious name.

"Conn's a businessman. Yes, there are things about his work that are not advertised, that doesn't mean they're interesting enough to print. And you know the rules, we don't go after our own, we just don't."

Though she would happily if Conn asked her to expose her father's misdeeds.

"We would if there was a story, if getting the truth out there was necessary."

Maybe they were made differently. Or maybe young Tulip had never been in a situation where sharing and not was the difference between life and death. Not hers, no. Even if she printed full transcripts of her interactions with the McDades, Conn wouldn't hurt her. It wasn't in him. How did she know? Because it wasn't in her to hurt him either. Physically or with words. Those conversations, the ones she had with him, and whatever she heard in the McDade sphere, were words she'd take to the grave.

"Do you have family?" More than just turning the tables, she genuinely wanted to know more about this woman. "Nearby?"

"Are you threatening me?"

The question wasn't asked in fear, Tulip seemed affronted, yes, but there was fascination too.

"I don't threaten people."

"Hmm." Tulip's disbelief came with contempt. "Because your fella does that for you?"

"Conn knows your name because I mentioned it. He has no reason to approach you or anyone connected to you. I'm curious about where you're from, the source of your interest."

"I'd never give up a source. The CI wasn't my source."

"I know that. Are you going to give me his name?"

"Are you going to tell me why Nicole McDade has a price on her head?"

Playing coy wouldn't get them anywhere. Tulip discovered that the contract existed on her own.

"Because someone wants her dead."

"Someone who?" Tulip asked. "I heard it was connected to Whisper Doherty-McDade, and she left the city in a hurry."

"What does that tell you?"

"A lot when the woman met with Biz McDade, Nicole's husband, alone. Were they having an affair? Is this jealousy?"

She frowned. "Was who having an affair?"

"Whisper and Biz."

Instant humor blasted out of her without finesse. It startled Tulip so much that she reared back.

"Want to talk about taking your life in your hands? Never let Whisper know you said that."

"She has a reputation too."

"And you never thought what that's like?" Her eyes widened in question; Tulip responded with a clueless head shake. "Everywhere you go, people think they know you. They watch. Stare. Gawp. Openly pass judgment, assume they know everything there is to know about you." From their current vantage point, it only took a slight gesture to turn Tulip's attention to the onlookers in the bullpen. "I've worked in this building for years, with a lot of those people for years."

"Now they're passing judgment?"

"With my heritage, people have always jumped to conclusions, built their own picture. Now I sleep next to a man with his own heritage, his own reputation. And it's a major contrast to what they thought they knew of me."

"Now they don't know what to think."

"They're as fascinated as they are terrified. All the questions, the supposition, they're desperate for info, but prefer to speculate in their circles than ask me anything direct."

"In everyone's defense, you don't answer direct questions. Not honestly. What would they get for asking them?"

She had to give Tulip that. "People don't understand. They put others in categories, label them good or evil, righteous or wicked."

"Doesn't everyone in your life fit into those categories?"

Oh, if only she could tell the full truth.

"No," she said. "Conn is a better man than any other I've known. Lachlan aside."

"Not your father or grandfather aside too?"

On a slow exhale, she held firm. "I didn't misspeak. Don't be fooled by appearances."

"So Whisper going to Biz in prison had nothing to do with the contract on his wife's head?"

"Whisper is a confident woman. She doesn't answer to me or do what I say."

"Which is what you said about Razer's social calendar." Tulip sat back. "You're wasting my time."

"Or you're wasting mine. This is your job, but it's my life, my guy's life. Do you have any intention of telling me who falsely fingered Conn?"

"Do you have any intention of telling me who put the price on Nicole's head?"

"It wasn't anyone I know," she said without blinking.

The moment that passed between them tugged at gravity, growing more somber. This was it, the faceoff had come.

"But it was someone, and you know who." A statement. "The McDades?" She didn't respond. "You have to give me something, Sersha. Was it one of the families?"

"Could be."

"Do you know where she is? Is Nicole safe? Is she still alive?"

"Last I heard." Though she hadn't asked with everything else going on. "Alive and safe."

"From everyone? You could only know that if she's with the McDades. Is she under their protection? Just because Ire's protecting her doesn't mean it wasn't a McDade that put out the hit. They aren't known for yielding to each other."

"Layers of intrigue," Sersha said and smiled. "Welcome to my world."

"Is she close by? Somewhere I can talk to her?"

"She's not taking visitors." No need for Conn's nod to confirm that. "You want to be careful about snooping."

"Why didn't you tell me about you and Ire? We went out, to Stag, and you didn't… say a word."

"I don't declare the details of my love life to everyone I meet."

"Yeah, but you knew I was interested—were you protecting them?

"You say that like we're your enemy."

"Aren't you?"

While it wasn't like her to be defensive, she had that same thread of suspicion in her. The curiosity made them good at their jobs. Tulip could be their enemy, if she played it that way, or she could clean up the misconceptions.

She got to her feet. "Come with me."

"Come with you where?"

"On an adventure."

As she went out, Tulip hurried after. Her three guys were in the bullpen, watching.

"We're going out," she said to Daly.

"We just got here."

Steeple leaped out of his office. "Sersha—"

"We're going out for an hour," she said. "I'll check back in later."

"Where are we going?" Daly asked, glancing behind her while keeping pace at her side. The not so happy expression on his face betrayed Tulip was in her wake. "Somewhere for lunch?"

"Actually, yeah," she said. "Can someone grab lunch?"

"Wait, we're your valet now?"

"You three are safe from menial duties," she said, entering the elevator with her First Team. "I know your names, you've got to stick around. Make room."

Wafting her arms in front of her, she forced her guys to the walls to give space for Tulip to join them.

"Not sure the boss'll like this," Hock muttered.

"Us this close to Bluebell?" Snuff asked to which Hock snickered.

"Very funny, guys," she said, bowing to press the lobby button. "You don't have to touch me to fear for your lives. Just pray I don't *tell him* you touched me." The guys stayed pretty flat, but she laughed and gestured at Tulip. "I'm kidding."

"Yeah, she could do it with a look."

She backhanded Daly's belly, still smiling at their guest. "Do you want something to eat? We can have something brought to us."

"So long as it's not from the deli down the road," Daly said as the doors opened.

She kept Tulip close as the trio surrounded them to cross the building lobby and go out to the street.

"Do these guys come with you everywhere?"

The answer to that question was complicated, if she overthought it.

"Aye," she said, and nodded at the black van behind. "And those ones." Daly opened the Bentley door. "Conn cares about my safety above everything else." She slipped in the back with Tulip not far behind. "Let me break down some of the mystery for you." Daly got in the front. "Take us to the club."

TWENTY-TWO

STAG IN THE DAYTIME wasn't intimidating. So she thought until Tulip stopped to look up at it after they left the car. The building was huge, dark, hiding whatever was within, cloaking its secrets. And, boy, did it have secrets.

Daly stopped next to her to side whisper. "Sure this is a good idea?"

"It's lunch. We'll show Tulip there's nothing sinister going on."

"Biggs is here already, guys are on their way with food." Good idea or not, he'd follow orders. "Problem though, you don't eat lunch."

"Tulip can eat. Just make sure there's coffee or booze."

"Never short of that, honey."

The club wasn't open for business, and Play was likely the one upstairs, alone or not. But they didn't have to draw back the whole proverbial curtain. The mystery came from the mystique of the family and its late-night dealings. If she could uncloud that mist, in the right crevices, and let the woman think she was just a little on the inside, maybe she could foster allegiance.

Dingo opened the door for them, lighting was low, and voices carried from the cavern beyond.

With full confidence, she stormed a path straight into the club. Those voices quieted. The many now-silent men around the room awaited her direction. Hers. They waited for her permission to continue.

Biggs stood up first and rounded the bar to plant his hands on it. "Safe Harbor?"

"Alcohol?" Tulip asked. "It's the middle of the day."

More than just a couple of guys laughed. Conventional rules didn't exist there. Tulip glanced around, maybe self-conscious. Yeah, it was funny, the guys meant no harm, but the point wasn't to ridicule the reporter.

"Can we have the room, please, guys?"

Without objection, the guys, other than Biggs and her First Team, tramped out through the various doors.

"They just up and leave like that? It doesn't piss them off you order them around?"

"I didn't order them, I asked them. Respect begets respect." In her book, not so much in Conn's. "And I've worked out here before; welcome to my office." Swinging herself into the VIP booth that jutted into the dance floor, she gestured at the next section. "Sit down, they'll bring the food here."

Biggs brought their drinks. "Milady."

"Thank you. Stick around, we'll probably want more."

"As you wish, mistress," Biggs said and winked.

Idiot, very funny. Playing to the myth could be fun too.

"What is the point of this?" Tulip asked.

"Buttering me up? Trying to be my best friend? If you really wanted to show trust, you'd take me upstairs."

Always looking for the angle. Tulip wasn't scared to open her mouth. Good quality in an investigative reporter.

"This is not about trust," she said. "These people, everyone you've seen or met connected with the McDades, they're real people, not characters in any plot or melodrama."

"And they work for you?"

"They work for the business," she said. "McDades look after their own. I want you to see what's good here. We're not evil. Stag contributes to the neighborhood, provides jobs, fosters community. You never heard of Irish hospitality? We look after our employees, keep people safe."

"People like Nicole? Is she here?"

She shook her head. "Why are you so interested in her?"

"No one can put the pieces together. There's one story and another. A woman's life is at stake."

"And she's a McDade, yet you suspect us? Why would we kill one of our own?"

"Her husband's in prison, he hasn't divorced her. There must still be feelings there. If it's one of the other families, what would their motivation be?"

"Maybe that's your clue, who has motive to want her dead?"

"It's not possible to figure that out without all the information."

"No one has all the information."

"It's sinister. Whisper and Raze show up, then disappear. Madison Byrne is in town. Word is Score McDade's on his way too. We're headed for a full-throttle showdown. Who'll get caught in the crossfire?"

"You have some interesting sources."

"You denying it?"

"No."

"Is it all connected?"

"To some degree, everything is connected."

"Sersha," Tulip groaned. "Are you giving me the runaround? Why has Nicole got a price on her head?"

"Who named Conn as my grandfather's killer?" Their eyes locked. "If I raise my voice—"

"Another threat?"

"I've given you plenty. I confirmed there's a price on Nicole's head. Told you she's still breathing, and that the McDades did not put out the contract. What else do you want to know?"

"Why she deserves to die."

"Given we weren't the ones to call it, I can't give you the right answer. I can make one up, maybe she's on Santa's Naughty List."

Four guys came to put out salad and sandwiches before disappearing without a word.

"This is serious," Tulip said, ignoring the spread. "I can't believe you'd be glib about a woman's life."

"And I can't believe you'd be glib in refusing to identify who wants to hurt my guy. His life is at stake in this too. If his life is at stake, so is mine, so is everyone on payroll. Why do you want to hurt the McDades?"

Startled again, Tulip mouthed nothing for a few seconds. "I don't want to hurt the McDades."

It wasn't a threat, but the woman had to be aware of their location. Intention meant nothing when there were so many heavies in the vicinity. Truth mattered less than her desire. Like she'd said to the guys in the Chronicler elevator. Around the McDades? Her words were orders, not requests. And no one would question them. Power, this was her kingdom. Conn had given her a crown and had no problem with her using it for her own ends. Not that she would, but the potential was intoxicating.

Honestly? She could ask Biggs or Daly to end the conversation, end her colleague's life, even just take her liberty, and Conn would handle everything else. A fawn in the forest, Tulip didn't know oblivion hung perilously close.

Conn wouldn't second-guess her. Would it be complicated disappearing a woman they knew little about? Yes. That wouldn't deter her guy. He'd handle it, like he handled all her messes.

Planting both hands on the table, she rose just a little to loom near her colleague. "Someone wants to hurt the man I love," she growled, possessive and unimpressed. "Someone whispered his name into the ear of an enemy," if the cops could be called that, "meaning him harm. Someone vindictive. Conniving. Callous. With a motive that hasn't been fulfilled. Anyone protecting that person means to hurt my guy too. Means the McDades harm. Me harm. And that's not something I take lightly. Do you take the imprisonment of an innocent man lightly?"

"I didn't know he was innocent."

"He was with me," she said, her head rolling a little. "Are you calling me a liar?"

"He's your lover."

"Yes, and the victim was my grandpapa. So I ask again, are you calling me a liar?"

Tulip shook her head. "I trust he was with you, he didn't pull the trigger."

"No, yet someone pointed the finger at him. Isn't that a more interesting story than some nebulous contract? What motivated the witness to insult the head of our family?"

"Money," Tulip said. "Revenge. Could be a power grab or protest."

Sinking down, she settled, picking up her glass to

swirl the liquid in it. "You want a quote?"

Clearly surprised, Tulip blinked. "A quote from… from you?"

"Or Conn," she said, assessing the woman as she raised her glass to sip the liquor. "A local entrepreneur cruelly ripped from his place of business in the middle of the night. Interrogated by hostile cops. A man related to the victim, by association. Who did the false witness want to hurt? Conn? The McDades? Maybe the McLeods? Could the snitch be covering his own crime?"

A glimmer of fog lifted, revealing a new glitter in the young woman's eyes. "I can write the story?"

She nodded. "Write it. Show it to me. We'll give you a quote."

"You… He'd really talk to me?"

"Providing your article highlights the correct wronged party."

"Should you check because I won't—"

"My word is as good as his."

Tulip slid along the seat. "I heard something else about you, something about Ire." With situation on top of situation swirling in her midst, that could point to any number of things. "Give me the inside track on—"

"I'll give you a maybe until you spill something. How do I know you even have this witness's name?"

"I have it."

She sipped her liquor. "So tell me."

"Do I have your word nothing will happen to him?"

"Contrary to popular belief, I'm not all-powerful. Something could happen to any of us any second." And what would happen to him was Conn's decision, she wouldn't dish out promises on his behalf. Oh, yeah, and there was a good chance she might slash the bastard herself. "The CI wasn't your source. Give me his name. Who's Wanstead got in his pocket?"

On a grumbled exhale, Tulip surrendered. "Sneddon."

"The security guy?" Wow, and he'd thought he had PTSD before? He ain't seen nothing yet. "Dick move."

Determining who was pulling Wanstead's strings was the next mystery.

"Sersha—"

Her phone ringing cut Tulip off. The screen said Imogen. She held up a forefinger to answer.

"Hey," she said without giving away the caller's identity. That it was Imogen increased the urgency, they'd got into some messes together in the past. Might be cueing up another. "You okay?"

"We can't get hold of Dad or Ford. I was at his apartment; Dad didn't go home last night. Tell me he's with you. Please."

"Not presently, but I know where he is and he's safe."

"Where? Please, Sersha!"

"Okay, okay." It wasn't like Imogen to freak without cause. "We're at the club having lunch."

"You and my dad?"

"Me and Tulip. You can come join us or we'll meet back at the office." Quiet lingered. "Hello?"

"Is Tulip... is she on the inside of... any of it?"

"No!" She snickered. "God, no."

"So why would you—"

"Reasons." She scooted along the seat. "I have to come back and talk to Steeple anyway. Meet us at the office." Hanging up, she bounced out of the booth and got going. "I have to get back to work."

Tulip followed. "Everything okay?"

"Yeah, will be." Landing a smile on Daly, he just glared. "What's up, friend?"

"You didn't eat anything."

Waving over her shoulder, she set the exit in her sights. "Yeah, I never eat lunch, didn't you know that?" Good thing this guy was under orders to keep her alive. "Let the guys have at it."

TWENTY-THREE

STRAT WAS ONE THING. She had no idea where Ford would be. With Tulip at her side in the car, calling Conn for an update wasn't possible. Almost as quick as they left, they returned to their Chronicler floor.

Imogen was pacing in Steeple's office. Back and forth, worrying her hands.

"What's going on?" Tulip asked. "Need any help?"

"You have a story to write." Maybe that was a little blunt, but she didn't have time for tact. Going into Steeple's office, from which he was absent, she retrieved her phone from her purse. "Imogen?"

"Oh my God, where is he?"

"Your dad was at Hustle last night."

Gasping, both Imogen's hands leaped to her mouth. "I knew it! I knew it. I said it to Jagg and—which hospital is he at?"

Probably not a good idea to tell Imogen about the whole kidnap and torture thing.

"Not one you'll find on any map," she said and

dialed. "I'll tell you everything, just give me a second."

"What for—"

"Macushla?"

"Baby, do we know where Ford is? Strat's boy?"

"Aye."

Okay, good, she waited for a location. Waited… and waited… "Mo Grá?"

"He's safe, unharmed. Working with us."

"Oh…" And Imogen's eagerness came ever closer, so she backed away a few steps. "Somewhere I can tell his sister who's standing right in front of me?"

"No."

Hmm, this would be an interesting dance. "What about Jagg?"

"He's downstairs in the car," Imogen said.

Sersha hadn't been asking the woman, and her guy got that.

"Was left behind to guard the daughter," Conn said. "If she needs more protection, Daly can divert some of the guys from the club."

"Imogen's just worried. Can I take her to…?"

"No." Clarifying, and awkward, given the woman was right there. "Tell anyone you care about to stay off the streets tonight."

Chilled, the awkwardness gave way to concern. "Mo Grá?"

"It's under control. And I'm proud of you."

Uh… "For what?"

"Your work with that reporter, playing by McDade rules. You're getting it, Cushla Machree. Exercise those muscles."

"The CI was—"

"I know who the CI was."

Her jaw loosened. "Why didn't you—"

"I know things." Something she should make a habit of remembering. "Told you it was handled."

"And we're just okay with—"

"We'll talk about it later. You're a good girl, Macushla."

And the line went quiet.

She exhaled. "Your dad is fine, your brother is fine."

"How do I know that?" Imogen asked. "Can I see them?"

"No, I'll ask your dad to call you. I don't have access to Ford, but he's working with us, he's fine."

"Working with you? As in working with the McDades?"

"Aye."

Every time she used that word, she shivered in a private place only accessible to Conn. Shit, just the thought of him…

"Jagg doesn't—he knows everything Ford's into," Imogen said. "He doesn't know anything about this."

"You and Jagg should look after each other. We'll take care of your dad and Ford."

Her reassurance didn't do its job.

Imogen couldn't shake whatever was putting the concern on her face. "After all we've been through, you don't trust me?"

"There's nothing to worry about. With technology these days, we get used to being connected, in constant communication, but it's not needed. You have my word they're good."

Because she trusted Conn's word.

"Dad's been off the radar this week, him and Lach," Imogen said. "I get they don't like that I'm with Jagg…"

"That's not what—no, that's not it. Don't read into this. Your dad, Ford, and Lach are completely…"

Except she couldn't finish that sentence because

she didn't have an accurate answer on the last guy. Just where was Lach exactly? Maybe she should take a page from Imogen's book and check her own backyard.

"Sersha?" Imogen asked.

Steeple came in. "Shit, you two are trying to kill me." He set her in his sights. "You got Tulip sucking Ire's cock too?"

That jarred her back to the moment, that and Imogen's accompanying shocked inhale.

"I missed that threesome." Wit was her only weapon, if she went for the other one—named Daly—someone would end up in jail… or hospital. "You know what it's like screwing bad boys. One orgy becomes like the next… they all run together."

"You can't say that to her," Imogen said, doing the offense thing.

"She wouldn't set the McDades on me for my idiot mouth."

Though when her boss's eyes met hers, they maybe weren't so sure about that. And, yeah, perhaps she let a sly smile slink upward, leaving him wondering.

"I don't mean because of that." Imogen got in front of her to challenge Steeple. "You think if you said that about me and Jagg, he'd be okay with it?"

Why would Steeple say that about Tulip? It wasn't an actual question, he was making a point, she got that. Still, it came from something.

"Because of the new story?" she asked her boss. "It's a good story."

"Yeah, and a good redirect from the whole contract killing thing."

"Contract killing?" Imogen asked, whirling around to take them both in. "Who are we killing?"

"You want someone dead?" she asked, sauntering over to prop herself on the windowsill. "What's your price range?"

Steeple stuck his fingers in his ears. "Ah! La, la, la, no back-alley handshakes in my presence."

"We should both be offended," she said as Imogen folded her arms. "What are you implying, Mr. Steeple?"

"Maybe that we have nowhere else to do these deals."

"Or he's dumb enough to think we have to do it ourselves when our men take care of these matters for us."

The quirk of Imogen's lips betrayed their tease.

Steeple's every muscle loosened. "How the hell did you two end up on my books?" he asked, rounding the desk to sit down. "How you doing, Sersh? Just checking in, not rushing you. Grief's got its own timeline. However many days you've got to take, weeks, whatever you want."

"Has Ire been with you?" Imogen asked, sitting at the guest side of the desk. "He hasn't been seen around much."

"At all." Not that Conn had a habit of being a man about town. "He's fine. Better than fine. Taking good care of me."

"You sticking with your grandfather's feature?"

She nodded at her boss. "I want to get down into it, really spend some time with the words."

Which was her way of saying concentrate on it at all. Despite doing almost nothing except write that week, she had nada for her editor. The promised range of features currently numbered zero, and that didn't print well on paper.

Steeple and Imogen looked at each other before laying her under their scrutiny.

"And the obit?"

"Oh, I get it," she said, mouth wide as she inhaled. "You're double-teaming me. Were you even worried about your dad at all, Im?"

"I was worried—I am worried."

"We're worried about you too," Steeple said. "Something's going on, tensions are growing, everyone's…"

"Everyone's what?" Had colleagues complained about her absence? "Who is everyone?"

"Uh, everyone we've interacted with," Imogen said. "There are rumblings, underground whispers…"

So this wasn't about her sabbatical or her colleagues' judgment, they wanted the inside scoop of what might happen in the city.

"Even before your relationship with Ire, you were our girl for the organized crime stories."

"Manzani stories," she stated.

"You shadowed Ire for a while too."

Deadpan, she couldn't believe they'd make her say it. "I was fucking him."

"Even when you—"

"Yeah, basically the whole time," she said because why hide now?

"You know there are rumors circulating. Score's heading to town, Ire's been in the shadows while Play runs things at the club."

"Right, and we're just wondering…" The two stole another glance. "What's coming down the turnpike? What's the McDades plan? How will this happen?"

"Exactly as my man wants it to." She pushed off the windowsill. "Get out your recorders and I'll give you every detail." One beat. Two. Rolling her eyes would be a step too far. "You seriously think I'd tell you what my boyfriend and I talk about in private?" She opened a hand at Imogen. "Let's talk about you and Jagg first. What do you talk about in the dark? Have you discussed the future? Marriage? Kids? How many cars is he working on this week? What does he think of all his clients? He can't be a best friend to all of them. Bet he's confided in you, told you things he trusted you'd keep secret. Spill! Come on, it's just us girls. Who cares if it ends up in print tomorrow?"

"Okay, we get it."

"This is the city, Sersh."

She settled against the windowsill again. "A city Conn loves. The McDades have put up with a lot of speculation, whispers behind their backs, two-faced everyone's who claim to be an ally but fail to follow through. Is this about the scoop or a genuine fear for the city?"

'Cause she'd had about her fill of righteous people claiming to love the streets they walked. The city had a lot to answer for if it granted license to anyone wishing to work under its name.

Before anyone was forced to reply, her phone rang. Damn thing had been going all day. This had to be what it was like to be Conn's phone. No, actually, it wasn't even close.

"Yeah?" she barked at the unknown number flashing.

"Bluebell…" The drawl was pleased, almost smug, with a smattering of charm. "We've gotta talk."

A happy voice. An unknown voice. Who'd called her?

Intrigued, she listened closer. "About what?"

"About what we can do for each other." Hmm, still intrigued? Yes. Wary Conn could never hear this? Definitely. "Let's have drinks."

Oh, wow, talk about balls. "Excuse me?"

"Drinks, at the club tonight."

The club? Their club. Stag.

Ah! Fuck. This wasn't some random letch, this was a McDade letch. Doran "Play" McDade, Razer's younger brother.

"Your cousin might take issue with us dating."

He laughed. "If I meant it that way my cousin would take my head off. Rightfully so. This is strategic. Trust me. Tonight, eleven thirty."

"I'll see what I can do."

Play was actually laughing when he hung up. Not like a full belly laugh, but more than anyone would get from Conn, even on a good day.

"Everything okay?"

"Yes," she said, her phone dropping to her side when her arm loosened. "I am going to get some work done." Boosting herself onto her feet to wander toward the door, she turned to go backwards, keeping her colleagues in sight. "Steeple, I will have something for you before midnight. And, Im, someone will put a cell in your father's hand." She pointed, phone in her grip. "No more distractions, either of you. As far as you're both concerned, I have no love life, no family, no knowledge on any subject, not until after I get into this. Thank you, goodnight."

TWENTY-FOUR

SHE WASN'T THE ONLY one working late. Though the lights were lower at that hour, the Chronicler office was far from abandoned.

If she could put together an outline for every one of her features, she could put the bones on each article. They'd need pictures. Comment. Did she want her father to comment? She could ask and then decide, or not, whether to use his words. Might be a better idea to make them up herself and just say they came from Ronald. Only a complete moron would argue with her these days, and Ron couldn't afford to piss off Connel any more than he already had.

Those who worked with her grandfather would have things to say. Would they be nice? Did they have to be? How much editorial control would she get? She and Steeple would need to have a discussion. Not about her social life, about what he expected these articles to achieve.

Her grandfather's house would be a treasure trove of his past. How much time did she and Lach have to clear the place before it was sold? A conversation she'd need to have with Conn.

Across the bullpen, Steeple's office door opened. "Sersh," her boss got her attention. Rather than pull her into his office, he came to her station. "Something happened at the Grand Hotel, it's on police radio."

"The Grand Hotel, why would you…?" Oh, shit, Nicole. "What did they say? What happened?"

Lach was her next thought, though if this was Nicole related, it wouldn't be a good idea to involve her brother. Many of her recent decisions put him in the shit. He deserved to live his own life, to make his own mistakes, rather than be tarred by hers.

"I don't know, sounds like an invasion, or a raid or a… The hotel called in about a disruption, violence, cops sent a dozen patrol cars."

Her pulse kicked up. "What room?"

"Don't know exactly. Eighth floor."

Nicole's floor.

Steeple wouldn't know that, so why was she his first thought?

"Why tell me?" she asked. "You came straight to me. Why?"

His somber, pale affect wasn't encouraging. "Irish down," he said. "The cops got there, and, on their radios, they kept saying—"

"Thank you."

Spinning on the spot, she snagged her purse and didn't even bother to shut down her computer. Her phone was in her hand when she joined Daly by the elevator.

"Bluebell—"

"You know about this?" she asked, selecting a contact while calling the elevator.

Daly took her phone from her hand before she could dial. "Bluebell—"

"I'll fucking kill him if he's got himself hurt." Her and the trio of men entered the elevator. "This is Nicki, isn't it? Give me my phone."

Why had he taken it anyway? Why had she let him?

Didn't look like the guys had been given any insight. "He won't pick up." Okay, so they had some insight. "We're on a blackout tonight."

"A blackout, what—"

"A communication blackout."

"Why?" she asked, but the guys just looked at each other. "Tell me what the—"

"We don't get the why, we just get the order. No communication."

"Why would we—"

"Usually, we're covering someone's ass," Hock said. "Can't be asked to testify about something we know nothing about."

"Doesn't it look strange, just suddenly no calls?"

"Calls are made, just… strategically."

"Where is he?"

That provoked a collective snicker. "We don't know." All three shrugged. "Think Ire McDade keeps us in his private loop? We're not in the inner sanctum."

She couldn't argue with that. Being his girlfriend, his lover, she was the epitome of his inner sanctum and she'd been blindsided. What chance did these guys have of knowing the plays?

"You know what it's like to love a man like him?" she muttered as they went to the street.

"No," Daly said, opening her door as the other two got into their respective vehicles. "And I don't guess he'd want you to tell us."

With a single exhale, she put a hand on top of the door sandwiched between them. "I'll tell you this…" Because she wasn't really going to bitch to his men, or anyone, about their relationship. "There's not a damn thing he could do that I wouldn't support him in. I'm his. Forever. So why is he determined to drive me nuts?"

Though Daly's lips thinned a little, their corners did upturn just slightly. "I'm thinking it takes some crazy to be part of this world."

And she couldn't argue with that. "Take me to the mansion."

That's where she'd last seen him. Was he likely to be there? Who knew? Drinks with Play were still an hour away. Maybe she could track her guy down before then to get some kind of explanation. Coercing him to share would be easier than doing the same to his cousin.

Irish down.

What did that mean? Nicole? If the cops knew the victim… Was there a victim? That hadn't been made clear. And now she was scared to use her phone. Not that she had it, Daly never gave it back. Didn't matter when she couldn't use the thing.

At the mansion, she got out as soon as the gravel stopped crunching. Running up the stairs, she didn't wait for security. This was about as safe as she'd ever get.

Office was empty, bedroom, closet. Damnit. Thinking Strat might have something to share, she went into his bedroom. Empty.

That set her fists on her hips. Both men were leading her a merry dance. Shit.

Going back downstairs, her guys were still loitering in the foyer.

"What's the plan?" Hock asked.

Without answering, she went to the dining room to stick her head around the door. "Anyone who—" And she noticed Strat, right there in the middle of the damn room, no shame. "You, Patient, get your ass out here."

Backing up, she waited there, just a few feet from the door until he came out to join her.

"You're pissed," Strat said, and spotted the guys somewhere in the background. "You ordered to keep her here tonight?"

She glanced back, then at her friend. "Don't talk to—" she spun to them, "did he order you to keep me here all night?"

"No!" Daly said. Hock and Snuff weren't so good at hiding their guilt. "Just until your drinks thing."

"Hear about what happened at the Grand?" Strat asked.

That brought her blinking attention back to him. "You knew about this? Oh my God…" She growled at the ceiling, then grabbed her friend's tee-shirt to drag him upstairs. "Why didn't you call me?"

"I got handed a phone to call Immie, then it was taken away. Thank you for that, by the way."

Striding into the office, she continued into the bedroom. "Thank me by telling me what the fuck is going on."

"Don't know. No one knows. It's a blackout though, so it's something."

"What the hell does that even—why are you out of bed anyway? I told you to rest, recuperate, you can't get better in one day."

"Think I never took a beating before, Scamp? No one pulled my fingernails out with pliers. This is fists and feet, standard stuff."

So it was okay providing no weapons were used? She could argue the men who attacked her didn't have weapons either and everyone went crazy about that. In contrast to Strat though, she'd never taken a beating before that night.

Forgetting the past, she went into the closet and flicked on a light. "Sit down." She kicked off her shoes and untucked her top, calling out to her friend in the bedroom as she got undressed. "How are you feeling?

What did the doctor say?"

"Nothing permanent. Looks worse than it is."

"Did you calm Imogen down? She was worried today."

"About her brother too."

She stuck her head out. "Did you speak to him?"

"Yeah, he's fine. Being looked after by all accounts."

"You spoke to him?"

"Yeah."

Huh, so her friend was allowed—obviously, that was his son. "I didn't know Ford was involved in any of this." Tossing her things in the hamper, she put on a robe. "How is he involved?"

She turned on the shower, then came out of the bathroom. Her friend was perched on the edge of the ottoman at the end of the bed. Feet wide apart, elbows on knees. Not the most comfortable spot.

"You can sit on the bed," she said, and gestured to the wingback seats by the window. "Or over there."

"If Ire McDade walks in here and I look too comfortable—"

"He won't care," she said, laughing. "He knows we're friends. Only friends."

"Don't think it matters if we're fucking. People aren't supposed to hang out in the head guy's space."

"This is my space too, and I'm telling you he won't care." Her head tilted. "You did this at the loft too."

"Think if Ire walked in here right now, you'd be more concerned with yelling at him than sticking up for me. We underlings are always the first forgotten."

"Would you stop?" Folding her arms, she rested a shoulder on the doorframe. "Where's Ford?"

"Stag."

"Staying there? Why?"

He stood up. "Ask the gaffer."

"If I could find him, I would."

"You get ready. I'll get dressed and come with you."

"No, you're hurt."

"Ah, it's cuts and bruises, Scamp. What good am I hanging around here? You've got your drinks thing, I want to check in with my boy. And you think I trust the three stooges with your life on a night like this? Hard for them to keep you in check when you ignore everything they say."

"I hear them."

"You rule them. They're too scared to say no to you."

"Daly says no." When he didn't know anything. She sighed. "Fine. We don't have time to argue. Twenty minutes, in the office. If you're not there, we're leaving without you."

"Think I'm likely to be the hold up here?"

She scowled at his laugh and backed up until he departed the room. Guy was right, unfortunately, all he had to do was shower and change. She had hair, makeup, nails, all things she hadn't planned to do, but now she was there, it seemed necessary.

Conn. Where was he? There would be a contingency for this, right? For what they'd do if Nicole was discovered by someone looking to claim the contract. "Irish down" could mean Nicole, or something else entirely.

Most might think if Nicole was dead, there'd be more of an uproar in the ranks, but it wasn't like she was the most loved McDade, not by a long shot.

As predicted, Strat was standing by the office door waiting when she emerged.

"Feel better?" he asked.

The swelling of his eye, the bruise on his jaw, the

cut on his ear… Yeah, he'd cleaned up, but the injuries weren't invisible.

"You sure you want to do this?"

"If there's a chance of trouble, I don't want you, or my boy, alone."

"Okay," she said and took his arm. "Then let's get to it."

TWENTY-FIVE

STAG WAS JUMPING. The line outside wound its way around the corner, not unusual for a weekend. At this time, it was doubtful many more would be admitted. Those inside wouldn't leave at the height of the party buzz, maybe that was for the best.

Did being in and around Stag improve these people's chances of safety and survival? Difficult to tell when she had no idea of the threat.

Door security parted to grant access to her and her entourage. Weird to think she had one, but her four guys stayed close, and they had their own tail of destruction. Entourage seemed more apt than "staff" or any other term that put her above them. These were her contemporaries, her friends, though they may not see their relationships in the same way.

Once upon a time, she'd worried when approaching Stag. Worried whether anyone would get in her way or obstruct her. God help anyone who tried that now.

She wasn't really aware of who was behind her as

she ascended the stairs to the office. None of her people joined her when she went inside. Boy did she immediately wish someone had got in her way.

Conn, yep, the guy she loved, standing up close to Madison Byrne. Was this what she was supposed to see? What a set up.

"Upstairs," Conn said to her, his fingers in Madison's hair.

Upstairs? Yeah, fine, she'd rather be anywhere but there.

"No," Madison said, her smile growing sly. "Why does she have to leave? Maybe she should watch." And that would empty her stomach fast, though liquor was the only thing in it, so… "Where's Play? Let's go upstairs and find him."

Being raised with position gave the Byrne woman confidence. Though that could also have something to do with knowing she was seducing this man away from his true love.

The curtain moved and Play appeared, glass in hand, moving at a slow, deliberate pace, yet exuding only masculinity. Strange how he could be delicate and overwhelming at the same time.

"Where'd you get to?" Play asked her like they were old pals, and completely alone.

"Traffic," she said.

That wasn't entirely true, they'd left the mansion late because it took her longer to get ready than—what did it matter? She'd arrived.

"Want to come upstairs?" Madison asked, threading her fingers through Conn's to guide him over to his cousin, who was granted the gift of Madison's other hand. "I have a secret to share."

Oh, a secret? Yeah, she'd still rather eat her own vomit than partake in anything that might involve.

"You don't care about secrets, Madison," Play

said. "Show your cards."

Her guy wasn't in the mood to screw around. "You know what we want."

This had been a day for quid pro quos.

"In exchange, I want…" Madison raised Play's hand to her waist, and twined Conn's arm around her. "Both of you."

Yep, that was exactly the enlightenment she wasn't in the market for.

"I have work to do," she said, getting a few steps closer to the curtain.

It flew aside with more flourish than she'd expect from—Nicole? Niall wasn't far behind with Razer and Whisper in their wake. Where had they come from? Nicole kept on going, marching right on up to the window that overlooked the clubbers below. The woman was alive, which was something. Maybe something. She wasn't clear on what actually happened at the hotel.

In a twirl, Mrs. Parker McDade raised her arms. "You people are crazy!"

"We people are your—hey, High Class!" Whisper swerved around her husband to pull her into an embrace. "Oh, baby, we've got so much to catch up on."

Whisper hooked their arms together and instantly she felt better, stronger. The connection reminded her that this was their domain, her domain. She kissed Whisper and slunk away from her, through the others to the man who shared her bed. His arm may still be around the Byrne, but her hands slithered up his body onto his cheeks. Without resisting, he came down to meet her kiss. Not only meet it but amplify it with the enticing dive of his possessive tongue.

He hooked her body, yanking it to his. Even though she bumped against Madison, she didn't relinquish the kiss. This was her man. No matter what might happen later, what he might have to do for the good of the family, he would always be her man. Mistress or not, no one would stop her showing him love.

"This family is…" Amped, Nicole dominated the stage. "Someone tried to kill me! I could've been killed. You people are supposed to be keeping me safe not making out like teenagers!"

Foreign words from Niall's tongue stole Conn's from her. Throughout his response to his lieutenant, his gaze stayed on hers, dark, aroused, tempting. Were there other people in the room? How could he hold a conversation when so much electricity zipped between them?

"I love this family, so friendly." Whisper closed in and caught her free hand in both of her own. "We look after each other, look out for each other. Making out like teenagers is bonus content, and our guys are all about the extras."

Turning her head to lay it against her man, she smiled at Whisper right there next to her. Nicole appeared just beyond.

"You told me no one knew where I was!"

"Shit, you're shrill. And you wonder why someone would want you dead, Pretty Nicki?" Whisper wasn't shy. "First time in my life I ever agreed with a Byrne. Feels icky, but I can't fight it."

"Peanut," came the warning from husband to wife.

"Why are we expending energy protecting the ungrateful slut?"

"Oh, Doherty, you are totally—"

The office door flew open. Before she'd even whirled around, a gunshot blasted the air. Her mouth opened but produced no sound.

The towering man just inside the door, arm straight, held a gun with just a trickle of smoke at the barrel. She jumped when his eyes cut her way, not to her, course not, they landed on the man against her.

"We'll take care of it," Conn said, ever calm.

Without a word, the giant of a man turned and walked out like nothing happened. Was it nothing? The shot, shit, who was—she'd heard someone hit the floor, had she? The—Nicole.

Conn cradled the back of her skull, not forcing her still, but keeping her close. On their rug, right in the middle, Nicole's still body, eyes fixed, stained the red of their already red stag head.

"All business, no pleasure," Whisper said on a sigh. "The things someone should do to that man. Only Fans was designed for guys like him. One picture and half the planet would be pregnant overnight."

"Contract's satisfied," Play said.

Whisper spoke next. "So you can toddle off back to Daddy, Madison and—oh, wait. Can she toddle back to Daddy, men?"

"Not a fucking chance," Play said.

With a single shouted foreign word, Niall commanded a half dozen guys to enter and encircle Madison.

Conn's other arm came around her, holding her close as Madison was forced to move with the current of the moving men.

"What is this?" Madison demanded. "Ire—"

"You just became a bargaining chip," Whisper said, heading the parade of others, traipsing back through the curtain. "A pawn. Score likes pawns."

Where were they going? Not downstairs. Where would they be—

Conn's embrace tightened, clamping her body to his. He wasn't going anywhere. Everyone else left the room, but he stayed right there, with her, holding her, staring into her.

"You're a fucking wonder, Cushla Machree."

She flattened a hand on his chest. "You are my kingdom."

He scooped a hand around the side of her head. "Act like it."

Their kiss carried them to the desk, she bumped against it, coming up hard against wood behind and in front. His was welcome against her core, desired, needed. Even before settling on the desk her hips were rising, writhing.

"Conn…" Her head fell back granting passage for his lips to trail down her throat. The pad of his thumb traced along her collarbone, stimulating each inch with the digit before his lips followed. "Yes…"

He unclipped her dress at the back of her neck and the two sections fell, though his hands did their part in sliding forward over her shoulders, pushing the fabric from her breasts to her hips.

The people who'd been in there had gone through the curtain. Would they come back? Would they be interrupted by—screw it. Shaking her feet to get rid of her shoes, the soles ran up his legs before her limbs coiled around him.

"Right here," he growled, dragging his teeth across her clavicle.

"Yes." The permission came from her mouth and her fingers battling with his fly. "Here."

Grabbing him out, she pushed away from his kiss to align their bodies and quaked when he slid into her. Them, together, the whole world existed for them to feel like this. The slow advance and quick retreat wasn't his usual rhythm, but the admiration in his eyes did almost as much to rouse her hormones as his stimulating body.

"Baby…" Letting her head fall back, she planted her palms on the desk and levered her hips up. "Mmm…"

God, he felt good. Without missing a beat, he

sped his thrusts until he pounded into her. Their lives depended on hitting climax, right then, right there. Grabbing her hip tight, his other hand slid through her cleavage and over her breast, curling his fingers into it, bruising force sent a barb of pleasureful pain to her clit.

Mm, yes, that was what she needed. His fingertips skimmed lower, the moment they brushed across her clit, she called out in climax as her body clung to his.

"Lord," she whispered when her peak of pleasure yanked his to its summit.

With him embedded deep inside her, she lost the tension of her arms and fell onto her back, right there, sprawled across the desk.

"Mo Grá," she panted, eyes closed. He slid out and righted her dress just enough to cover the sensitive parts. "If I stay right here, will I get in the way of your business?"

As he sat at the desk, she opened her eyes. With her head on the angle of his side, she smiled at him upside down.

"You're never in the way."

He touched her shoulder and kept on going until he held her breast beneath the concealing fabric. Her arms weren't in the dress, but she didn't care. She did care his mouth was so far from hers.

"Everyone went through the curtain, is there a party going on upstairs?"

"Basement," he said and opened a drawer to retrieve a stack of paper.

"Basement? The stairs through there are up."

Reading, he didn't give her his full attention. "There's a concealed stairway access through the playroom."

So much she still didn't know about the building. Breathing out, holding the dress to her chest, she gave in to the inevitable and sat up. That was the "oops, shit," moment. Nicole still lay there, on the rug, dead.

"Oh, God."

"It's handled," her guy muttered behind her.

"We just had sex in front of a corpse." And hadn't she just been thinking they hadn't done anything freaky in a while? Yeah, that definitely qualified. "I can't believe she's really dead."

"Not much more proof I can give you than what you're looking at."

"Who was he?" she asked, looping her arms into her dress while twisting on her butt to sit in the middle of his desk, legs curled at her side. "The shooter? How did he get past security?"

Without furor or panic. If he'd fought his way in and up the Stag stairs, shouldn't they have had some warning in the form of sound at least?

The cigar box sat back in its place. Huh, how had that happened? Did it still have—

Conn's heavy hand closed the lid before she could open it more than an inch. "I don't know," her guy said, still reading, until his eyes rose to hers above the document for a second. "We'll look into it."

Yeah, right, like she believed that. But she wasn't supposed to, his gaze said it all. When he was reading again, her mind went to work.

"You let him through security. You must've. No one would get into Stag without…" she whispered. "How could he know Nicole would be right there, right then to—who was he? Was it him at the hotel earlier? Did he follow your people here?"

"Our people. And no."

"I don't understand."

"All players saw what they needed to see. Everything went according to plan."

Not enough that Nicole was just dead, the whole

thing had been orchestrated by...

"You're incredible," she whispered. "The cops said 'Irish down' on their—"

"We're not the only Irish in the city." More than incredible. He put the paper aside. "You haven't eaten dinner, do you want to go out?"

"It's after midnight."

"Free choice, pick any restaurant in the city."

"Shouldn't we do something about Nicole?"

When her head started to turn, he grabbed her hand, stalling it. "Macushla, you trust me." That wasn't a question, didn't have to be when he knew the answer. "It's handled."

TWENTY-SIX

A FOREIGN CALL from behind the curtain got her guy to his feet.

"Come on," he said, clipping her dress closed, then hooking her waist to help her from the desk.

Holding his hand, she went where he led. "Where are we going?"

She didn't expect an answer, and he delivered on that assumption. At the top of the stairs to the apartment, usually, they'd flip a U-turn and go to the bedroom. This time, at the opposite end of the space, the round dining table was occupied. Huh, was that the first time she'd seen it used? Now there were butts in seats, Whisper, her husband, Razer, and Play McDade.

Conn funneled her into a seat, pushing it in under her before sitting next to her.

McDades.

A Doherty.

A McLeod.

Talk about unlikely bedfellows.

"Are we gonna vote?" Whisper asked. "Mine's

worth two, I vote for me and Shyla. McDade wives stick together. And PJ's vote is mine as well. He likes me more than he likes any of you. Score's vote should be worth a half point, since he didn't bother to show up."

"Talk of him showing up did its job," Raze muttered.

So Score had never been on his way?

"Vex is in the basement," Play said, ignoring the Doherty. "Madison's in the cell beside him. Superintendent's at the end of the hall under lock and key. We're headed for a full set. Should we grab a Gambatto to balance it out?"

Her father was imprisoned in Stag? Oh, he'd love that so much. How had he ended up there? It must've been with Lachlan's approval. Unless Conn strongarmed her brother, but if that confrontation happened, she'd have heard about it… wouldn't she?

Raze kept things on track. "What's next, Ire?"

"We eliminate the pest."

"Biz hasn't lost any of his arrogance," Whisper said. "Should've seen his face when I walked in."

"Didn't he know you were coming?" she asked.

"Probably didn't believe I'd show." Whisper's smile glowed with mischief. "He was never my biggest fan."

"Anything from Burl?"

"Sources say there's been an increase in activity," Conn said. "Expected. I'm not concerned."

Play pushed back in his seat. "Miami won't be safe until we take care of the Manzani problem. Think Vex will help us out there?"

"Vex Manzani is useless, a dickless piece of shit barely worthy of the air he breathes." Far as she could tell, only Whisper noticed the shiver of arousal that went through her. Conn shouldn't be allowed to talk like that with others in the room. "Only way Vex leaves this building is in a box, unless Silvio agrees to the terms."

"Gotta take care of the Byrnes too."

"Man loves his daughter," Play said. "She's the ticket."

"So we hold her until Rick Byrne severs his connection to Biz?"

"Severing the connection matters less than leaving the man isolated and hated. He cannot be allowed to believe he has any chance of rejoining the family." Conn's gaze cut to Whisper. "Dohertys loyal to the McDades get a bump in the ranks and receive a cash bonus for every Byrne head they collect. I want them off the board."

"'Bout time they were wiped out."

"I like that," Whisper said and bobbed her brows at Sersha. "I get it." She just smiled while the men stayed all business. Whisper cleared her throat, almost mocking their seriousness. "What are we gonna do with Nicki's head?"

"Her husband put out the contract, the Byrnes were a conduit. Send her head to Byrne. Tell him to expect Madison's next if he doesn't get in line." No one at the table responded, someone behind them did, in an Irish tongue. Shit, Niall could sneak with the best of them. "Rick Byrne wanted the woman dead, he deals with the fall out."

"And that won't get us in shit with…"

"Man wants his money," Conn said to Whisper. "Delivering Nicole's head is proof of completion."

Whisper rose to go to the bar. "Those guys don't need to do jobs, they could just show up and demand money." The murderer, he's who they were talking about. "Everyone would give it to them. They could just sit on their asses and collect until they die."

"Their power comes in the myth, Peanut. That rep would change fast if they became beach bunnies."

Play snickered. "Imagine any of those guys in Speedos."

Everyone else enjoyed that, she didn't quite follow. "Those guys?"

Whisper put a glass in front of her. "The Huntsmen. That was your first brush with the Reapers."

"Our people off the street tonight?" Razer asked. "Everyone accounted for?"

Whisper went around the table, pouring whiskey into each glass. "They don't vanish when they're not working. They could be in any city, any time."

"And if we know they're close, we clear the streets."

"Why?"

As Whisper sat again, she glanced at each guy. None of them were in a hurry to answer.

"They're feral," her friend said.

"Meaning…?"

"They weren't raised like…" Whisper leaned over the table, lowering her volume. "Word is they didn't come from any human, hell itself bred—"

"Peanut." Razer did a lot of warning his woman. "They're human."

"I'm not so sure." Whisper tossed her hair, then the whiskey into her throat. "They're nocturnal."

"Yeah, that's been proved," Play said. "They are only seen at night."

"Maybe they're vampires!"

"Enough," Conn said, obviously tired of Whisper being… Whisper. "Madison and Vex stay here. I'll take care of Silvio."

Razer blinked, his eyes stayed heavy. "His allies in the city?"

"What allies?" Conn asked. "We have the inside now. Harvest will proceed without obstruction. The Manzani threads are stretched. His people leave Miami, and he severs his link to Biz, or his son won't breathe another day."

"Vex isn't his favorite," Whisper said. "He might be okay with that."

In Silvio Manzani's position, she'd be okay with it. No, she didn't like being in the same building as the sleaze, but she trusted her guy's chains to hold him.

"How does he prove it? We can't take his word for—"

"His contacts will vote in favor of the Harvest rezoning."

"That vote could take a while."

"With the right pressure, it will happen when we want it to happen."

"We may not need Silvio's support," she said and waited for Conn to meet her eye. "The Carlyle."

"What about it?"

"I recorded it," she said, sort of squirming.

"We'll destroy the footage."

"No," she said, grabbing for Conn's hand. "On purpose. I recorded it on purpose. I didn't know what I would get until… The johns, the fire, we got the evacuation."

Slow pride lit his gaze. "Bet some of those guys vote on the council."

"I bet they do too," she said, aroused by pleasing him.

"Vex stays where he is."

Good. The streets would be safer. Saner.

"Silvio won't like it."

"I don't care. Something else is more important," her guy said, his hand slipping onto her thigh beneath the table. "If Silvio shows his commitment to shunning Biz, we'll support Hell's bid for freedom."

Parole.

Silence.

That wasn't something she'd expected him to say, and apparently the others were of the same mind.

Incredulity filled their Doherty. "Hell Manzani is dangerous." Not something that had to be stated, Whisper's unusual solemnity was a testament to just how risky the move might be. "If you let him out, he could bolster Manzani strength. They could become a serious threat. The man's been in prison for two decades, I doubt he spent that time knitting booties."

"Score came out a changed man," Conn said with a tinge of duplicity. "Isn't everyone worthy of a second chance?"

"Helios Manzani is no joke," Whisper said. "That man is—"

"Agreed," Play said, eyes locked to Conn's. "It's time."

"It is," Razer backed them up.

Shit, this was about more than anyone's virtue. Clarity filled her lungs. It was a rescue mission.

Whisper's head moved as she gaped at one guy, then another, and another. "What the hell is this?" Something Whisper, apparently, didn't know about. "Since when are McDades in the habit of unleashing powerful enemies?"

Curling her fingers around Conn's on her leg, she gave her support, if it counted for anything. "I agree too."

"What the fuck?" Whisper exclaimed.

"We bring McDades home. All McDades."

Dorsey, Conn's young cousin, may be a McDade by name, but she'd lived her whole life imprisoned by Manzanis. What was left of her loyalty?

"Do we have the facilities for her?" Play asked. "Is she better here or elsewhere? I'd say we should ask her, but I'm not sure she…"

"Has the capacity to make decisions for herself,"

Razer said and nodded her way, though his concentration stayed on Connel. "Use your woman."

That got her the attention of everyone.

Whisper's wide eyes would be amusing in any other situation. "Who the fuck are we talking about? Do we have the facilities for who?"

"Helios Manzani went to jail, in part, due to evidence betrayed by a McDade," she said. "A four-year-old McDade."

The go-ahead to explain wasn't necessary. This was Whisper. Her explanation saved Razer from telling the story during their sex time later.

"A four-year old?"

"She's been in Manzani hands since then," Play said, sweeping up his glass. "As long as Helios was imprisoned, she was too."

"Shit," Whisper said, slapping a hand on the table. "Your father agreed to that?"

"Her father agreed to it," she said for Conn. "Kept everyone alive."

It didn't bear thinking about that the Manzanis would consider killing an innocent child. Despite society's progression, in the right circumstances, the possibility of murder still existed.

"You'll meet with Silvio Manzani? Arrange it?"

"Not yet," Conn said. "Timing is everything. Nicole's head goes to Byrne, send the rest of her to Manzani."

"Let's dirty everyone's hands, damn right," Whisper said. "I've got to say, for a McDade, you know how to plan an operation."

"Enough from you," Razer said. "We have business downstairs. Ladies, want a ride back to the mansion?"

"No, we have business of our own," Whisper said and leaped to her feet. "High Class is gonna fill me in on all the McDade lore I missed.”

Everyone was leaving the table.

“She can tell you about the Manzanis too,” Play said. “Especially Hell. They exchange love letters.”

“Not love letters, just letters.” She pushed in her chair. “And if you make the margaritas, I’ll tell you whatever you want.”

“Cheap date.” Whisper came over to steal her hand. “I love it! Bye, boys, behave yourselves!”

The guys went downstairs, she didn’t know what floor, but down there somewhere. And she happily took her seat at the bar while Whisper went around to the other side.

“I want to hear about your prison visit with Biz too.”

“Then we better call down for more tequila. This is gonna be a long night.”

The wink was punctuation Whisper always carried. Aggravating or accommodating, Whisper Doherty-McDade made no apologies, which was just the way a McDade wife needed to be.

TWENTY-SEVEN

"OKAY, OKAY, GEEZ, husband," Whisper said into her phone then hung up. "We're going back to the mansion, want to come with us?"

If they were the only ones left, Conn may prefer just to stay at Stag.

"I'll wait," she said, accepting her friend's hug. "Have fun."

"No doubt about that."

Whisper rushed to the door at the back of the room to exit. The one to the club balcony, not the office. Hmm, must be a reason she was avoiding it, could be she didn't want to step on any toes. They didn't know who might be working down there. If Raze was heading out, Play might be too.

She washed up her and Whisper's dishes, dried, and put everything away. Time trudged on, tiring her. Washing her face, brushing her teeth, combing her hair, she went through the motions of getting ready for bed. Whether it was there, at the mansion, or the loft, she couldn't imagine there would be any need to be social before she and Conn crashed.

If Strat was still there, he might have hung around under the misconception he had to be there so long as she was. Her friend didn't have his phone, and her purse was in the office. With what he'd been through in the last couple of days, last couple of weeks really, Strat deserved a break. At the mansion, he'd be looked after, though he may prefer staying at Stag if Ford stayed.

Music still pumped from the club, bass rocked the walls, maybe some of those stragglers got in after all.

She'd check with Conn before going down to the basement for Strat, just in case. Vex would be restrained, but she still preferred to let her man know her location. Anywhere he was she was safe, something she'd assert to him any time he forgot.

"…simple as that."

The words carried at the same time she opened the curtain to the office, so she didn't know if it was the voice or the face she recognized first.

"Lach," she said to the man in the middle of the chesterfield, fingers linked on his head, legs outstretched, crossed at the ankle. "What are you doing here? Where the hell have you been? I haven't heard from you for ages."

Conn was propped on the front of his desk, whiskey at his lips.

"Yeah, and if it wasn't for this guy…" Lach nodded toward Conn. "I wouldn't even know you're still alive. Talk about dropping off the fucking map."

"Have you seen Dad?"

"Do you care?" Lachlan asked, making eye contact with Conn as he put the glass on the desk. "Want to finish this later?"

"Aye."

Lach stood, but she rushed over to the rug, extending an arm toward each of them. "No, not later."

Uh, from Lach's face, her attention went to the stag head under her feet, then to Conn. "Are we okay?"

"Aye."

How many secret conversations could the man have at once? Nicole's body was gone, and there was no sign of blood or death. Didn't mean there wasn't forensic evidence lying around. Guess that was why they needed a hush-hush basement stairway in the playroom. Getting rid of a corpse in a crowded nightclub may be a little awkward without discretion and secret passages.

"Why are you meeting at this time of night?"

"Never notice your boyfriend does a lot of business in the dark?" Lachlan asked, though there was a glimmer of a smile behind those words. "We're just keeping things steady."

"What does that mean? What is 'keeping things steady'? What is that?" She went to sit, pulling her brother down with her. "Conn said he's talked to you about the dad stuff."

"Yeah."

"And you're okay with…?" No way her brother would be. Conn could've coerced him, not that she didn't trust her guy, but he knew how to get what he wanted. "He'll stay as Superintendent."

"Yeah," Lach said, no hesitation.

"Do you know what that means? He'll keep his job, his position, his power—"

"And use it for McDade ends, I know the drill."

Who was this guy? Her brother, her Lachlan, could never be relaxed and okay with the implications of that.

"You're okay with… What's going on?"

"It's late." Conn tossed the last of his liquor into his throat and discarded the glass. "We'll pick this up another time, McLeod."

No snark or hostility, the men's relationship had

changed, and she'd missed the whole thing.

Lach smacked a hand into Conn's and they shook quick. "I'll be around in the p.m."

"You'll get all the access you need. Need a ride?"

"No, I'm good." Her brother came to kiss her head. "Be good, little sister."

"Be good?" Without responding to her question, Lachlan left, giving her only Conn to gape at. "What is going on?"

"It's late. You need rest."

"Why don't you need rest?" Though that was beside the point. "Why was Lach here?"

"You want to bar him?"

"No! He's my brother—"

"Your brother, exactly. Family means a lot here. Do you need anything from upstairs?"

"No," she mumbled as he got her purse from behind the desk to hand it over. "Where are we sleeping tonight?"

"Where do you want to sleep?"

"Don't you want to have breakfast with your cousins at the mansion? Is Score coming at all?" Maybe that was a reason to avoid the family home. "He has a toddler." She smiled. "Not sure I can see you tolerating a little person, without manners, running around."

"McDade children are taught manners," he said, slipping off his jacket to put it around her.

"Taught manners?" She blanched. "You don't mean…?"

He tucked her hair from her face. "Have I ever raised my hands to you?"

"No."

"And I won't to our children either. I lived that upbringing, and we do things my way now. Respect comes long before discipline."

Why, in that moment, did it feel like she had so

much to learn from him?

"Is Strat still in the building?"

"Yes. He's staying with his son, with your permission."

She nodded. "As long as someone's keeping an eye on him. Is Ford in trouble?"

"Ford is ideally suited to his role here."

"Because…?"

"His relationship with Vex has tenure, adds an extra layer of torment. And allows Ford something like payback."

"As jailor?"

"He's in the position of power now, leveraging his own retribution."

That was impressive. Such a simple choice would make so much difference in damaging Evander's spirit.

"Can you make sure Strat isn't going out by himself for a while?"

"If you think he's at risk, that puts you at further risk—"

"He's not at risk for being him, he's at risk for what he means to me. That's why Vex went after him, isn't it? I told you, people around me are in danger. It seems like every way I turn—"

"You're a McDade." He caught her chin on a finger to lift it up. "Aye, we have targets on our backs. The intensity of the threat level will increase the more our power grows." And it didn't concern him one iota. "Now, where do you want to sleep tonight?"

"The loft."

The flash in his eyes may have been surprise, but she saw caution too. Their space, where they'd shared time and bonding, meant a lot to her. But they hadn't been back there, not together, not since the night they'd gone to her grandfather's only to be ripped apart.

"Are you sure?"

"If you don't want to, we don't have to. I understand if you want to spend time with Razer and Play."

"I don't care about time with them. You were given the choice, and this is the one you made."

He linked their fingers to guide her downstairs. A car waited for them on the curb, and they were quickly on their way to her selected destination.

"I want to forget it happened." Lifting his arm, she wrapped it around herself and closed her eyes to lean against him. "I want us to sleep there, wake up, make love, and be together like we should've been. We should never have gone to my grandfather's. I'm sorry I asked you to come with me. I know we've said this before but… I think about it. How we could've told him to go to hell and just curled up together, safe. That's the fantasy I want to fulfill."

"Hmm."

Curious about the tone of the sound, she peeked up. "What? What is it?"

"You swallowed those pills in that bed."

Oh, God. Their heads were in completely different places. "And you don't want to—I never wanted to kill myself, Mo Grá. I wanted your attention."

"An extreme way to go about it."

"You're an extreme kind of guy. I'd go to any lengths to be with you. Do anything to be at your side. I understand if you don't want to go back there. I'm sorry, I wasn't thinking. Is that why you put it in my name?"

"I put it in your name when I thought you'd take the out. You gave up your apartment to your brother. I wouldn't see you on the street."

Her brother wouldn't have seen her on the street either. Still, it was nice he'd been considerate. Funny, so many people were surprised Conn wasn't violent with her, yet no one knew how thoughtful he was, or how much time he spent looking after her.

"I love you," she said, relaxing and closing her eyes again. "Mo Grá. Forever and always, I'm yours."

And she loved that. Just belonging to him was a buzz. The depth of his security, the stability he gave her, no one would understand. Few people found love so strong and sure. She had it and planned to cherish it for the rest of time.

TWENTY-EIGHT

FINISHING WITH THE blow-dryer alerted her to the phone ringing.

The phone. A phone.

On the closet vanity. She boosted up from the stool to get it and dropped onto her ass as she answered.

"Good morning!"

"It's almost noon."

She smiled at the Irish accent. "So still morning. Miss me, Lieutenant? Your boss would have a problem with you calling me up like this."

"Your team are waiting for you."

"Meaning you'd like me to leave? I'm not dressed yet."

"Boss'd have a problem with you going out like that."

Yes, he would. "Are you calling to tell him something or to steal him from me?"

"You've had him half the day."

"Not yet, but I would if he'd let me." Wearing only a towel, Conn appeared from the bathroom, wet from the shower. Mmm. "We'll have to come up with some kind of shared custody arrangement." Standing up as he put on a watch, she dropped her robe. "Otherwise you'll never get him back."

Conn wasn't paying her attention, though he must have noticed her hand snaking around to loosen and discard his towel.

"You got him tied down?"

"No," she said, kissing his arm. "Just tangled up." She raised the phone. "It's for you."

Glad to free her hands while he took the device to his ear, she kept on kissing. God, he felt good, everywhere, all the time. And that foreign tongue. He could be ordering breakfast and she'd still be coming all over the place.

Pressing her lips to his chest, her fingertips played on his flesh. They'd barely put each other down in the hours since they got back from Stag. He'd pleased her in the shower, and curling her fingers around his cock betrayed he was ready for his. As she lowered to her knees, his voice kept going. Their eyes met and his permission seeped into her with a heat only he could provoke.

With all the experience they had together, he should be over the sensations of her mouth devouring his cock. Her palms skimmed up his thighs, massaging him, her thumbs lifting and resting until her hands could squeeze, her lips could taste, her mouth could suck.

His sharp inhale revealed the phone was forgotten and both his fists locked in her hair. Either he'd hung up on his friend, or Niall had a ringside seat to this radio show.

The cursing was expected as he thrust into her throat, those foreign words, the gritted teeth that she glimpsed as tears watered her eyes.

Even though he had control, all the power was

hers. She was doing this to him, for him, and he took it, like it could be the last time.

The impact of his climax showered her throat with the truth of his possession. Forever more, his purpose, and his pleasure were hers.

And the phone rang again. At least that gave her a clue Niall hadn't been listening in.

Conn grabbed it from above his watch drawer. "Yeah?" His eyes came to hers again. "Looking right at her." Not in the most respectable of positions. He tipped his mouth from the phone. "Strat's downstairs."

Well, that was no kind of subtle. "You're excusing me? You've never done that before."

Not in their private space, where she had free access to every other part of him.

He caught her hand to jerk her onto her feet. "Your brother's never called while you're giving head before." And that shock statement provoked a groan from the other end of the line as she got a slap of horror. "Strat's downstairs."

Yeah, he'd said that already and she appreciated the reminder. Conn kissed her hair and smacked her ass when she bent over to swipe up her robe. Seriously? He'd just said that with Lach right there?

Still in something of a stupor, she tied her robe while crossing the bedroom and heard the cherry on top.

"Not a problem," Conn said, she guessed to Lach. "I finished. Talk."

Her mind was still underwater, gasping for air, when she got to the kitchen. Strat seemed in a good mood, though still bruised and, she had to believe, tender. Wounds didn't heal overnight, she knew that from personal experience.

"What's that look for?" Strat asked and immediately corrected himself. "Never mind. Forget I asked. I don't want to know."

Coffee would help, right?

Yes, coffee.

"You don't want to know?" she asked, going to the coffee machine.

"When you answer my dumbass questions, I end up making plans to hock my car so I can pony up bail."

"Conn would pay my bail."

"Missing the point there, Scamp."

Maybe she was, yeah. After pressing a few buttons, the scent of the coffee pouring released some of her tension.

"You spent some time with Lach," she said, turning to lean on the counter. "When you were looking for me?"

"Yeah," her friend said, wary. "Some."

Had to be more than that. "Did you notice anything weird about him?"

"Weird how?"

While holding her own, she took a mug of java to him. "Like he's changed. Not as… Lachlan, as he was before."

Strat scooped up the mug. "I didn't know the guy that good to start with. Sure, him and Immie were hot and heavy, but we were chalk and cheese… Least I thought we were."

Interest piqued, she lowered into a seat by him, leaning in close. "You thought…? You thought he was good and wholesome and—"

"Teacher's pet? A blue-eyed boy? Detective Do-Things-by-the-Book? Yeah."

"And that opinion's changed?"

"We were on the road together for the better part of a week. Guys get to know each other when they're pissing together in the bushes."

"What do you think of him now? What did you think of him on the road?"

"Guy's got a lot going on in his life. Grandfather's dead. Father's a wrong 'un. His life's in the hopper."

Didn't help that his relationship with Imogen ended not long ago, and his ex just got with another guy. Not just any guy, her brother's best friend, which kinda made them keepers from the get-go.

Oh, yeah, and his baby sister was screwing the city's most dangerous crime boss. She couldn't forget that one.

Her up wasn't up. With Conn back, it was getting close. Or it had been until her brother… Lachlan didn't have any anchor, anything to keep him on course. Where was his up?

"I'm worried about him."

"Yeah, that's what you're supposed to do with family."

"No, I'm… It's not just any worry… He's different, changed, something's… something is going on with him."

And she'd been so caught up in her own shit that she hadn't noticed it happening.

"Guy's got a lot to process. He hurt you?"

"No!" Offense hit hard and fast, even more than it did when people suggested Conn was violent with her. "Lachlan would never hurt anyone. Not unless it was absolutely necessary." Like in the line of duty when some fucker had a weapon trained on him. Even then he'd hesitate. "Lachlan is a good man."

"Good doesn't have to mean good. You're friends with me, and your boyfriend's not exactly…"

"Not exactly what?" Conn asked, startling them both.

Damn the McDades and their stealth. She spun on the chair to see her guy entering.

"We're talking about Lachlan," she said as Conn

went to the fridge. "I'm worried about him."

"That's what you're supposed to do with family."

Some of Strat's concern gave way to a smile. He'd used exactly the same words. "Guy knows what he's talking about."

"You two don't know him, not the way I know him."

"Could be argued…" Strat started.

Conn closed the fridge, glass of juice in hand. "Finish."

With her, Strat might refuse. When it was her guy giving the order, Strat had no choice.

"Little sisters don't always know everything about their older brothers."

"Imogen and Ford didn't live together growing up, not full time. You can't use them as your example."

"I'm just saying, you don't know everything about your brother."

"He's been my touchstone for as long as I can remember. I never knew mom and my dad…" She exhaled because no one had time for ancient history, both men knew the details already. "He's never been like this."

"Like what?" Strat asked.

Conn's dark, brooding stare enchanted her. "You trust me?"

"You know I do." She clutched the back of her chair. "I love that you and Lachlan communicate, it means a lot to me. I love you both. The closer you are, the more security I have because you two can watch each other's asses. I want both of you coming home at the end of every day."

"So what's the problem?"

"I don't want him to lose who he is."

Strat put his coffee down. "You've always been a stubborn mare."

"Thanks, Strat, that really contributes to the current discussion."

Her friend snickered and touched her hair. "We used to sneak around together, you remember?" She nodded. "You kept us quiet, on the dl." Which meant? "You protect your brother, as much as he protects you. Me, the boss," he semi-nodded Conn's way, "your father being dirty, you expended a lot of energy keeping secrets, projecting the illusion of life you thought the cop wanted to see. You wanted him to be proud of you, so you hid anything that could hurt him. Shit, after your attack, you sent him out of the room, you sent every McLeod out the room."

And asked for Strat. "I remember."

"You don't see the irony in that versus this? You hid who you were to protect him. Ever think maybe he did the same thing? Hid anything maybe… unsavory about himself?"

She didn't want to believe there were things she didn't know about her brother, but Strat was right. And it wasn't just her. Everyone, in some way, could be accused of hiding things about themselves, keeping secrets.

"He doesn't have to hide anything," she murmured. "I love him."

"Yeah, he'd probably say the same about you, but there was plenty he didn't know." Strat's hand slid over hers on the table. "You love me, and I'm about as shady dealings as you can get, you never had a problem with that. And your boyfriend… think it's safe to say he lives in the gray."

She got it. Her friend squeezed her hand and Conn was still there, glass near his lips.

"Lach's hurting and being a guy about it, he has nothing to hold onto right now." Guilt, worry, she couldn't just switch them off. "His whole life is… He worshiped our father, everything about him constrained Lachlan. There was a mold, one shape, one way to be. Now he's learned my father never fit the mold he was forcing on his son. Everything Lach held dear was a crock of shit…"

"How did you feel when the truth about us came out?" Conn said, slow, shrewd. "Tell Strat."

It was a sentiment she'd shared with Lach. "Liberated," she whispered the word Conn used to give clarity to her feelings that night. "It freed me."

Strat bobbed his head. "Could be that mold forced your brother into being something he's not."

"But he always was—"

"Doesn't matter, maybe he is exactly like that, maybe he isn't. This, all the truths out, gives him a chance to learn what's important to him. Without those lines tying him down, he's free to figure out who the hell he wants to be."

She picked up Strat's hand to hold it on her cheek for a second. "I can still look out for him, right?"

"He's family, Macushla." Those words from her love's lips meant so much. As she relaxed into a smile, he put his glass in the sink and strode from the kitchen. "Strat can stay."

And there was her best friend, now terrified.

She laughed. "He's kidding."

"He does that?"

"Sometimes." She stood up. "I'm going to get changed, I want to set up a meet today."

"Set it up yourself? Is it my birthday or something?"

She bowed a little to murmur, "You may think so when you see who we're meeting."

TWENTY-NINE

HIS DAUGHTER. What father didn't want a surprise meeting with their youngest child? Not that her friend knew who they were waiting for just yet.

At Vyne, they ordered drinks and waited.

"Im loves this place, talks about it all the time," Strat said, scanning the space. "Have you eaten here?"

"Uh, yeah, maybe."

"Maybe?" he asked. "You're not listening to me."

"No."

She didn't expect to be stood up, but a question hung in the air over how sane it was to set this up. Not because it was Imogen, she was a fan of the woman. Now she was. It had taken a while for them to get together and actually find common ground.

Her apprehension came in the subject matter, it could be dicey.

"Good," Strat said. "'Cause I'd rather you didn't listen to me when I tell you the rumor I heard last night."

Last night? Wait, did he say rumor?

Suddenly, Strat was her whole wide world. "What rumor?"

He laughed. "You're predictable, Scamp."

"Tell me."

"Word is, there was a Huntsman in town last night."

Okay, so, humph.

"Cool," she said and fixated on the door again.

She'd asked Imogen to come alone. Maybe she thought it was weird they weren't meeting in the office. Or maybe she was reluctant to come to a place she'd frequented with her ex. So long as those were the reasons for the tardiness, they were okay. If something happened to Imogen, if she had to tell Lach the woman he'd loved was hurt or in danger… Loved? Was it past tense? How fast did someone fall out of love after being dumped?

"Yeah, that's what I thought."

Her friend's acceptance was curious in itself. "Thought what?"

"Figured I'd say it out loud and your reaction would tell me if it was true or not. Ire told you?"

"Not exactly."

"Just be glad you didn't lay eyes on him. Word is they never leave witnesses."

"To their existence?" Okay, slightly scary because she hadn't just seen an intrepid Huntsman, she'd watched him murder for money. "It's a myth."

"They're a myth. How do you think they stay that way?" He flattened a hand on the table. "By never leaving witnesses."

"I'd check your sources."

Damn sure she'd be checking hers.

"Still haven't told me what happened at the Grand last night. Guys downstairs thought it was something, you know, McDade related."

"We're not the only Irish in the city."

"And there's more to that story."

"I didn't ask specifics," she said.

"Wow, maybe you got hit on the head, or…" He leaned in. "Are you a doppelgänger?"

"Ha, ha, ha." Why hadn't she asked Conn for details about what went down at the hotel? She would. As soon as she circled the wagons around her brother. "Maybe I'm holding off until you give me a full rundown of what happened in Hustle the night you were abducted."

"I told you what happened."

"You told me up until Conn walked in, what happened after that?"

Damn fate would choose that moment for Imogen to arrive.

Spotting her, she stood up, and the woman diverted to approach, about three seconds later Imogen and Strat noticed each other.

"My daughter?" Strat said. "You couldn't give me the heads-up?"

"What do you need the heads-up for? Are you afraid of her?"

Strat adored his daughter. Despite that sentiment not always being reciprocated, Strat held true. Nothing could dent his love for his baby girl.

"Switch sides with me." Both of them left the booth. "Immie."

"What the hell happened to you?" Imogen reached for her dad's bruised face, but he ducked out of the way. "What's this about?" Strat directed his daughter to sit then slid in after her, facing the door. "Has something happened? Where's Ford?"

She slipped in at the free side of the table. "Your brother's fine."

The server brought drinks and Imogen ordered too.

"Are we eating?"

"Are you hungry?" Strat asked. "Sersh hasn't

eaten breakfast." Though she had got a shot of protein. "And I'm ignoring the smile on Scamp's face right now."

"I want to see Ford. If I'd known you were—Jagg's outside, he's been crazy protective since Ford disappeared. Is he safe?"

"Your brother hasn't disappeared," Strat said. "He's working for the McDades."

Imogen paled. "What? Since when? No offense, Sersha, but I thought my brother was free of that crap."

"This is…" Strat lingered. "It's special circumstances."

"Nothing will happen to him," she said, "you have my word."

"Is that what you said to my dad before he got beat down?" Imogen's concern was devoted, pained, and didn't that just pile on the guilt. "You said he was at Hustle, but I didn't know… Dad, why are you getting mixed up in this again?"

The man had once been free of it. Until not long ago actually. Her connection to Conn, her relationship with him, dragged her friend back in, against his will. He'd never say it, but that's what happened. This wasn't a path he'd chosen, it was one she'd put him on. Forced him on. Had she done the same to Lachlan?

"This was a bad idea," she said and pushed to the end of the booth. "I'm sorry, both of you, I—"

"You're not going fucking anywhere," Strat said and grabbed her wrist to keep her seated. "This makes sense, what you're doing, it's a good idea."

Imogen's focus yo-yoed between them. "What's a good idea?"

"Kinda touched actually, you do pay attention when I talk, Scamp, what d'ya know?"

"You're really on fire with the jokes today, old man," she said, deadpan, but gave up her escape attempt. "I'm worried about Lach."

"Was he beaten up too? Is he working for the McDades?"

Pushing for answers on that subject hadn't been fruitful, though she should've tried harder. Imogen didn't know the truth about the superintendent, about him murdering his own father, about him being on the take.

"Lach's not handling this well."

"The alderman's murder?"

"Yeah," Strat said. "Let's go with that."

"What does that mean?"

"Nothing," she said, flashing a glare at Strat. "I wanted to ask if you'd noticed any difference in him."

"Lach? I haven't seen much of him, he's… unhappy."

That much was obvious. "My brother, he's important, he's a good man. I don't want him left behind. You've got Jagg, I'm with Conn, and… Lach looked up to my grandfather, and my dad isn't exactly the type to put his children first. We have to look out for him."

"I'll reach out, talk to him, but… he doesn't trust me like he used to."

When they were a couple.

Strat straightened a fraction. "Shit," he exhaled.

"What is it?"

"Trouble at two o'clock."

As she turned, it arrived.

"Lach?" she asked. Shit, how did he do that? "What are you doing here?"

Except he didn't answer, just grabbed her arm. "Excuse my sister and me a second."

Dragging her out of the booth, he pulled her to the door though they didn't go through it.

"What are you doing?" he hissed.

"What am I doing? My job as your sister. I'm worried about you."

"Little late for that, don't you think?" he asked only then releasing her arm. "Imogen is my business."

"You broke up."

"Doesn't matter. I don't want her involved. Don't want any of our family crap tainting her, you hear me?"

"What are you talking about? Where is this attitude coming from?"

This hostility, the frustration, it wasn't the Lachlan of old, this was exactly her fear, that he'd be hardened by events.

"She's not to know."

Not to know? What? The list of "could be" was long.

"About Dad?"

"About Dad, Vex, Byrne." What the fuck? "None of it."

"How do you know about Byrne?"

Vex was another question mark, but Lach would be more likely to come across information about him than a man, and contract, almost a thousand miles away.

"Baby sister, you made your choices, I'm making mine. Stay out of it."

"Out of it?"

"My life. Your choices are yours, mine belong to me."

"No deal, sorry. I love you. Haven't we looked out for each other all our lives? You can't ask me to stop now. Is that your plan? To give up on me?"

"I'm not giving up, I'm playing the hand, seeing this through to the end."

What the hell did that mean? End of what?

"I need you more now than I ever have in the past. I need you, Lach."

"No, you don't," he said and stepped back. "You got it so right. All those years we..." His jaw moved, something was on his mind, and from his lack of eye contact, it wasn't something he wanted to share. "Look at where we are, Sersh, and how we got here. All my life, everything I worked for…"

"I know," she said and caught his hand. "I know how screwed up things are, and I'm sorry for my role in how we got here."

He extricated his hold from hers. "We're past the point of apologies. The game has changed, there are new rules now, for both of us."

"They don't have to be different. You can't let yourself be—can't let dad's choices, my choices, dictate who you are."

"Isn't that what I've always done? What am I? In this fucked up mess, what the fuck am I?"

An identity crisis? Strat was right, her brother was riding these rapids. Any drastic choice made now may be irrevocable later. If he felt this way in six months, a year, fine, changes could be good, but not now, not in a hasty reaction to shock.

"You're mad." Staying calm was kind of condescending, but yelling wouldn't accomplish anything. "Lach, please, talk to me. We can figure this out. I can help you figure it out."

"Stay out of my life, Sersh," he said and opened the door. "Go back to your huddle, but if I find out you told Imogen any of this, that you involved her…" He shook his head almost like he didn't recognize her. "This isn't a game."

As he marched out, the words rattled in her skull. It wasn't a game. Her impulsive, selfish actions endangered people she loved. Wasn't that the same thought she'd had over and over? Why didn't she do something about it? Instead of sitting around on her ass, she needed to grab control.

THIRTY

NOWHERE WAS EXEMPT from distress or rubberneckers. At work, people whispered. At Stag, everyone watched. Her apartment wasn't her apartment. The loft echoed with trauma's past. And the mansion… didn't fit without her guy.

After insisting on dropping Strat off at the mansion for some respite and a checkup with the doctor, she and the rest of her team drove for hours. Not far. Just around the city, up one street, down another.

The sun set before she called a destination. Her grandfather's house. Wasn't home, it was practically foreign to her, so why was she drawn there?

Lupe.

Having lost the love of her life, it was a wonder that her grandfather's housekeeper kept going. They'd been together seven years. On first talking to the woman, after her grandfather's death, she'd pitied her. Not in a sad, pathetic way, but keeping their love a secret for so long seemed cruel. Her own relationship with Connel had just become public at that point. Like an idiot, she concealed the freedom of the revelation to spare Lupe's feelings.

Maybe she'd got it all wrong.

Lupe and her grandfather kept their relationship a secret and everyone kept their lives, kept their alliances, played their roles, for seven years. Seconds into her selfishly announcing her relationship to Conn, lives and connections started to wither.

"It's not a game," she whispered, standing on the sidewalk gazing up at her grandfather's house.

"You okay, Bluebell?"

"Security still here?"

"Our people."

She nodded. "Good. I'm going inside."

Stranger and Familiar stormed a path up the stairs to open the front door. No one hesitated to accommodate her.

Daly stayed close, which, as she went into the office, was reassuring. The couch, the desk, everything was in place. And in the nook by the fireplace was his chest. Her grandfather's chest.

"What are we doing in here?" Daly asked.

Hock passed by to go to the opposite door, the one her father dragged her out when—no, she wasn't going back there.

The chest. Crouching by it, she touched the lock and twisted to look up at her bodyguard.

"Can you open it?"

"Aye." Hunkering with her, he retrieved his lockpick and got to work. A couple of seconds later, he opened the lid an inch. "Done."

"I don't know what's in here."

"Are we betting?" Hock called from the other end of the room.

"It's gotta be something sex related," Snuff's voice came around the corner. Her guys covered all access points. "Could be a crossdresser."

"Wouldn't that shit be in the bedroom?"

"We're not betting, this is a somber moment for me, respect maybe?"

"Shit," Daly said and backed off a few paces. "Serious faces, guys."

If whatever was in the chest was sensitive, she shouldn't want others to see it. Still, when it came to being in that room and being protected, not only was she unwilling to take any risks, but her guy would tighten her collar if he believed she'd gambled her safety.

"Your boss shares my bed, you know."

"We'd heard that scandalous rumor. Can't be true. Snuff still thinks he's in with a chance."

Hilarious. The fools who teased her would also give their lives for her. Love came in many forms, some of them unspoken.

"Are we friends?"

"Are we—what?" Daly asked.

"Friends. Would you call me your friend?"

"I'll call you any damn thing you want, or your boyfriend will slit me open."

Semi-groaning, she lurched a little his way. "Forget that, I'm asking. Honestly. Are we friends?"

"Not if you want to bitch about your boyfriend or wax together."

When had she ever done that with a friend? Strat wouldn't be interested in either. So much for a straight answer. Wise guys could talk their way into, or out of, anything.

Her hand skimmed the varnished wood. The chest had been there, in her life, as long as her grandfather. She'd never once wondered what was in it or given it more than a passing thought.

Stop procrastinating.

No one would open the box for her. Whatever

was inside, Conn would deal with it. If it required discretion, her guys were perfectly placed to handle it. She trusted them to be diplomatic.

Lupe's insistence rang through her as she lifted the lid until it locked into place. Framed pictures were scattered on top, her grandmother, her father as a child, her and Lachlan seated together in a window. Lupe was right, this was worth looking at, and something she'd never imagined existed. A chest full of memories, of a love the McLeods weren't the best at expressing.

Even if it wasn't always overt, her grandfather had—

Under the pictures were folders, spines upward, labeled each with a series of years. Blue and red. One then the other. What was…?

Sliding out the first, she opened it up and… "These are Lach's cases."

Newspaper clippings, notes, his transcripts. Pushing the plastic pockets aside, one after the other, they presented a record of her brother's life.

And the next one, the red…

"Bluebell?"

"These are mine," she whispered.

Her articles for the school newspapers, clippings from the early newspapers and magazines that printed her words. Contest pieces that won, and those that didn't. He'd kept notes and scraps of paper she thought she'd thrown away.

Every folder, every year, her grandfather had collected their lives, put them in order. Was this pride? Wasn't that what Conn said? Her grandfather loved the city, but this? This was proof he loved them too.

Putting one folder down, she took off her jacket and removed her boots as she settled down on her ass.

"You boys should order food, we could be here a while."

She didn't take enough time to read and reflect. Hadn't she been looking for inspiration for her features? Good old Alderman McLeod kept on giving. She'd make sure the city would never forget him.

THIRTY-ONE

PICTURES, STORIES, drawings from when the McLeod kids were young. The floor was covered with folders, paper, photographs. Oh, yeah, and pizza boxes, half eaten sides, and a bunch of empty cups too. Three fully grown men, as ripped as her guards, needed nourishment to get them through. Gotta keep up, all night long.

No, ah, laying unfair requests on them would be, well, unfair. Snuff's third yawn reminded her of the time.

"Shit," she said, stuffing things back into a transparent pocket. "I'm sorry, guys."

Daly hunkered down next to her to pick up a photograph. "Sorry for what?"

"It's late, you've been with me all day."

"It's almost two a.m.," Hock said. "Doesn't mean nothing when you never go anywhere before noon."

When the boss was in her bed, sure.

"We're here as long as you need us."

"Does anyone live close by? We can drop you

off. I want to go to the club. Anyone know if Conn's still there?"

Standing up, Daly took his phone from his pocket. "He's still there."

The mess stretched far, putting everything back in its place took a while.

"Do you think someone could pick this up and take it to the mansion?" she asked. "I don't want it to get lost in the shuffle of everything when we clear the place out." And Conn may appreciate one or two of the pictures, like the one still in Daly's hand. "Hey." She snatched it from him. "What are you doing with this?"

"Something to stick on the noticeboard for the guys," Daly said without hiding his amusement.

"Yeah, the boss would love that."

A high school picture? Yes, she wore the uniform like a good little girl. Had it really been that revealing? She didn't remember now, but it seemed a little risqué for homeroom. Hock and Snuff bumped her while peering over to get a good look at it.

"Nice."

"You three go drool somewhere else," she said, giving each of them a shove to break up the huddle and slipping the picture into her purse.

"We'll get guys to pick the chest up," Daly said. "It's in safe hands."

Of that she had no doubt. McDades were thorough, and careful, and aware how their leader would respond if they showed her any disrespect.

"Ask them to look around for a key too. It would be good to keep everything secure."

"We don't find it, we'll replace the lock."

Though who would care to steal the sentimental stash? She'd have to reach out to Lupe, thank her for the prompt to check it out. And to ensure her grandfather's former housekeeper was enjoying her new role with the

McDades. She hadn't followed up since Conn made the suggestion. The woman was her grandfather's significant other in the last years of his life, she was practically family.

On the way out, the couch stalled her. That, the desk, the room… she swallowed disgust, anger, terror, it couldn't happen again, and she didn't want any reminders.

"Bluebell?" Hock asked.

"Have a bonfire."

"A bonfire?"

"The couch, the desk, the drapes, anything in this room that burns, I want it gone. Permanently gone." Her stern eyes met Daly's. "You understand?"

"You got it."

Some of it could be priceless antiques, or it could be cheap tat made to look old. Whatever the case, she was adamant. None of those things, those memories, had a place in their lives.

Overall, it had been a successful night, and she didn't want to lose the high. Staying positive, she wouldn't let her father influence her mood.

"No one answered my question about digs," she said as they got to the street. "Can we drop anyone off? I don't mind taking the long way round if it gets you guys home sooner."

If Conn hadn't chased her yet, he was still in the midst of his agenda, whatever that was. Hers still wasn't completely clear. What she did know? She needed to go to the club and ask her guy for help.

Better him than her, but still, her heart hurt a little when she thought of it.

"Home soon?" Hock asked. "We sleep at the club, the mansion, wherever you need us to sleep."

As Daly opened the car door, headlights swung around the corner and a vehicle came to a stop nose-to-nose with her ride.

"Get in the car," Daly said.

She only got a step before the driver's door opened. The height of the guy would betray him even if she wasn't familiar with his silhouette.

"Swerve," she said as he strolled onto the sidewalk. This was no coincidence. "What can we do for you?"

"Need to talk."

"These are my guy's office hours, he'd be happy to accommodate. Do you need directions, or a note from the teacher?"

"I need to talk," he said, jerking his head toward her grandfather's stoop.

"Okay, I'm not going in there with you."

He held up his hands. "Packing nothing."

Hock and Snuff went to check. Not that it mattered. A guy of his stature didn't need a weapon, not to take down someone of hers.

"You want to talk to me? Come to Stag." Going around the door, she didn't care Swerve wasn't happy. "We'll talk there."

"I want to talk alone."

"And we will, at Stag… if my guy agrees to it."

"Need his permission for everything?"

And it was funny he thought that would spur her into complying. She had nothing to prove. Did Conn do business and have conversations without her? Yes. As she did in return. But Swerve? No. No way. Divide and conquer wouldn't work. She and Swerve had no personal relationship, so whatever he wanted to talk about, it was business. McDade business.

"Are you afraid, Swerve?" If he could taunt, so could she. "Is Ire the Big, Bad Wolf? Don't worry, I'll protect you… if you're nice to me or have something I want. Otherwise, you're on your own."

She got in the car and Daly closed the door. It wasn't only the location that put her off getting cozy with Swerve. The guy was crazy, sure, and they were holding Vex, one of his allies, under lock and key, neither of those were points in his favor.

"You're fearless, Bluebell."

"What do I have to fear with you guys around to keep me safe? Let's go to the club," she said, though that had been their intended destination anyway. "And keep an eye on him."

Strength. Commitment. Loyalty. These were McDade qualities. Supporting her guy meant supporting the family. His family. Their family.

After sifting through the memories in her grandfather's chest, she had to wonder if they'd have the same for their children. Any time the subject came up, Conn spoke like it would happen. Business got in the way, family drama got in the way. They'd had little time to discuss how either of them saw their future together.

Would they ever be secure? Would their children? Though she didn't doubt his resolve to keep her safe, Conn never made any promises about his own life. Raising kids alone would be tough. Raising McDade kids… If Conn wasn't around, would she have the ability to protect them?

At Stag, she didn't wait though a car pulled up right behind her. Daly and Hock took her inside while others corralled Swerve.

The guys on the stairs up to the office made way for her and her guards. They'd maybe think twice about letting Swerve by, except he was with McDade security already, they could take him down if necessary.

In the office, Conn was at the desk with a half dozen other guys in the room. Strat, on the couch, Niall, of course, a couple of others she didn't know. They were high enough in the ranks to hang out with Conn, so she guessed they were safe.

"Hi, honey, I'm home," she declared and dumped her purse on the desk to bow and kiss him. "I brought company."

Snuff and Stranger led Swerve into Conn's office with Familiar at his heel.

"Vermin?" Conn asked. "You take pity on the mangy stray? Need me to put it down?"

Swerve actually snickered. "Thinks she's being smart, she's too scared to meet with me alone."

Conn's hand slid up her leg, as he pushed out the chair, he directed her between his thighs to sit on one.

"No, she's a good girl, does as told. She's McDade property, you don't approach her. Need another lesson in manners, Manzani?"

In that busy room, any hostile confrontation could get violent, and Swerve's odds weren't great.

"I'd ask you the same. Stepped up in Hustle when no one wanted you there, Irish."

"That why you're here? Fighting the baby's battle for him?"

"No," Swerve said, sauntering up to the desk to toss a flash drive down. "Figured I'd give her the dignity of seeing it first."

"It?"

Niall snatched up the drive and plugged it into a laptop, dropping into the chair at the end of the desk to load it up.

"Fun times, McDade. You and your perfect little bluebell," he said with a sneer. "Want the world to know how depraved you are?"

THIRTY-TWO

SHIT, WAS THIS the…? Their sex tape? It wasn't a big deal, she and Conn had talked about it. Well, she'd told him there was a chance of it being out there. Niall, and other McDades had seen it before. And with her father locked up and her brother on a… whatever he was on, a sex tape was the least of their worries.

All true.

But did it have to be revealed in this room filled with guys? She'd prefer to put on a live show than sit quietly while their grunts and moans littered the air. At least if Conn was actually inside her, she'd have him to focus on.

And, yep, without preamble, the panting started, a moan, a gasp. She couldn't be self-conscious. If Conn was staring this one down, then so was she. They could take it. The screen wasn't faced their way, and Niall did lower it some, so no one was really watching it.

She stole a glance at Strat, her friend looked more amused than disgusted, thank God. He'd tease her about this forever.

"Yes," Sex Tape Her said. "Oh, yes, baby!"

"Like that?" came his response. "Feel good?"

"Oh, yeah, just like that. Fuck!"

"Full steam," Swerve said. "No hesitation."

Yeah, so either the footage had been cut to miss the foreplay, or they were hearing a select part. She'd never actually watched their sex tape in full. Conn had it, then Strat did. And she was there, it wasn't like she could forget how incredible it was to be in bed with—

"Oh, fuck, Ire! More! Please, oh, fuck."

"Call it out, baby. Fuck, yeah."

Her smile came as Conn's chin rose.

His hand dropped to her lap. "Release it," he said to Swerve, then switched to Niall. "You got it there? Send it to every news outlet. Post it online. Sell it to the porn sites."

Swerve wasn't the only one confused by Conn's smug confidence.

"That how the Irish treat their women?"

Her smile became a grinning snicker she had to muffle against Conn's neck. He yanked the drive from the computer and threw it at Swerve.

"Take your smut and get the fuck out of here. Approach her again and you'll get your own sex tape, got a lot of guys on payroll who'd love to ride your ass. Fuck off."

Pissed, Swerve stomped out and slammed the door. Maybe wasn't a good idea to irritate a man not known for his restraint, but her guy wasn't on that list either.

"You'd really be okay with it being out there?" Snuff asked.

"Scamp?" Strat asked with concern.

Wasn't so funny now, not for him. No one else understood.

Still tucked against Conn, she shifted the angle of

her head to see her friend on the chesterfield.

"Nothing to worry about."

"You get it?" Conn asked Niall.

"Aye."

"Send it to our guys, back trace it. I'm more interested in the who than the why."

Because that was kind of obvious. And he always said learning the who revealed the why.

"Can you send it to me too," she asked, "please."

Of course the lieutenant got the nod from his boss first. "Aye."

Conn boosted her to her feet as Niall excused their guys and got closer to talk to his superior. While security and the unknown guys filtered out, she went to sit next to Strat.

"I left you at the mansion for a reason," she said to her friend.

"I cadged a lift."

"Apparently. You're supposed to be resting."

He opened his hands in the air by his thighs. "You see me sitting? This is resting. How come you're giddy 'bout the sex tape?"

"It's funny."

"Never thought there'd be much comedy between Ire McDade's sheets."

"You might be surprised." Taking his hand, she rested her head on him. "But that's not why it's funny."

"Then why's it funny?"

"It's not us," she said, bouncing up to kiss his cheek. "You need to get back to the mansion, and the doctor. I'm thinking we should tie you down or sedate you for a couple of weeks."

"You'd never survive that long without me." Probably true. "Better staying here. My boy's here." His frown deepened. "How'd you know it wasn't you on the tape?"

"I heard the words."

"Things we say in bed don't always stick later. Could be you."

She laughed and got up, stealing his hands to hoist him up too. "No, it couldn't." She leaned in to whisper, "I don't call him Ire in bed."

"Never has."

That Irish-American drawl widened her smile again, and it was close, so close that its owner's fingertips drifted up her arm.

Not just in bed, she never called him Ire, except with other people.

Strat was a lot more serious than her hormones. "It's a fake?"

"Without a doubt. And who do we know with experience in the porn industry… Hmm…" She feigned wonder. "Let me think… Someone who knows Swerve…"

"Shit, it's…" Strat trailed off and glanced above her to Conn. Niall went somewhere, she didn't know where, but he wasn't around. "You asked who."

"The actors," she answered. "The people doing the screwing."

"Weakest links in the chain."

"Might be Silvio's project, but what does he plan to do with it. No way he did it just to embarrass us. We're together, the world knows we're together now. Kinda follows that we have sex." She bumped back against her guy. "I thought it was the original."

"Every copy of that is in the vault," Conn said, relaxed as always.

"Except my copy," she said and snagged her friend's hand. "Strat has that."

"That's what the flash drive is? Fuck, am I happy I never got curious."

"You were always curious, just not that curious."

"You weren't exactly in with the McDades then. Could've been anything."

"Give it to Conn, or Niall, they can put it with the others."

"Doesn't matter," Conn said, sort of distracted.

"Does if it's the only copy out there. If it gets out, Strat loses his head."

Her friend blanched. "Good point, I'll get it."

"It's blank," Conn said when her friend moved sideways. "The drive you were given is blank."

Slowly, jaw loose, she turned to him. "Months. How did it take you months to tell me that?" Though it was confusing. "What if I watched it?"

"You didn't."

"Yeah, because I was attacked on my way out. If I hadn't sent Strat after it, I'd have been terrified that… Baby, why did you do that? How did you know I wouldn't watch it?"

"You would've watched it, if the attack hadn't happened, you would've watched."

"Probably, and I'd have seen it was blank, that there was nothing there…"

That was when Conn's dark emeralds sank to her gaze. And that was all the more shocking, because that meant…

"I'd have come back," she murmured. "I'd have demanded to see you."

God, that changed everything. Absolutely every little thing about—grabbing his face, she forced him down to accept her mouth. Back then, they hadn't been over, he was never done with her. What she'd said to him, after the attack, how she'd pushed him away, all of it was misguided.

Easing from their kiss, she sailed on their permanence.

"I get what I want," Conn said.

Her lips curled as she bowed back to meet his eye. "Yes, you do. I exist beneath you, under you."

"Aye."

When she tried to kiss him again, he resisted. "I have a meeting."

"I don't know if I care about that."

He'd let her sit in on business plenty and after what he'd just revealed, it didn't feel like a moment to leave him. Didn't feel like a moment to have company either.

"I care," Strat said, heading for the door. He stopped, holding it open. "Coming or not, Scamp?"

"I'll find you in a minute."

Strat went out, leaving her and Conn alone.

She pressed herself against him. "I made a decision and… have to do something that might break his heart."

"*You* don't have to do anything. Say what you want, I'll make it happen."

"Well, when you say things like that, I want you to kiss me."

And he was bold in catching her cheeks, pressing his thumbs under the angle of her jaw to position her just right for their lips to meet.

As he withdrew, she moistened her lips again, the rush of blood in her ears reared up.

"What about your favorite little nook?"

Stooping lower, he kept her head, thrusting it back to bare not only that nook for his mouth, but her throat, her cleavage.

"Conn…"

The desperation in that whisper closed her eyes and—

"Just what a guy wants to see this time of night." Lach's voice shattered her reverie. "You want to talk or get it on with my sister?"

So that was why Conn tried to excuse her? Lachlan?

"Private time, I guess," she said on a sigh. "Where are we sleeping tonight? Should I go or wait?"

"Play's at the mansion. We can stay here."

Suited her, she tossed him a smile that faded a little when she saw her brother's stern expression.

Why was he pissed with her? Not a little pissed, like a lot pissed? Her Lachlan looked out for her, loved her. This guy couldn't stand her.

"What happened with Imogen?" he asked before she'd even taken a step.

"Nothing happened with her. I asked her to look out for you, that was it."

"She know about Dad?"

"No. Not that I've told her, and I don't see Strat exposing something like that to anyone let alone his little girl. How would that knowledge benefit her?"

Burden her? Sure.

"Ford know?"

"I haven't spoken to Ford, haven't seen him since…" forever ago, now her guy was glaring too. Though not at her. "Are you two going to tell me what's going on with you?"

"No," Lach said without giving Conn a chance to utter a word. "Because protecting the people we care about is important."

"You think protecting me starts with lying to me? Doing the right thing never starts with doing the wrong thing, brother. Wonder who told me that."

"Who's lying?"

"Right, because an omission isn't a lie. Never thought you'd adopt that McDade stance."

Any McDade stance.

"You sleep with him," Lachlan said. "Why do that, why trust him, if you don't believe in him?"

"I believe in him and the McDades, all of them, everything."

"So why question my loyalties?"

"To the McDades? Because your loyalty has always been—"

"With you, dad, and both of you walked away from that. The McLeod name is nothing now."

"Dad's still Superintendent, no one knows he's a murderer. There's no reason your life has to change."

"Except it's a lie. Dad isn't Superintendent, he is." Lach jerked his chin toward the silent, assessing Conn. "You think I want a career based on that? Based on a lie? No promotion will ever be honest, no bust scrupulous. The guys on the streets, these families…" He shook his head. "Your world has changed, your views, you're a McDade." Which she wouldn't deny. "And Dad, whether he likes it or not, he's dancing to their song too. He has no one to blame for that, no one except himself."

"You don't have to follow him. Make your own choices."

"I am," he said, raising his chin. "Maybe I don't want to march to the blue beat. Maybe I never did. I conformed, did what was expected. No need to do that anymore."

This was her issue. It wasn't her brother's. Why was she pushing at him? Poking? Arguing? She didn't want to tarnish him; like she'd tarnished others. If this was the path Lach really wanted, she'd support him. But how could she know for sure?

"No, you don't." Setting her sights on Conn, she chose to be as decisive. "Take Strat off payroll, Ford too. They'll always have access, be welcome and protected, but they won't be on our books."

Conn half-nodded, sort of, he did one of his twitches, in acknowledgment.

Her brother may be taking a McDade wage or

not. She'd dragged the Stratfords into this, she could set them free. Lachlan wasn't so easy to free when he seemed determined to rush in headfirst.

Her fingertips met Conn's jaw. "I like everything I'm wearing…"

"Then you know what to do with it."

The clothes were irrelevant. The message was clear.

When was the last time they'd slept at Stag? She remembered the last time she'd been in that bed and, boy, that was a memory that needed replacing.

"Sersh," her brother said. She paused at the curtain. "People make their own choices. Everyone makes their own choices."

She smiled at no one and bowed her head. "Not in this house, Lachlan. What our leader says is law." She exhaled. "Don't be long, Mo Grá."

THIRTY-THREE

"YOU'RE TROUBLED. Talk to me."

Conn didn't have to say out loud what she already knew. Oh, but her guy did know her, and never shied from giving her an opener.

Sated, strewn across their Stag bed, this was when she did most of her reflecting. Being with Conn, connected to him physically, in the quiet, in the dark, somehow it leveled her yawing mind.

"'What's in your head belongs to me.'" She repeated his words. "That's what you said. All of me belongs to you."

"Aye.

His certainty was always absolute, he was never unsure or undecisive. God, she could use a little of that, a lot of that.

"How do you know you're making the right decisions?"

"Strat?" he asked. Good guess. Her friend was on her mind, but he wasn't the only one. "It's handled."

"I know, you handle everything. I never have to

ask twice." She wasn't worried about her guy following through. "Just… do it delicately."

"He's been good to you. It's loyalty, Macushla."

Which, in the past, he'd accused her of not having or understanding.

Rolling onto her stomach, she cupped her face, supporting it with her elbows on the bed. "My decision to take him off our books isn't about that. I still love him and trust him as much as I always have."

"You think he feels different about you?"

"No, I'm not severing our relationship. With everything that's happened recently… When Strat had the chance, he chose to get out of this life. He wanted a quiet existence, not one like this."

"And Ford walked away from the Manzanis."

"Will you love me any less if I come without the excess baggage?"

"*Excess*" was relevant because even with protecting the Stratford's, they still had her father, Vex, and everything else she dragged in her tail of destruction.

He drove his fingers into her hair. "Macushla."

Just the word reminded her he'd support her through anything.

Her eyes dropped before meeting his again. "Will you tell me what's happening with Lachlan?"

"Trust your brother."

"Do you trust him?" An honest question. With Conn, she wouldn't shy from asking the hard ones. "I love my brother, and I love you, but I never thought you'd play nice together."

"You think it's a con?"

"Hard to say when I don't know what you're doing together. I know him as a man strict about his career, about his morals. Seeing him with you in secret talks, it's strange, but…" she held her breath a second. "If he wanted to corner or incriminate you, I'm not sure he'd take his current stance with me. Wouldn't it be easier to keep me sweet? Maybe then I'd inadvertently help, soothe your potential suspicions or something. Maybe it's a double bluff, or a double, double bluff. I don't know."

On a groan, her hands went up through her hair as she face-planted on the bed.

This wasn't her ratting on her brother. She had to be honest with Conn and hope they'd never be in a situation on opposite sides. If Lach was in, he was in, great. If he wasn't, and he planned to prosecute the man she loved, or his underlings, Conn could only follow one line of action: annihilation. She couldn't lose her brother, but she couldn't lose Conn to twenty-five to life either.

"You need to breathe, Macushla."

Just his voice was enough to loosen her clenched muscles. "When did life get so complicated?"

Crawling up the bed, she climbed on top of him, rubbing the inside of her knuckles hard up and down his abs, avoiding his scar.

"This isn't complicated," he said. "You make it complicated by layering everyone else's crap on yours. Stick to this, baby."

"This has always been easy." Her head tilted. "Straightforward? Simple?" None of the words seemed right. That was it. "Right. This has always been right. Even all the times I said it wasn't, being with you is right." Lowering to kiss him, she tucked her head under his chin and relaxed. "People don't understand us. How can we be such a puzzle to others and such a breeze to ourselves?"

"Other people are insignificant. They don't interest me." His hand went behind his head. "Focus. One thing at a time."

And he'd take care of the big picture. Having a safety net like Conn almost felt unfair. Whatever happened next week, next month, he'd be there, looking out for her, keeping her safe.

"I focus on you as often as I can." She took a beat. "Why didn't you tell me about the flash drive? Ours? I brought up the sex tape and you never said a word about the one I had being blank."

"You don't like lies." And, technically, giving her a blank drive that was supposed to contain something was a lie. "Not revealing a truth is—"

"An omission not a lie." At least his rules were consistent. "You wanted me to come back. Telling me we were through… you didn't mean it."

"Cutting ties was the smart route."

Not one he could commit to fully if he'd given her the blank drive hoping it would reconnect them.

"At mine, after the attack, when you came to me. I told you I needed people who'd be around a long time. You let me talk to you like… Why didn't you tell me the truth?"

"I let you down. You weren't protected in McDade territory. If I wasn't capable of looking after you, I didn't deserve to have you."

For a man who lived in the "gray" as Strat put it, Conn dealt with a lot of guilt when it came to her safety. And if she'd been a casual lay, he wouldn't have placed such a premium on his role as protector.

"You know…" She sighed. "I think I can't love you anymore and then you just…" With a smile, she kissed him then rose, wriggling her hips. "You're the one thing I always rely on. Never ask me to live without you again."

Skimming his palms up her arms, he caressed her for a few seconds then cradled her breasts in both hands.

"I'll talk to Silvio tomorrow."

Divert the conversation, take it to work. Man, her guy knew just how to untangle her webs.

"About the tape?"

"No, I won't give him the satisfaction of asking direct. That game isn't important to me."

If it was them, he'd care someone had access to their private moments. That it was a fake? This was child's play her guy didn't have time for.

"Does Silvio know we have Evander?" she asked. "And about the shooting? Is the tape a shot across the bow?"

"If that's the best he's got, destroying him won't take long."

If not about the tape or Evander… "You'll talk to Silvio about Hell?" she asked. "Hell's last letter said he had a parole hearing coming up. That was a while ago though. With the murder and Dad, I haven't had a chance to write back. Do you think he knows about us? That I'm with you?"

"He knows."

Could be why he mentioned parole, he'd know about the Dorsey deal too. Being close to Conn, she had the facility to convey messages, to whisper in his ear. Hell had never asked her to pass anything along, or mentioned Conn. That didn't mean he wouldn't imply or suggest.

"Should we be worried if he hits the street again? What's he really like? Is he hungry for it? I can only learn so much through writing."

Evander wanted to steal the Manzani empire from under his father. With him locked in the Stag basement, that plan wasn't exactly what she might call "progressing." If Hell got out and wanted power, would he challenge his father? His brother? His enemies?

"All we get are rumors, secondhand reports, guards intel."

"You get reports from prison guards?" she asked.

"I get reports from anyone I want."

For twenty years both Hell and Dorsey had been locked away. How much contact they had with others was unknown, though it was safe to say it had been limited. These people couldn't know themselves, not as they'd be on the outside. What was important? Was freedom enough?

Dorsey had more than paid her dues. Twenty years she'd been locked up, basically her whole life. And Hell couldn't have spent much time with savory types. She dreaded to think how that would've changed a man already colored by darkness.

Their family, the Manzanis, had the potential to hurt the McDades, to hurt Conn. There, in their bed, she didn't want to give the opposing family too much airtime.

"I opened the chest in my grandfather's office," she said. "The one Lupe told me to check."

"You were out late. Wasn't too happy when I heard where you were hanging out."

"The guys were with me. I wouldn't go in there alone. Swerve showed up outside when we left, how would he know we were there?"

"Any place belonging to you or your family will be monitored. The Manzanis will do regular patrols."

So she shouldn't read too much into it. They're on the ball, keeping tabs, much like the McDades would. It didn't freak her out Swerve showed up, might actually work out for them in the long run. By refusing to deal with him alone, and forcing him to come to Stag, she and Conn sent the message they were a single unit.

She stroked his stomach. "Why were we deepfaked? Why us? What did they hope to achieve?"

"It's game playing."

"Silvio was the one making porn, not Vex," she said. "This has to be him."

"We'll fire back but leave him playing in the sandbox." Because the McDades were focused on building their empire. "Once he learns Vex went behind his back, they'll go through their own civil war."

And could be in the midst of it when Hell reappeared. Yeah, okay, there was a little schadenfreude in that. It would also give the McDades a chance to gain ground. There would be less of the pie to go around by the time the Manzanis got their head back in the game.

Taking pleasure in another family's misery was somewhat hypocritical. Her own doorstep wasn't exactly shiny, clean, and faultless.

"My dad still here?"

"Aye."

When was the last time she'd slept under the same roof as her father before this recent palaver? A long time ago.

"Will he be here forever?"

How could he keep his job if he was never seen? People would ask questions eventually.

"Until he understands who is in control," Conn said. "Who he has to thank for his freedom and his position. It's time for an attitude adjustment." Which was probably something her father said to her back in the day. "We'll keep him on a close leash, provide private security." McDades who'd watch his every move. "And we'll pull him back in every time he steps out of line. He breathes free air because we allow it. He breathes at all because we allow it. He'll figure that out fast or it'll be taken away. He breathes while he's useful, not a second longer."

"And my grandfather's house?"

"It'll be cleared and sold."

"You told me that already. I mean when will it happen? I asked the guys to burn everything in that office. That okay?"

"You don't need my permission to give orders, but I grant it. Whatever you want, Macushla, whatever you want."

What she wanted was to enjoy being intimate with him in the dark. "Are you sure you want to sell a house with a secret exit?"

"Think the mansion has none of those?"

She laughed. "We're blocking them before we have kids."

"Think so? How will we escape them?"

Maybe not straight comedy, but her guy had a sense of humor. Parenthood. Conn was so busy as it was, would it be fair to pile on more responsibility? Why was she so mired in the thought of reproduction? It kept coming back. Something to do with her own position as child to a father who'd wronged them in so many ways. She'd do it differently, Conn would too. Illegality aside, she wasn't lying when she'd dubbed her love a better man.

They could just stay there, like that, together and safe. Her breathing slowed and though his fingers tangled in her hair, they quickly stilled.

Quiet. Calm. Safety. Love. She'd never been happier than when she was right there, anywhere, existing with him.

An almighty crash shook the walls. The colossal sound reverberated through the floors and furniture, quaking her atoms.

One shout followed another. Movement. There was movement and—

"Stay here," Connel said, leaping out of bed to rush out, sweatpants in hand.

Oh, geez, this couldn't be good, wouldn't be good. Whoever was visiting hadn't got an invite. Would they leave quietly or make themselves known? Seemed they'd already made that choice.

THIRTY-FOUR

MORE VOICES, a shout, a ruckus. Shots, she definitely heard gunshots, quick, slow, some louder, some too close for comfort. She wanted to do as told and stay in their bed, but, at the same time, didn't want to be naked if someone burst in. Grabbing clothes from the closet, she dressed and threw her hair up. The second her butt hit the bed, Niall materialized in the doorway.

"Come."

A man of few words. She followed him down the stairs and round into the playroom. Without turning on the light, he grabbed her hand and pulled her through a door to the left. Then they were going down. Huh, so quick welcome to the basement stairs. At the bottom, there was another door, and a turn.

"What's going on?" Her heart pounded. "What happened? Is someone hurt? Where's Conn?"

"Taking care of business."

Niall opened another door and shoved her into light. The glow burned her eyes, as she shielded them, a door closed, the one behind her.

"What the…?"

"We're here."

"We?"

Was that Strat? Yes, he put her in a car, drove up a ramp, and then they were out, on the road.

"What's going on?"

"Incursion," Strat said.

"What does that mean? What incursion? I don't—what the hell is going on?"

"Heard we're breaking up," her friend said.

Wait, did he mean…? How could he possibly know about that already?

"We're not breaking up," she said, "I'm giving you back your life. Go back, what do you mean incursion? Who's incurring?"

That didn't even make sense. Nothing did. She'd been lying with her man, warm, sleeping, comfortable, and now she was out in the night. Her head couldn't catch up.

"Byrnes," Strat said.

And, shit, if that didn't put the danger into immediate perspective. "Oh my God, Madison! They've come for her, haven't they? They want her back! If they get her…" Would they snatch the woman and run, or stick around to dish out a little payback? "This isn't good. This is bad. Really bad. Really, really bad."

She'd been obsessed with her choices hurting the people she loved, now she didn't even have a chance to speak to Conn, to find out his plan.

"Byrnes can want, they won't get," Strat said, shifting his hands on the wheel. "Shit, did I sound like a McDade there? Better turn that dial if I'm out on the street in the morning. Bet the Gambattos have a few want ads in the paper. Think Ire'll write me a reference?"

Could there be a crappier time for this to happen? What made it worse? He wasn't even mad. He wasn't sad or bitter or spiteful, there was a blade of anger, one sliver, but it was matter of fact.

"No one was ever throwing you in the street. I love you; I'd do anything for you. I want you safe, to have the life you want, and this isn't it. You chose to leave this life already. You're my friend, my best friend, and you only got into protecting me because I took you to Conn, I put you in front of him. I need to fix this for you. I have the ability to do it, Conn trusts me on this. No penalty, you get away clean."

"Know why Ire trusts me to guard you? Me? The old, fucking, washed up has-been?" She tsked at him. They might tease, but he was worth any other two men, three, sometimes four, depending on the guys. "Do you?"

"Because you love me."

"That's damn right. Irish doesn't have to tell me to protect you, it's automatic. He doesn't have to train me how to fight or warn me to get in front of any bullet meant for you. Why? Because you're my girl, you're not a daughter, you're not a child, you're smart, capable. When you're not griping and you're thinking straight, we make a helluva team. Quit trying to make everyone's choices for them. Live your life, not mine."

"My brother hates me."

"He doesn't hate you."

"And he's right. He should hate me. Every person I love has been touched by my decision to be with Conn."

"Immie's decision to be with the cop influenced my relationship with her. Jagg, the same. Just like me and Bette's choice to break up influenced Ford and Im. We're a part of each other's lives, we're family."

"Strat—"

"The day I came to Stag with you, when you were in trouble, I chose to be there. You said it would out us and I walked in anyway. Remember that? 'Cause I fucking do. I made that choice. *I* made it. I'm not ashamed of you. You ashamed of me?"

"No!"

"Take me off payroll, won't make a difference. I'll still show up, I'll still get in front of that bullet. Just means I'll have to couch surf, but there's plenty of beds in Stag."

If Stag was even still there. God knew what mess they'd left behind.

"My brother hates me." Didn't he get it? How many different ways could she say it? No one understood. Yes, pathetic, but she'd never displeased Lach before, not like she had by being with Conn. And her father, it almost felt like her brother held her responsible for that too, somehow. "I don't know how to make it right."

Strat frowned. "This something to do with Vyne? You cut things short after he showed."

"He's always supported me. Always been on my side."

If Strat couldn't help her make sense of this, no one could.

"He's still on your side. Love doesn't go away just 'cause someone's angry."

This wasn't just anger, it went deeper than that. "He's spending all this time with Conn."

"Yeah."

"I don't know what they're doing, neither of them will talk to me."

And she wasn't used to being so far out of the loop with either of them.

"It's business."

Did he just—he better not… "Do not tell me you know what they're—why would they tell you and not me?"

"I don't know. Believe me, I don't." Telling Strat would be tantamount to telling her. He'd share if he knew, wouldn't he? "The guys have noticed Lachlan's around the place when he never has been before."

Was that a first? "Did you just call him Lachlan?"

"Yeah, shut up. If he's going to be on the team, we'll have to get used to him."

Was that it? Her brother would be around long term? What did that mean for his job?

"Can he be a cop and—he'd never do it dirty." The Lachlan she'd grown up with wouldn't. The one who'd raised and nurtured and… she breathed out. "Shit."

"What?"

"Shit. I figured it out. Damn, I'm slow. Spending so much time with my father killed a few hundred brain cells."

"You figured it out? What did you figure out?"

"Will you take me to Lachlan's?"

"We're supposed to go to the mansion."

"I don't have my phone." Strat was lucky she was dressed; clothes very nearly hadn't been part of the deal. "You have to take me to his apartment so I can talk to him."

"It's the middle of the night."

"And I have no patience. We left Conn behind, I don't know if you noticed. You tell me the Byrnes are bringing down the roof, then expect me to toddle off to bed and get a good night's sleep? That ain't happening."

"I have to follow orders. Boss says I'm close to my pink slip."

"You'll be closer to God if you ignore me."

A phone rang. Strat's phone. He dug it out of his pocket to answer. "Yeah…? Yeah, I got her."

"Who is that?" The Stag situation couldn't have been resolved already. That couldn't be Conn. "Strat?"

He put the phone on speaker and dropped it into the center console nook.

"You're on speaker," her friend said.

"Sersha?"

"Lach!" It was a good sign he cared enough to check she was okay. Though… "How did you know—"

"I'm with Dad," Lach said. "Are you safe? Are you hurt?"

"Not hurt, and yes, I'm safe. You're with Dad?" Wasn't he still at Stag? "I don't get it. How can you be with Dad? Is he at your apartment?"

"Your brother's not at his apartment," Strat said.

Hmm, another reason her friend might've been reluctant to take her there, couldn't he have just said that?

"Where are you?"

"On the way to the mansion."

"Whoa, wait, what? What mansion?"

"Strat," Lachlan said.

"Yeah, yeah," her friend drawled. "We'll meet you there." He stabbed at the screen to disconnect the call. "I told you he'd been around."

"Around like at Stag around? Like with the guys? Like underground?"

She didn't even want to utter the word basement. Shocking though that was, she didn't quite know where to settle her outrage.

Was it that her brother was so "tarnished" now that he could hang around with wise guys and low lifes as equals? That or he was deep in the McDade family intending to collect and share evidence of misdeeds with his law enforcement superiors. Did Conn trust him enough to allow him inside? If he trusted him like that because of her, the McDades could lose everything because she loved her brother.

Her friend shrugged. "You could say that."

"I can't believe any of this, I can't… What is he

doing with Conn?"

The question was rhetorical, in that moment anyway. An answer would come from elsewhere… maybe. Now she needed a strategy, something to tempt Conn into divulging details. She'd never had to turn it on like that for him before, not for such a crucial reason. Was she confident? Maybe, he'd ask if she trusted him and—

"Fuck."

The word was a whisper on her friend's tongue; his tone delivered a shot of alarm.

"What?" she asked. "What's fuck? What is it?"

Brow low, he glanced up, down, at the side mirror, then the rearview. "We have a tail."

"A tail?"

"We're being followed."

THIRTY-FIVE

"WE'RE BEING—what the fuck? Followed?"

Twisting, she grabbed the shoulder of her chair to peer out the back.

"Stay low," Strat muttered. "Seatbelt."

Was she wearing a seatbelt? Nope. Grabbing it, she quickly put it on and slouched low.

"Why are they following us? The mansion?"

Could they take trouble there? Should they?

"To find out where we're going. The prisoners are being moved to the mansion. We can't risk these guys getting hold of anyone. If they follow us there, we'll lead them right to what they want. Give them a way in. Might as well set off a flare."

Okay, they couldn't do that. That had to be the Byrnes goal, to follow someone from Stag to confirm where their prize was being taken.

"So we don't go there. Where?"

"Hold on," Strat said and sped up. "Call Ire."

"I can't." Her friend did a double take, his frown deepening. "If I call him now, he'll drop everything to get here. We can't let him—the family has to endure."

"Right."

And everything Conn planned would be shot to shit. The others needed him there. Niall needed him there. If the Byrnes were launching a full-scale op to get Madison back, which they had to be, there would still be fighting going on. There was no one she trusted more as a strategist than Connel McDade.

"There's a gun in the glovebox and a couple of clips." Before she could open it, Strat reached over to yank her seatbelt tight. "Hang on."

As he increased his speed, he took a corner fast, thrusting her both back and to the side at once.

"Can we outrun them?"

"Not in this," her friend said, narrow eyes on the road until flicking to the rearview for a second. "How bad do you want it?"

It? Being her? That wasn't a question for her, it was intended for whoever was in the vehicle behind them.

"They want me." She was the bonus prize. The toy with the meal. The backup plan if their first failed. "Don't they? That's what this is." On another tight corner, she grabbed the door and console. "Shit, Strat, what are we—"

"Good."

"Good? What's good?" Because that long drawl was more daring than happy. "Strat?"

"They're sticking with us."

"And that's a good thing?"

They sped along a straight, weaving in and out of any traffic that got in their way. Was the point to get the cops involved? Shit, if they did that and the Byrnes meant business, they'd end up with dead LEOs whose only offense was showing up to work.

"If they get you, they trade you for Madison."

"That's something, they won't kill me." Except the moment their eyes met, she finished the thought. "Me." Apprehension shook her throat. "They'll kill you."

"Least then you won't have to fire me."

"Strat—"

The quick turn of the wheels stole her words to a gasp. They shot down an alley, past a dumpster and Strat slammed on the brakes, turning the wheel to bring them around at an angle in a screeching stop.

Thrust one way then the other, her head spun.

Strat was alert. "Get out your side, stay behind the back wheel."

"Stay behind the—what?"

Brakes squealed, not theirs, the Byrnes.

Strat grabbed a gun from his waistband and threw open his door. "Go!"

Her butt hadn't left the seat when the first gunshot echoed. Didn't take long for her to hit the asphalt after that. Another shot followed, and another. Glass shattered and scattered, she heard every sliver hit the ground and sheltered her head.

How many assailants were there? And why was she leaving Strat to the battle? On her hands and knees, she crawled on the ground to reach in for the gun in the glove box. Scooping out the clips, she stayed low.

Damn, she should've practiced at a range. Guns had always been a part of her life, she'd just never been interested in honing her aim.

"Shit," Strat said. Another shot, and another. "Fuck!"

"Strat!"

That sounded like pain. No, she couldn't—Strat couldn't lose his life. Her friend was hunkered down behind his door, dumpster providing some cover. The window above him was gone. The next shot hit the windshield. Strat returned fire, around his door, and through the window space.

"Give us the girl!"

The girl? Is that what she'd been reduced to? Fuck that. Gun in hand, she couldn't just cower.

"Suck it, Byrne," Strat called back. "Want her? Come get her!"

More shots, her side, theirs, her friend, the enemy. God, her heart hammered, and it wasn't fear, not for her life. Slamming her door, she reached the front tire when there was another shot, then silence. This felt different than before. Different to—no more shots, quiet, footsteps.

"Scamp."

Above her, Strat grabbed her arm to haul her up and pull her around to the trunk.

"What happened?"

"We're moving now."

He opened the trunk to pull out a bag and—

"Shit, you're bleeding." A bloom of red on his sleeve tightened her chest. "Oh my God, what—"

He thrust one bag at her and collected up the clips scattered on the ground. Not only hadn't she got a shot off, she'd dropped their ammo too.

Pushing her down, he put her in a crouch. "Stay here." He paused to show a hand again. "I fucking mean it. I will tie you up and toss you in the trunk if I have to." Her boyfriend wouldn't like that treatment, yet she smiled as tears gathered in her eyes. "Don't start that shit."

Stomping off, he went around the hood. She peeked up to watch him check the other vehicle. Where were the guys? Did they just leave? Was there—boosting a little higher, she saw the body on the ground, one at the door, a leg at the back suggested there was another.

When Strat turned to come back, she ducked down, returning to the same position he'd left her in.

"Can't follow instructions for shit, girl," Strat said as he passed their hood. "Fucking move."

Leaping up, still holding the bag, her friend had another, its strap cut across his torso as he reloaded his gun.

"We should get you to the hospital."

"Hospitals ask questions."

Yes, they did, but he was her friend. Her friend who'd killed for her.

"The mansion then," she said, "the doc will be there."

"Doc has his hands full." They went to the end of the alley, to a dark parking lot she hadn't known was there. "We get you safe first."

"You're bleeding. Bleeding takes precedence over—"

Her friend stopped and raised a fist. "You hear that?"

"I hear what?"

Moving faster, Strat went to a car in the corner and dug something from his bag. In one slick move, he popped the lock and opened the door to drop side on into the driver's seat.

"You're—we're—"

His scowl silenced her. As she sucked her lips into her mouth, he leaned back to do something beneath the steering wheel. Something? Yeah, he was hotwiring it, as proven when it revved to life.

"Get in," he said. "Fast."

Running around, she jumped into the passenger seat. The door wasn't even shut and already they were moving.

"I didn't know you could still do that to cars."

"Gotta know what you're doing."

"And I thought Ford was the car guy."

A slanted stare. "Where'd you think my boys got

their skills?"

"You shouldn't be—you're bleeding, Strat."

"It's nothing," he said again.

With the blood on the opposite side, she couldn't check how much of nothing it was.

"They were Byrnes?"

"Yep."

"How many?"

"Three."

Their eyes met again. "Strat, I—"

"Don't. What did I say about that bullet?"

That he'd always get between her and it.

They trundled through the city, not at speed, vigilant instead. Strat's attention went everywhere. Her friend was on high alert, determined to keep her alive. After only just saying he'd protect her life with his, he'd proved it in real time.

"Are we okay?" she asked, glancing around. "Anyone else following?"

"No, and we left the phone in the fucking car." He slammed his hands on the steering wheel. They had weapons and ammo, no form of communication. "We don't know if the mansion is safe."

"If we were followed, others might've been too. The mansion could be under siege, caught in an attack of its own. We could circle back to—"

"No, if the Byrnes didn't put out a message before we engaged with those assholes, their silence will have brought others out. We can't take the risk they'll get the jump on us."

"Where's safe?"

"Maybe nowhere 'til sunup."

And even then, there were no guarantees.

"So we keep driving? In a stolen car?"

"We'll get out of the city. Dump it."

"Out of the city? Strat, Conn'll—"

"Want my head? Yeah, probably, but you'll be alive." Her friend flashed her a smile. "That's gotta earn some points with him, doesn't it?"

Her guy would be angry because that's how his fear manifested itself. But Strat was doing what he thought was right regardless of any consequence for him.

"Wait," she said, struck by an idea. "Go to Imogen's."

"You want me to bring my daughter into—"

"Not Jagg's, the apartment she shared with Lachlan. Their old place."

"They still have that?"

"Conn does. Can you pick a lock?"

"Be embarrassing if I couldn't," Strat said. "Why would Ire keep—"

"I'll tell you when we get there." Because how deep into the truth she'd get depended on what they found. "No one will find us there."

And no one would think to look either. Except Conn. If the cameras were still active. Even if they weren't, maybe she could link them up.

"They have a hard line?"

She shrugged. "Only one way to find out."

As soon as they could, she'd reach out to Conn. Call or—that is if he wasn't bleeding too. Her blank stare went to the road ahead. Her love stayed behind, and she'd left him there.

The Byrnes wanted blood, the redder the better. Would they leave if they got Madison? Would Conn give her up? No, he'd never do something that could be construed as weak or afraid. She'd never been a fan of Madison's and now the woman could cause Conn's demise.

Was he hurt? If he was, safety wouldn't matter, Strat wouldn't have to protect her. He'd once said he couldn't protect her from the man in her bed. Her friend couldn't protect her from herself either. What would the morning bring?

THIRTY-SIX

THEY DID A FEW extra laps, taking the long way around to get to her brother's place. His old place. After he and Imogen broke up, he'd moved in with her. Imogen was now living with Jagg, her new boyfriend.

The only reason they still had access was Lachlan's efficiency. He paid rent in advance, and hadn't asked the landlord for it back after his relationship fell apart. Until the keys were returned, the apartment was still technically Lachlan and Imogen's. Had her brother returned his keys? She didn't know. Imogen's keys? Yeah, the woman gave them to her to return to her brother. She might have, sort of, accidentally, on purpose, forgotten to do that.

Instead she set up a safe house for the woman she'd rescued from the Carlyle fire... yes, the fire she kind of started too.

"Lachlan not ready to give it up?" Strat asked as they traversed the hallway to the apartment's front door. "Immie's pretty set with Jagg."

Yeah, she'd have to be given the waves of turmoil

that relationship caused.

"Imogen gave me her keys to return to Lachlan."

"And you didn't?" he asked, crouching at the lock. "You don't have the keys with you?"

"I gave them to Conn."

Her friend twisted to frown up at her. "Because…?"

She glanced back down the corridor, hyperaware of their illicit actions in the reputable building. "Can we just get inside, then we'll talk?"

Strat got to work. She'd have to ask Daly to teach her to pick locks. Why Daly? Strat already thought she was a danger to herself; doubtful he'd facilitate adding to her repertoire of unlawful skills. Daly might think the same, but, on balance, he'd be more afraid of Conn finding out he'd refused her anything.

Her friend swung open the door and stood to curve an arm around her, directing her in first.

Breathing out, she turned on the light. "Maybe I shouldn't have—" There were dishes on the drainer. Why would there be…? A door opened, she whipped around to find another weapon pointed at her. And the bearer… "Marseille?"

The woman's tension loosened a little. "Sersha?"

"Jane Doe… Shit."

Marseille swung her aim to land it on Strat.

"No!" she said, leaping in front of him. "He's a friend, my friend, we can trust him."

Strat dropped the lock on the door. "Now it's a party."

Marseille was still there. Conn hadn't moved her. He'd have his reasons, but the woman's presence was turning out to be a dangerous variable.

"Will you put the gun down?" she asked, arms out in front of her as she gestured calm. "Please, Marseille."

The weapon dropped to her side. In a nightgown, hair loose, she must've been asleep… and terrified.

"I'm sorry." Sersha dumped her bag. "We didn't know you were still here. Why are you still here?"

"It's safe here," Marseille said, putting the gun on a side table. "Why did you come?"

"Because…" Going into the kitchen, she grabbed a couple of things and put them on the coffee table. "Can you get me the med kit from the bathroom, please? It's—"

"Under the sink. Lachlan showed me."

Without thought, the woman disappeared into the other room. Her mouth fell open, and her wide eyes rounded to Strat.

Cradling his arm, he came to sit with her. "The cop wasn't supposed to know she was here, huh?"

She helped him ease his shirt from the sticky wound.

"I told Conn, he said he'd handle it." And for some reason, that meant sending her brother over? How had that come about? So many questions. "I guess this is his way of… that." She winced at the injury on his shoulder. "I'd say it's just muscle, but…"

That wouldn't lessen its pain.

"So I shouldn't work out so much, I'm too jacked, that what you're saying to me?"

Still smiling. Even in pain, Strat was more interested in ensuring she was okay than he was in looking out for himself. Not just physically, but the smile meant to ease her heart's pain, her guilt's too.

Marseille came rushing back in and put the kit on the table. "Can I do anything?"

"Boil some water."

The woman went off to do that.

"I'm nowhere near capable of—"

"Dig out the bullet," Strat said, "sew up the hole. It's as simple as that."

"Says the patient to the reaper."

He laughed. "Just muscle you said, you can't kill me. No, I take that back, you, Scamp, if anyone could find a way to—"

"Don't make this worse."

She cleaned around the wound, trying to find the edges and figure out how the hell she'd do this. Hurting her friend would break her heart. Like she'd said his would be if the McDades revoked their need of his services.

Where would she be if Strat hadn't been the one with her? Daly would have skill, Hock, Snuff… But Strat didn't blink, he spotted their tail, knew how to tear up the streets and lead them exactly where he wanted them. The length and width of that alley were no coincidence. She'd bet it was no coincidence the shady parking lot was there either, in the dark, far from cameras and prying eyes. Filled with cars he could easily jack.

She forgot just how long, and how deep, he'd once existed in this underworld.

"I've got it," Marseille said.

"Pour some into a long, shallow dish, it'll cool quicker."

"Is that like seventh grade chemistry?" Strat teased, and she glared, fine, anything to keep them both from falling apart.

"I need a couple of clean towels too."

Otherwise she'd wreck the couch, owned by… someone. Not her. Marseille went into the bedroom.

"Who are you pissed at?" Strat asked.

Shifting, she opened the med kit her brother kept well stocked. "This'll probably hurt."

"It will hurt, I've done this before. Answer me, who are you pissed at?"

"Why do you think I'm pissed at anyone?"

"If it's supposed to be a secret, tell your face," he said, extricating his arm when she tried to distract herself with it. "Your brother? Your boyfriend? Or the girl?"

"I brought dark ones," Marseille said, delivering the towels.

With their hostess just standing there, their conversation couldn't continue. Thank God. Strat was right. She didn't know why, but rage simmered in her belly. Cleaning his wound with the water, catching it with the towel, concentrating kept her mind from racing.

"Okay, this is the hard part. Marseille, you have any liquor?"

"That's my girl," Strat said, sinking into the couch. "Bring on the booze."

"There's scotch."

Marseille went toward the kitchen as her eyes met Strat's.

"He be pissed?" her friend whispered.

"Better Scottish than American." Again, she shrugged. "We just won't tell him."

That was holding onto the hope they'd see Conn again. Pretending this was all okay, that they could joke and enjoy each other, comforted both of them. Probably more her.

Strat squeezed her leg. "He's fine."

Damn, the man didn't even need her to speak to know her mind. Marseille came over with the alcohol, holding the open bottle out to—she intercepted it and gulped some before giving it to Strat, the guy who was supposed to be, you know, injured and in need of dull senses.

"Okay, breathe in, old man."

"You've done this before?" Marseille asked, looming over her shoulder.

"No guts, no glory, right?" Confidence went a

long way, yes, but she'd never fool Strat. "I'm good at improvising. We'll be fine."

She wasn't the one bleeding.

To his credit, Strat made little sound and hardly flinched. And to hers, she didn't breathe. Helping her friend was paramount, it wasn't time to be squeamish or nervous… or terrified. Still, it didn't feel good to be rooting around inside him looking for—

"Got it!" Holding it up between the tweezers, triumphant, her relief vanished when blood trickled down his arm. "Shit."

"Oh, God, what is—that's a lot of blood."

"It's not a lot of blood," Strat said to Marseille, snatching the gauze from the table. He pushed her away to apply pressure himself. "Get the needle."

"Sewing kit."

Prepared didn't cover it. Lachlan had a sewing kit right there in the med box.

After she splashed some alcohol over the needle, Strat moved the gauze. She took a deep breath.

"Are you okay?" Marseille asked. She didn't even know which of them the woman was talking to. "Do you want more liquor?"

The bottle was thrust into her peripheral vision.

"No more," Strat said. "I'll have to drive later." They could crash there, except Conn would eventually get word she wasn't around. Then what? He'd tear up the city if she didn't put herself in front of him. "And I might not be done shooting."

Her friend wasn't the macho type. Refusing wasn't his way of showing his toughness, it was a signal the danger may not be permanently gone.

"You… you were shooting?"

"Do you have a way to contact Lachlan?" she asked Marseille while still sewing. "A number you call or…?"

"Uh, yeah, I… I'm only supposed to call in an emergency."

In a static beat, her eyes met Strat's. With the needle still in hand, propped on Strat, she gestured at the medical supplies and blood stained… everything, unable to hide her incredulity.

"What do you think this is?"

Getting angry with Marseille didn't help the situation. Conn. Trouble. Danger. All she could think about was her man. Wasn't so long ago she'd gone through the same thing after he was shot. If she wasn't killed by a wicked Byrne, high blood pressure would end her.

Self-conscious, Marseille disappeared into the bedroom.

"Go easy," Strat said in his forever calm father voice. "Woman just woke up to this."

"We all just woke up to this." Clenching her teeth, the frustration didn't go anywhere. "Didn't we just get over the last time I lost him?"

"You never lost him, kid. And, I'm sorry to say, this is the life." The one he'd told her it wasn't easy to live. "It ends this way, one day, for both of you."

She couldn't doubt the wisdom in his eyes. "I'm destined to be dead in an alley somewhere?"

"You won't get dead, not so long as I'm around." He'd proved not only his skill, but his commitment to her too. "Ire's not so easy to protect."

Marseille came in, phone at her ear. "Yeah, they just showed up and I—"

"Is that my brother?"

"Your brother?"

Finishing with the needle, she knotted it and cut the string. She'd dress the wound after getting an update from the man who'd raised her.

"Give it here." Snatching the phone from

Marseille, adrenaline drove her mood. "What is going on, Lach? Why have you—where are you?" Checking he wasn't in imminent danger took precedence over complaining. "Are you still with Dad?"

"How did you end up there? Everyone's going crazy. Terrified to tell Ire you're missing."

"I'm not missing just… temporarily waylaid. Where is he?"

"Still at the club, last I heard."

"Last you heard? What does that mean? Last you heard?"

"What happened?" He ducked the question. "Tell me why you're with Marseille."

"It's a long story," she said, pushing her bangs up from her face. "Strat got shot."

"You shot him?"

The exclamation was meant to wind her up, trust her brother to be her brother.

"*I* didn't shoot him." And she wouldn't tell her cop brother what happened to the real shooters. "He's doing okay, I patched him up, but I want him to see the doc. Are you at the mansion?"

"You'd be okay with that? With me being there?"

"Lach, I don't even know where to begin," she said, breathing out. One battle at a time. "You're safe?"

"I'm safe. Get to the mansion before Ire finds out his guys are hiding your disappearance from him."

Did it count as hiding anything? If Conn was still caught up with whatever was happening at Stag, no one would interrupt his line of concentration. It wasn't hidden news, just deferred until it was relevant. Which it never would be because she wasn't missing.

"Did the Byrnes show at the mansion? Is it safe?"

"It was when I put Dad there. Don't know now, I'm on the road."

"On the road? I thought you were safe? Where's

Dad?"

"At the mansion, locked up tight, where I left him." And her questions about that situation would have to wait for another time. "I'm on my way back there."

"You were at the mansion and left? Where did you go?"

"Back to Stag."

"Why?" To help or make some arrests? "Niall asked me to track you down. Easier than I thought." She smiled. "Meet me at the mansion."

"But what if—"

"If there was a problem at the mansion, Niall would've told me to avoid it. Instead he told me to get you there, to Ire's suite. I'm guessing you know where that is. Can Strat drive?"

"I can drive."

Except maybe she shouldn't with their current vehicular situation.

"Put him on."

And in her melee of madness, she handed the phone to her friend.

"Yeah," Strat said, frowning for a beat before laughing. "Yeah, you got that right… I'll take care of it." He hung up. "Get your shit, we're going."

THIRTY-SEVEN

SHE REFUSED TO LEAVE the mansion's foyer until laying eyes on her brother. Lighting was low, the house should be asleep. It probably was before the alarm was raised, maybe, the guys there didn't follow a typical timetable.

Her bare toes chilled on the cool marble, feeble against the beat of boots running in and out of the building.

A stream of men left, then the front door swung shut.

"There'll be more of them," Whisper's voice echoed above. Swirling around, the woman's smile came with an almost laugh as she leaned over the balustrade. "Looking for your pop? He's downstairs with Vindictive Vex and Marvelous Madison."

"She's here?"

Keeping their female prisoner increased chances the Byrnes would hit them again. They'd stay on their hitlist… though no matter who won the night, that wouldn't change. Still, something about the McDades triumph stirred her pride.

"We have reinforced security here," Whisper said.

"Security that just ran out the front door?" Strat asked, folding his arms as he leaned on the newel post. "Might be the Byrnes plan."

"Some of those guys are patrolling the perimeter, and we have a posse in the basement, taking care of business. Ire predicted this. Man's got a talent, can't deny it. And I'm here! I know what to do when I see a Byrne: kill it."

"Why did this happen tonight?"

"Was gonna happen eventually," Whisper said, strutting along the upper floor to slowly descend the stairs one at a time.

"Byrnes aren't known for their brains."

"All muscle, no hustle," Whisper said, reaching her level. "Said your guy was smarter than a lot of others at the top, didn't I? I'm good at being right. Want a margarita?"

"Where's Raze?"

"Working."

"And you're okay with that?"

Seemed to be a regular thing, Whisper staying away from the action. The why still perplexed her.

"Thing with Zay is when I'm around, he doesn't keep his attention where it's supposed to be. Most of the time, it's on my ass. So do I mind when he does the heavy lifting? No. It's the fucking middle of the night, why do I want to go out there and shoot Byrnes...?" Whisper paused; her lower lip betrayed a pondering. "Okay, the shooting Byrnes part is no problem. But with the strength of McDade numbers around here, I'd probably shoot the wrong guy." Funny until the prophecy came true and Conn found out. "Someone has to stick around to do the bail and lawyer thing if necessary. Where are we on the margaritas?"

"I'm waiting here. Right here. Until my brother shows." Or her boyfriend, but she doubted that would happen first. "I need to find out what the hell is going on."

"He's cute, your brother, guy like him coming to the dark side? There'll be a helluva lot of soaked panties, uh huh, all the way through, mark my words."

Disgust wrinkled her nose. "Okay, now I need alcohol, strong alcohol, to erase that mental image."

Whisper swung around Strat at the foot of the stairs only to spin and face her again. "Heard you've been stressed about it, your righteous brother hanging out with the villains."

"Oh yeah? From who?"

Whisper shrugged. "Word travels. And here's my wise, learned opinion… go with it."

"That's your advice?" Having expected something sage… and useful, she sagged. "I thought you'd back me up."

"I am backing you up, High Class. I'm with you all the way. You're tilting at windmills, baby. Go with it!"

Raising an arm, Whisper sauntered off to disappear through a door.

"Want to go to the basement?" Strat asked. "Check out the prisoners? Don't know how long your brother will be."

"Lach has to show eventually. And I'll be right here when he does."

Transporting their dad at least kept her brother safe from the initial fight at Stag. Didn't save her lover, but she couldn't dwell on that.

"Don't want to see your dad?" Strat asked.

"I'm Cushla Machree. I don't take meetings at that level."

Despite the locks and chains, her father would

still attempt to condescend her. What did he have to say? Nothing of interest.

No, it was the younger McLeod that troubled her. Her brother's return to the club after escaping deserved an explanation. Demanded one.

"Relax, Scamp, Ire knows what he's doing."

"We ran out of there too fast. Niall showed and I—why did I run out on Conn?" Something she could remedy. They'd driven their latest stolen car onto the grounds, but there would be others, non-stolen, around somewhere. "We have to be with him. Stick with him. I should never have left."

Intending to go outside was one thing, actually getting out was another. After her best friend, a guy twice her size, put himself in her path, fleeing wasn't so easy.

"Calm the fuck down. Where do you think you're going?"

"To the club. My club. Where I'm allowed to go. Where I'm safe. Where Conn is."

Did he need any more reasons? She'd keep going if necessary.

"You heard what Whisper said. She leaves her guy to do his thing 'cause if she was around, she'd fuck with his head. You want to fuck with Ire's head?"

"No."

Wasn't that why she'd refused to call him in the car? Conn needed a clear space, safety to strategize. Worrying about her would steal his focus unnecessarily.

"Trust me, from a guy's point of view, he needs to know you're safe or nothing else matters."

Such a double standard that no one seemed to acknowledge. "Everyone's so worried what he'd do if I was missing, why can't anyone see Conn's missing? I don't know where he is. If he's hurt, if he's—"

"He's in the thick of it." Lach's voice brought her around. "He's at the club. Alive."

"How do you know?" she asked, flashing a look back, then forward. "Why did you come that way? You came in the back?"

"Checked on Dad first." Oh, nice, so the murdering patriarch was more important than her sanity? "Because this isn't the time for him to be pushing McDades. There's a reason Ire put me in charge of him. Turns out, our dad's a difficult prisoner."

"No shit." Ronald McLeod was used to being the one carrying the keys. "I don't care what happens to him right now," or at all, "but you… You brought him here then went back to Stag?"

"That was the plan," Lachlan said. "Your guy's been preparing this strategy for a while. I took point on Dad."

Strat added a little clarity. "Other prisoners had other… jailors."

Like Ford with Evander, maybe Play with Madison. Arrangements hadn't only been for their enemies and assets either. Niall transporting her to Strat and getting her out of there pronto was no coincidence. Shit, even if he hadn't known the when, Conn had been fully prepared for the Byrne invasion.

"When did he tell you—how did you—"

"You want to have this conversation here?"

In McDade territory, it didn't occur to her to be vigilant. This was deeper inside than Stag, more than the loft in some ways too.

"It doesn't matter where we have the conversation," she said, though sailed past her brother to ascend the stairs. "You want somewhere private?" Resting a hand on the banister, she looked back to her friend. "Strat, you don't get off easy. You're in on this too."

"Because I haven't shown my loyalty enough tonight?" he asked, smirking, following her brother on his approach. "I don't referee my own kids, why do I got to referee you two?"

She went into the office and propped herself against the desk while the guys came in and closed the door.

"Talk."

"That an order, little sister?" Lachlan asked, half-smiling. "Look at you, in the big chair."

"I'm not in any chair. I want to know the man I love is safe. What is so wrong with that? I want to know what happened to our home. I want to know why anyone would think attacking us would be justified."

"Ire has something Byrne wants."

Someone actually. "Blasting into Stag like they did—how did they get in?"

"Drove right through the front of the building."

That was more horrific than anything she'd imagined.

"They drove into the building? Into it?" That suggested losses. "Who was hurt?"

"Don't think anyone's done a body count yet. Ire's busy rounding up Byrnes. Turns out bringing Dad and others here was a good idea. Ire's going to need the space at Stag."

Sliding her ass onto the desk, she threw up her arms. "Explain this to me. How do you know so much about Stag?"

"Think the cops only know what the families share? There's been stories of the McDades basement for years. Generations."

"So you're just guessing? I don't want to be..." Her eyes met Strat's. "What do I do here?"

"Find out what he knows," her friend said. "I don't know what he knows."

"You knew he was hanging out in the basement. I didn't know that."

Lach interrupted. "You don't need to know everything."

That attitude wasn't appreciated. "Is it genuine? Your time with the McDades? You really want to be part of the family?"

"This is my sister's world. You think I want her living in it alone?"

Though he didn't seem as angry, his motivation still worried her. "I figured it out, you know," she said, slipping off the desk to go to the decanter in the corner to pour drinks. "Your mood recently. I thought you were pissed at me."

"I am pissed at you."

"Yeah, but that's not why. None of this is that."

"No?"

Taking a drink to Strat first, her friend welcomed it. Shouldn't be any need for him to drive again, he could drown in liquor if he wanted. After what he'd done for her, the least she could do was keep his ass safe in McDade World.

Her brother was next.

She put the glass in his hand but didn't let go of it until he met her eye. "You're pissed at you."

"That I didn't see this coming? Sure." He plucked the glass from her fingers. "You and Dad do have something in common, your secret lives."

No longer so secret.

"I chose Conn. This life comes with the man I love."

"Yeah. And this life comes with the sister I love."

"You think you let me down. The way you've been with me, it's not 'cause you're pissed at me for falling in love with Conn. You think something you did, something in the way you raised me, did this to me."

"I trust Ire wouldn't hurt you."

"No, he wouldn't."

"But as long as you're in this family, so am I. We're all each other has, our only link to our past. You're my blood, Sersh. The only blood I'm proud to have."

Even in spite of her life choices?

Kicking him out of the McDades, demanding he live a righteous life, she'd be isolating him. Lachlan couldn't rely on their father; they'd never been able to do that. Accepting her meant accepting how she lived, who she loved.

The sting of tears in her eyes diverted them. "I didn't mean for this to happen. I love you. I'd do anything to keep you safe and happy. Anything."

"Don't you see that's what I'm doing? Keeping us together, you and me, we stick together. Didn't I always tell you I'd never be mad?" A tear skittered from her lashes, another blurred her brother's features. "You call me and I'll always come get you, I'll always be there for you. I'm never mad. It's my job to protect you, to support you."

Just as hers was to Conn. "I care about the McDades. About Conn. They may not be the most virtuous, but they have integrity. Doing the right thing matters to them. It's just... the right thing for the family." Even if that meant breaking laws or bones. "Conn loves me, Lach. Honestly loves me."

"If I didn't believe that, I wouldn't be here. I'm not spending time with him, and the family, to trip them up or call them out. Dad's taught us there isn't a virtuous path. Even those we think are on it are ultimately out for themselves. Sometimes doing the right thing is about love."

Love for a sibling. He was there for her.

"I thought you were mad at me, and I couldn't— it wasn't that. You thought you did something wrong, that in raising me, you'd let me down, set me on this path."

"Whether I meant to or not, I did. We're here—"

"Because of us." She linked their fingers. "I love you, so completely… Don't give up your career for—"

"My little sister?" He smiled. "Isn't it all about family? Ultimately, we are what matters. Losing Henry showed how we neglected each other. We have to change the way McLeods do business. That starts by acknowledging the law, and enforcing it, don't grant us any favors. It's an illusion, completely false. Smoke, mirrors, and bullshit. There's nothing superior about that path. I never did what I did to be whiter than white, I wanted to help people. To do the right thing. And now I know, *right* has nothing to do with the law, or punishing those who break it."

"Lach—"

"It was naïve and lazy. I conformed, followed in the footsteps of those before us. If I continue to do that, I end up dirty just like Dad."

"Are you going to quit?"

Being a cop, presently or formerly, put him at more risk of harm than most other McDades.

"I don't know yet. I do know the loyalty I showed to my colleagues wasn't returned. I can't trust anyone there. I couldn't trust my own father. Do you know he was the one pushing Wanstead's buttons? That CI, Ire being pulled in for Henry's murder, that was Dad's doing."

And they knew why that was, to divert attention from himself.

She snickered. "I'm sorry I didn't see his face when he found out about me and Conn."

"I wasn't in the room either, but the building shook."

"I'll bet. Really screwed up his plans."

"If Henry could thank you for that, he would. I

thank you for it too."

"Thank me for—"

"We could've put Ire behind bars for Henry's murder. Without you, Ire McDade would've spent his life paying for our father's crime. We may never have known… I rethink every second, kick myself for not noticing. What kind of cop was I that—"

"I didn't see it either and investigation is my livelihood too. Dad started the con young, he groomed us to believe him all our lives. We didn't think to question it, question him."

"You got it, know it or not, you knew from the beginning he wasn't so righteous or honorable."

"There are plenty of people I don't get along with, doesn't make all of them crooks. Wish I could take credit for figuring it out, but it wasn't me. The McDades told me the truth. Well, Dad's actions revealed his murderous streak. But being in league with the Manzanis, with Silvio, Conn got that long before I did."

"He told you?"

"Yes. We have communication, respect. I didn't tell you immediately because I didn't want to lay that on you. What could you have done? If I told you a crime had been committed, that our father committed a crime, you'd investigate. That put you at risk. If you'd brought it up with Dad—"

"It would've tipped our hand." Our. What a relief it was to be cradled by her brother's support again. "If nothing else, uncovering these truths, you and Ire, Dad's duplicity, it sets us free, all of us. You did what was right, regardless of the personal cost. The bravery and honor it took you to stand up for Ire, without knowing how the situation would play out, it gave us all courage. You showed me what real integrity is, Sersh. And I'm so goddamn proud of you for it. We have to stop getting caught up in labels and lanes and start standing up for the people who stand up for us."

"You did once tell Conn you could be allies."

"And I was right. We're allies, Sersh. Anyone who loves you gets a pass, gets my support."

Strat, in the corner, raised a hand. "I love her less today than I did yesterday."

"Not my fault you got a bullet in you, old man. It's amazing I'm still alive with the way you drive."

The easier mood gave them all a little breathing space.

"Got sticky for a minute," Lachlan said. "Ire almost lost his chance at that pass. How could he love you if he didn't give a shit?"

"I don't understand."

"Niall reached out, he called me," her brother said, "the night you went missing."

"You never told me that," Strat said.

"Yeah, 'cause no one can trust you to keep your trap shut around my sister."

As she'd thought, telling Strat was tantamount to telling her. Something was different about these two men, so important in her life. Lach would never have spoken to Strat this way when he was with Imogen.

Not that Strat was ashamed or offended. "You've got lessons to learn about women, boy. Even your own sister."

Weirdly… she liked their banter.

"How did Niall calling mix up your view of Conn?"

"Pissed me off that your boyfriend didn't care enough to contact me himself."

"He was injured," she said. "Dad shot him."

Her brother grew more solemn. "I wouldn't believe what Niall said, any of it, not until it was confirmed by you or Dad."

"You told me you hadn't seen Conn."

"I hadn't. I thought the McDades were playing me. How could Ire love you so much and delegate your wellbeing to a goon?"

"Niall's no goon," she said, her gaze bouncing to Strat. "Anything you didn't tell me?"

He held up a hand. "I said I hadn't seen Conn either…" He sipped his drink and kept his mouth behind the glass. "Mighta talked to Niall. And, you boy, don't forget to tell your sister I told you the only reason Ire wouldn't reach out direct was if he was incapable."

Lach's head bobbed. "He did tell me that."

"More than once. If he wasn't bleeding and drugged up, Ire would've led the charge to track her down."

"Strat's actually smarter and more astute than we give him credit for." She sighed. "Except tonight he was dumb enough to get himself shot, that wasn't so smart."

"Was when you play it forward," Strat said. "Only way I don't get shot is if I handed you over to the Byrnes."

"Hmm, yeah, shot would be nothing to what Conn would do to you if you surrendered me to our enemy."

So maybe he was smart, but the teasing was too much fun.

"And Niall was damn clear he didn't want you to know about the communication, or that we should mention it anywhere near Dad."

"Ire wasn't out the woods in a hurry," Strat said. "Found that out afterwards. Word is he shouldn't even be on his feet now. But it's not like anyone can tie him down."

Pushing back her shoulders, she played that through her head. "Someone can."

"No one in this room wants to know that."

Their disgust and her smile united them.

And then it happened, another crash, not like the one in Stag, this was way closer.

Lachlan stepped aside to turn and there was Conn, just inside the room, concentrating completely on her.

THIRTY-EIGHT

READING HIM THERE, eyes hooded with the fury he was named for, she stepped past her brother.

"I wasn't missing. I wasn't hurt. We were followed from the club and had to divert." Still, he said nothing. Anyone else, namely her brother and Strat, might be pissed she told the truth. What she gleaned, that they may not have absorbed from her lover's energy, he already knew. Conn knew, lying wouldn't get them anywhere. "Strat got shot protecting me."

"Aye," Conn said, not in question, he already knew that too. On the spot, he turned to her friend who leaped up from the couch. "You're in charge of her security."

Strat's head tipped a little forward. "I'm… I'm what?"

"Head of security, take whatever guys you need. Train them. Give her the best. Every second, you know where she is. Manage the schedules, the discipline. You've proved you'd give your life for hers."

"Yeah."

"From now on, you make sure no one has to."

As Conn's attention moved, Strat took a step forward. "At the scene where—"

"It's been handled." Whatever that meant. "Macushla, the Stratfords will be protected by this family." Like Strat protected her, yeah, but that wasn't what he meant. Her guy was telling her Strat wasn't getting a break, or a pink slip. "That's final."

"Your boy's downstairs," Niall said to Strat.

She'd barely noticed the lieutenant, her eyes stayed locked on Conn's. Her heart beat faster, her throat hurt, her love grew.

That suit, the clear expression, his hair just a fraction damp. He'd showered and changed. Good. But what did that mean? He'd showered before coming to her, was that because his clothes could be used in evidence against him?

"What happened? At the club, Byrne—"

"Was no threat," Conn said as she got closer. "I handled it."

Yeah, like he'd handled Marseille.

"They wanted Madison," she said.

"They didn't get her."

"I know. Won't they come again?"

"Hard to come at me when they're under our control."

"All of them?"

"Enough of them."

The thinning Byrnes ranks had been decimated at the same time the Dohertys lost almost a whole generation.

"And the club? Stag? The damage to—"

"Damage will be repaired," he said, pinching her chin to raise her head. "We're unshakeable."

Which was his way of telling her to grow a pair.

"What about the authorities?" she asked. "The

press? Want me to call Steeple?"

Steeple would know more, her editor always did. Except she couldn't risk calling him from Conn's phone, or the club, or from their secret location. Damn caller ID and backtraces.

"Has he called you?"

"My phone's at the club."

"Niall," Conn said without turning.

"Aye," Niall said.

"Strat's phone was left in the—"

Niall tossed something to her friend in front of the couch. He held it up, his phone, huh. Guess the scene really had been handled, just like they said.

"Doc's waiting for you," Niall said to Strat, who looked to her.

"Bluebell patched me up. I'm good."

"No, you're not," she said, actually turning Conn as she leaned against him to lay eyes on her friend. "Go see the doctor. He'll give you painkillers and antibiotics. And he'll have something to knock you out. You need rest."

Before he claimed the Bluebell Brigade.

"Now."

The single word from Conn dispelled any notion of objection. Niall opened the door until Strat trailed out, then said something in his foreign tongue, to which her guy replied.

Oh, how his words dampened her panties. When Niall left a second later, Conn's attention landed on her brother.

"Handle Jane Doe."

"I will," Lachlan said.

"Handle her? What does that mean 'handle her'? What's going on with her?"

Before opening his mouth, her brother got a nod from Conn.

"I've been working with her, learning what she knows, what she saw, trying to track it down… unofficially."

"So she'd never have to testify? Because you know if this got to a court—"

"She'll help your brother as long as she can," Conn said.

"Then Ire's got a whole new life waiting for her," Lachlan explained. "She'll be safe."

"No Manzani will touch her."

And if in the interim some Manzanis were brought down by what Marseille knew, all the better. She might not topple the regime, but any harm they could inflict on the Manzanis was positive.

"I trust both of you. There was no need to keep it a secret, I can be helpful if you tell me things. Keep me in the loop, I'm a familiar presence to Marseille, if she's unsure—"

"Oh, she was pretty sure," Lachlan said, slipping his hands in his pockets. "About the *women* who rescued her. The plural was a surprise."

"I have chips to play with the Manzanis. Conn and I weren't together, but Imogen would've made an easier target than—"

"I know." Lachlan bowed to kiss her head. "Showed me we don't have to be doing the blue thing to be doing the right thing."

And that was a big admission from her brother. Turning to hug him, she held tight. He hadn't changed, they hadn't changed. Okay, maybe a few details had, but at the core of them, they were still them.

He'd never put her in the middle if this was an undercover sting. If he disliked, or distrusted, Conn so much that Lach thought he should be in jail, he'd never let her sleep next to him every night. If for no other reason than when the McDades discovered the double cross, she'd be an immediate, and vulnerable, target.

Backing away, her hand found Conn's, who gave her brother a side nod. Yep, time for him to read her the riot act.

Lachlan didn't seem concerned as he sauntered to the door.

"Oh, hey," he said, turning back to them. "Seen that picture kicking around with the guys."

"Picture?"

"That picture—shit, I'll fucking kill him," she said. "You've seen it?"

"Yeah, and it's not a uniform," he said, smirking. "It's a costume."

"You let me go out like that?"

"You were nineteen." Shit, did her brother remember everything? "Didn't give me much say."

Not that she ever had when it came to her apparel. "How do you even remember that?"

He laughed. "Don't think you want me to tell you that in current company." Saying that necessitated his answer. "That was the night you met Vex."

She shivered. "Burn it."

"Already did, little sister." He opened the door. "I'll check in with Marseille."

Alone with Conn, she rested her face against him. "I'm sorry I left you at Stag."

"It was my order. I would never have let you stay."

"Because your head isn't in the game when I'm around?"

"That and you'll have to get used to it."

"Leaving you?"

Stacking his hands on the back of her head, he bowed to kiss her crown then skimmed them around until the pads of his thumbs pressured her jaw upward. Much as he had on the night of their reunion in his office.

One soft kiss followed another. Right there in the middle of the office, he sampled her mouth from this angle and that, giving her something while he took. The reassurance of each other's safety demanded they celebrate in that intimacy.

Used to it? Yes, he was right. She would have to get used to him being in danger. His life was always at risk, as was hers, as they always would be.

"Mo Grá," she whispered between kisses. "Take me to bed, Mo Grá."

"I'm going back to the club."

She laid her hands on him to put some space between them. "You're leaving? Why did you come here just to leave me?"

Sweeping her hair from her face, he scooped it higher, admiring her features down the line of her throat. "You know why I came here, *Cushla Machree.*"

To lay eyes on her, to prove she was safe, to gather the strength he got from her.

"I could come with you. Back to Stag."

"McDade wives stay in safety."

"Wives? But I'm not..." A harsh edge to his determination broke through. "When?"

"Soon. You need the McDade name. It's long overdue."

Her smile flourished and she pulled him down for another brief kiss. "Taste's good, doesn't it?"

"Yes," he said on the whisper of a snicker. "Told you, didn't I?"

"You did. Damn, am I happy I insulted you."

"This is your kingdom."

"Act like it."

Accepting his next kiss, their need would have to be sated before he could go anywhere. Everyone she loved under the same roof, she could get used to that. As long as she existed under her McDade's roof, she'd never wake lonely again.

Thank you for reading this tale!
If you can, please take the time to review.

~

Ask your local library for more Scarlett Finn novels!

~

For all things Scarlett Finn check out:

www.scarlettfinn.com

www.ingramcontent.com/pod-product-compliance
Lightning Source LLC
Chambersburg PA
CBHW051247210726
48287CB00002B/380